LOVE
AGAINST
THE LAW

LOVE AGAINST THE LAW

A NOVEL

JUSTINE KLAVON

atmosphere press

Part One

Chapter One
Criminals

It was Christmas Eve and the mall was packed, even more so than Sammi and her friends had been expecting. Sammi walked through the crowded two-story building, scoping everything out and making sure she was aware of the entire layout. Her crew was in the underground parking garage in a black Chevy Tahoe, waiting on her word.

Sammi didn't start this crew of thieves, but she was the mastermind behind their heists. Eli had found her in a bar four years prior and they had been inseparable ever since. Eli, who had two years on Sammi, was the glue of the group so, naturally, his twin sister Shay was desperate to be included. Shay's boyfriend, Howard, was a computer genius and probably the most important member of the crew with his hacking abilities. And then there was Sammi's best friend, Kodi, who shared Sammi's abandoned childhood and was a naturally gifted thief.

Sammi continued her mission through the busy New York mall and headed for the security office. As soon as she turned down the small hallway where the bathrooms and security office were located, she made extended eye contact with a passing man. That eye contact was a huge mistake because that guy was going to remember Sammi and her unforgettable ice blue eyes. Even worse, Sammi knew who that guy was.

Mack Johnson was a greatly decorated New York police officer who was recently promoted to a detective after being made famous for singlehandedly stopping a terrorist attack while not even on duty. He was a modern-day John McClane and he clearly wasn't afraid to bend the rules for the job. He was nothing but bad news for this crew.

Sammi and the cop locked eyes for a few seconds too long as they passed by each other in the narrow hallway. Mack was initially intrigued by the twenty-six-year-old's body. Sammi was wearing a pair of slim-fitting light blue jeans and a low-cut black tank top with a tight black leather jacket that she had left unzipped. She had her long blonde hair pulled back casually in a ponytail, which only accentuated how elegantly slender her body was. But as she returned Mack's gaze, he saw darkness dancing in her shining sapphire eyes and knew she couldn't be up to anything good.

As soon as Sammi was alone in the isolated back hallway, she put a small bean-shaped earpiece into her right ear. Each member of her band of thieves had an earbud just like hers, which allowed them to communicate easily during a heist. They were expensive little electronics and the team had worked many jobs without them before having enough stolen cash to afford them. But the benefits of the tiny earpieces made them worth every penny.

"We've got company," Sammi announced to her friends. "Mack Johnson is here."

"Mack Johnson?" Eli questioned his girlfriend, making the immediate connection. "We can't handle a cop like that."

"Calm down. There's five of us and one of him," Sammi all but scoffed. "Besides, he's probably leaving as we speak."

"I've got eyes on him," Kodi chimed in before anyone even knew she had left the parking garage. "I'll follow him and make sure he leaves."

"Good plan, Kodi. I'm entering the security office now," Sammi told everyone and slipped quietly into the cupboard-sized room.

The security office was just a dark, square room with a stack of outdated monitors displaying delayed footage from security cameras around the mall. There were two office chairs placed in front of the screens and a guard fast asleep in one of them. Sammi took the handgun from the waistband of her jeans and brought it down on the back of the guard's head as hard as she could. The guard woke up on the first hit so Sammi bashed him again, this time rendering him unconscious.

"I'm in," Sammi gave the cue for everyone to move into their next positions.

Sammi was shutting down all of the security cameras when Eli arrived at the office less than five minutes later. He gently placed two machine guns against the wall before changing into the guard's clothes and tying up the still unconscious man. Sammi tucked her pistol back in her waistband, shouldered her machine gun, and tried to wait patiently for nine o'clock. Her pacing by the door and jittery hands didn't faze Eli in the least because she got like this during every heist. She was excited; she lived for this.

As Sammi continued pacing, she caught Eli watching her with desire in his aquatic green eyes and couldn't help but think back to the passionate kiss they'd shared just before leaving their apartment earlier that evening...

*

Eli's and Sammi's apartment was technically home base because it had once been everyone's home, so that was where the five of them met up before and after each of their heists. That particular night had been extra festive, with Christmas lights throughout the tiny, one- bedroom apartment and a tree that was too large for the space stuffed next to the television set and decorated with Tiffany & Co. ornaments that Kodi and Sammi had snagged off a display at their Fifth Avenue location. Eli hadn't been happy with them that day for committing such an unnecessary theft, but they were so pleased with themselves and Sammi's smile was probably the brightest he'd ever seen it, so he couldn't stay mad at them.

With upbeat holiday tunes playing from the television speakers, Sammi danced around the apartment in a Santa hat while sipping on an energy drink. Her job of planning the heist was already done, so she was overseeing the others. Howard and Shay checked on Howard's technical equipment while talking quietly between themselves, and Kodi helped Eli make sure their guns were locked and loaded. But Kodi quickly got bored and the two blonde best friends wandered off into the kitchen to get a moment to themselves.

Kodi and Sammi had been the last to join the group of five and they more often than not felt unwelcome when the whole group was together. Eli had invited them in because of his immediate attraction to Sammi without checking with the others first and there was obvious resentment from Shay because of that. But Shay was also visibly jealous of the friends' head-turning good looks, so the guys of the group chose to ignore her judgement for that reason. Even Howard sometimes preferred Sammi's brilliance and Kodi's cheerfulness over his girlfriend's constant bitterness. But Sammi and Kodi still appreciated their space away from the others most of the time.

Buzzing with caffeine and excitement, Sammi hopped up onto the kitchen counter, keeping a hold of the can of Monster in her hands and took another swig of the bitter drink. Kodi pulled the Santa hat off her best friend's head before taking the spot beside her on the counter and tossing the hat on top of the fridge. She grabbed the can from Sammi, wanting a sip, but was disappointed to find that it was empty and stuck her bottom lip out at her bestie.

"There's another one in the fridge," Sammi told her with a giggle, just as Eli walked into the room and right over to his girlfriend.

"Is this what you're wearing tonight?" Eli asked Sammi, raising his eyebrows curiously at her as his right hand ran up her thigh. "Were you hoping to pick up the security guard?"

"Why? What did you hear? Is he hotter than you?" Sammi teased, giggling some more.

"Not even possible," Eli grunted confidently as he hoisted Sammi down off the counter by her butt. "And he'd have to have a death wish to try and take you from me."

With those words, Eli brought his hands up to either side of Sammi's angelic face and held her gently against the counter as he pressed his lips to hers. They kissed each other like they'd never kiss again and Kodi scurried from the room out of total discomfort. Not that she was surprised by their grossness, though, because that was how Sammi and Eli prepared for every heist, just in case one of them didn't make it out with their life...or their freedom...

*

"Hey, Kodi, can we get an update on Mack Johnson?" Sammi asked as the clock reached nine.

"He's gone. I watched him drive away," Kodi responded.

"Game on."

The mall closed at nine o'clock, so all of the customers had left the building, but employees were still in their stores with all of their Christmas Eve cash. Eli shut all of their gates from controls in the security office so that nobody could leave. He, Sammi, Kodi, and Shay divided up the keys to manually open the gates and rob each store at gunpoint while Howard took over the security controls and kept an eye out for any trouble.

Less than thirty minutes after nine, Sammi exited her third store, stuffing cash into her duffel bag. As she stood up after manually closing and locking the gate, she felt something smack hard into the back of her head. She stumbled forward from the force of the blow and turned around to find herself face-to-face with Mack Johnson.

"I knew you were going to be a pain in my ass," Sammi snarled, dropping her bag of cash on the tile floor. Her first instinct was to swing her machine gun at his face like it was a baseball bat.

Johnson staggered backwards toward the second-floor railing overlooking the floor below them. He covered his face as blood poured out of his nose and Sammi smirked; they both knew it was broken. Taking advantage of Johnson's moment of weakness, Sammi ran at him at full speed, shoving him hard in the chest upon impact. Not quick enough to brace himself, Johnson toppled over the railing and hit the ground on the first floor with a thud.

Hearing the commotion, Sammi's team hurried to her aid, except for Howard who remained in the security office. Sammi told them what had happened with Johnson while everyone quickly counted their hauls. Howard collected their totals and Sammi knew right away that she was short compared to the others.

"I'm not getting less than everyone else," Sammi grumbled, grabbing her machine gun and walking over to the next store in her row.

"Sammi, we're splitting it all evenly," Kodi tried reasoning with her.

"I'm not a failure," Sammi replied more to herself than anyone else as she opened the gate and aimed her gun at the two remaining employees.

"Sammi, you threw a cop off of the second floor. You are not a failure!" Eli called after his girlfriend.

Sammi ignored everyone and continued with her robbery.

She knew that they were dividing all the cash evenly, but as the designer of the heist, she owed it to her team to provide just as much as the others, if not more. So, she forced the two young women to empty the single cash register into her open duffel bag. They were crying and visibly shaking as Sammi continued waving the gun around. Once Sammi was in possession of all their cash, she retreated from the store and locked the gate behind her. The rest of her team was waiting, and they turned simultaneously to head for the security office to meet up with Howard. Standing directly in their path was Mack Johnson with his police-issue handgun aimed at Sammi.

"Bitch broke my nose. Now it's personal," Johnson hissed as the four thieves raised their guns at him.

"There's four of us and one of you. What are you going to do now, cop boy?" Sammi taunted and took a step toward him, keeping her gun aimed at his face.

Johnson began firing his weapon as he ran directly at the bad guys. The band of thieves scattered, Kodi taking all four duffel bags with her. Sammi stood her ground and fired back at Johnson, giving her team enough time to get away.

Suddenly, both Johnson and Sammi collapsed to the floor at the same time. It looked like Sammi had shot Johnson in his right shoulder. And he had gotten her in her left thigh. The wound burned so she closed her eyes as her leg seared in pain.

Sammi couldn't believe it. She had never even come close to getting shot before. As she lay on the cool tile floor, internally begging for the pain to stop, she replayed the entire heist over in her mind up to this point. This was her fault for making eye contact with Johnson. And she was either going to jail or going to die for her mistake.

Sammi's eyes shot open as someone grabbed her right arm to help her up. It was Johnson. He got Sammi to her feet and handcuffed her wrists behind her before steering her toward the nearest exit. He had a hold of her right arm, but she was still having a difficult time walking on her injured leg. Every step she attempted to take on it shot another flame of pain up her entire body. Her left leg finally gave out from under her, ablaze with agony, so she and Johnson both had to stop so they could readjust. Before they could go any further, Eli and Howard appeared in their path with their guns raised.

"Drop the guns!" Johnson yelled, putting his own gun to Sammi's head.

"Let her go! You're not gonna kill her; you're a cop!" Eli hollered.

"Maybe so, but she's bleeding out. She's got about an hour to get medical attention. Turn yourselves in and I'll take her to the hospital myself," Johnson tried negotiating.

"Yeah, right. You gotta do better than that," Eli replied.

"Always gotta do it the hard way," Johnson mumbled.

Within the blink of an eye, Eli aimed his gun at Johnson's face and fired. Sammi heard yelling and cursing in the distance but couldn't understand why she suddenly couldn't see anyone. The blackness surrounding her begun to swirl around her and, the next thing she knew, her face was on the cold tile once again. It felt nice despite the new flash of burning pain in her right side. She welcomed the soothing touch of the cool floor until everything went quiet.

Chapter Two
Wicked Game

When Sammi woke up, she didn't even want to open her eyes. Her whole body ached and there were shooting pains all over. The burning from the pain was so intense that she was afraid to move. The last thing she could remember was her idiot boyfriend shooting her instead of the cop who had been arresting her.

As Sammi lie there in pain, she was abundantly aware of the silence surrounding her. Shouldn't there be some kind of noise—the beeping machines of a hospital or the clanging and banging of a prison? Anything. Then it dawned on her, maybe she didn't hear anything because...maybe she was dead. In a panic, her eyes flew open.

Sammi found herself in an unusually large but weakly decorated bedroom. She was tucked into the center of a king-sized bed with soft grey blankets. There was a nightstand to her left with just a lamp and a picture frame on it and a door to the left of that. To her right was an enormous window with the dark shades drawn, keeping the sunlight out of the room but not enough to keep it from peeking through. Directly across from the bed was a generously sized flat-screen television mounted to the wall and closed doors on either side of it.

Confused, Sammi forced herself to roll out of the bed and she gingerly hobbled over to the giant window. Both sides of her body were in an equal amount of pain, so it didn't matter which side she favored. She pulled one of the curtains back to take a look and was surprised by the sight. She was definitely still in the city, but she had to be at least thirty floors above the ground judging by how tiny the cars stuck in traffic looked below.

Before she could think too much about where she might be, the pain in Sammi's leg became too much to bear and she had to sit on the edge of the bed to get her weight off of it. It was then that she realized she wasn't wearing what she had been when she was shot. Instead of the jeans and tank top that had gotten her into this mess, she was just wearing a navy blue t-shirt that was three sizes too big for her with the NYPD logo over her left breast. If the New York Police Department was involved, she was in serious trouble.

Sammi's legs were bare so as soon as she sat down, the shirt rode up and the gunshot wound on her thigh was exposed. The wound had been cleaned and stitched up, but Sammi still cringed at the sight of it. It looked gross and something about looking at it made the pain intensify. Realizing this, she really didn't want to see where she had been shot the second time. Her right side, just above her hip, slightly burned and felt sticky and stiff. Her imagination ran wild with the thought of how bad the injury could be, causing her to only panic more. Giving in to the need to see the damage, she lifted up the t-shirt and had to choke back vomit. The second bullet wound had also been cleaned and stitched, but it was still oozing gore.

Sammi covered the wound back up and took a more detailed look around the room to try and keep her mind off of the pain. The bedroom was very plain and very neat. It could have passed as not belonging to anyone if it weren't for the single picture frame on the nightstand. Sammi picked up the frame to investigate and her stomach instantly knotted. It was a photo of her nightmare from the night before, Mack Johnson. Also pictured with him, in a forced family pose, were a pretty woman his age and two children. It was Mack Johnson's family, so was this Mack Johnson's apartment?

Now even more confused and wondering if this was some bizarre kidnapping, Sammi tried leaving the room for the first time. The door next to the nightstand was unlocked so she let herself out into the nicely carpeted hallway. She explored the entire two-floor, three-bedroom apartment, looking for some sort of explanation of why she had been brought here but found nothing and no one. The front door was only locked on the inside, so it seemed that the homeowner was out, but that Sammi was free to leave.

Sammi started to exit the apartment, looking forward to getting home and back to familiarity. She hadn't even closed the apartment door behind her when she realized that she couldn't leave because she wasn't wearing any pants. She hadn't seen her own clothing anywhere at all while looking through the home. Still not entirely certain where in the city she was, she couldn't risk going out in the street dressed the way she was, especially considering how guys looked at her when she was fully clothed. Defeated, she slowly let herself back into the apartment and crumbled to her knees, one hand still on the doorknob.

Frustrated by not knowing what was going on and not being in control of the situation, Sammi began sobbing on the floor. Tears started to roll effortlessly from her eyes and landed in tiny splashes on the hardwood floor. Sammi lost track of how long she remained like that before finally composing herself and deciding her next move. Even though her injuries were throbbing and she looked like a walking disaster, she had no choice but to get out of there.

Back on the second floor, Sammi returned to the bedroom where she had woken up and started throwing drawers open, looking for a pair of pants or a long coat, anything that she could wear to cover herself up just to get home safely. In the very last drawer, she found a pair of navy-blue sweatpants, also emblazoned with the New York Police Department logo. They were huge, but they had a drawstring so she hiked them up past her waist and tied them as tightly as she could, hoping the string and the elastic would be enough to hold the pants in place over her flat little bum just long enough for her to get across the city.

Fully clothed and with adrenaline now masking the pain in both of her gunshot wounds, Sammi dashed down the stairs and right out the apartment door. She hadn't even made the complete turn out of the doorway before she came to a halt in front of Detective Mack Johnson returning home from work. Caught in his soulful blue eyes, Sammi was trapped, unable to break free from their extended eye contact.

"Oh, you're still here," Mack muttered as he tore his own gaze away, breaking the connection.

"I was just leaving," Sammi replied quickly before making her run for it and tripping over the doormat that she didn't even see under her feet. Luckily, she caught herself on her hands and knees, but bursts of pain shot through her injured thigh and up into her side, causing her to let out a slight whimper.

A hand reached down to help Sammi and she looked up, back into the detective's soft eyes. She took Johnson's hand and let him help her up as he kept an arm around her to make sure she was steady on her feet. As she stood, she caught a glimpse of the badge on Johnson's belt and a breath caught in her throat. Being that close to law enforcement was making her understandably nervous.

"Careful," Johnson whispered softly, keeping a hold of Sammi's elbow. "Would you mind allowing me to check on your stitches before sending you out into the world? I must admit, I'm not a pro."

"I guess," Sammi gave in without a fight because of how much her thigh was burning after her fall. "The one on my side was bleeding when I woke up."

Johnson grimaced for her as he guided her back into the apartment, still not letting go of her elbow. Sammi was torn between the warm feeling in her gut that she got from the cop's closeness and the anxious feeling that she was about to be placed under arrest. She hated not knowing what was going on.

"Why didn't you just take me to the hospital?" Sammi stuttered after swallowing hard as she followed Johnson through the apartment and upstairs to the master bedroom again.

"They would've asked too many questions. Then you'd be going to jail, and your friends would keep all the money they got away with," Johnson explained matter-of-factly, waving his free hand out to the side as if his point were obvious.

"So, you're hoping I'll get the money back for you?" Sammi asked, raising an eyebrow in shock.

"What? No! If anything, I think you yourself should keep it all after that fight you put up last night. But when your brilliant team leader accidentally shot you instead of me, I couldn't just leave you there to bleed out."

"My team leader? I think you've got it all wrong. I was in charge that night."

"Sorry. I must've misread the situation."

By then the two of them had reached the bedroom and Sammi leaned against the doorway, watching Johnson as he quickly remade the bed from Sammi's slumber earlier. Johnson was wearing a pair of tan khaki pants that hung perfectly on his waist and a tight black t-shirt that had to stretch over his bulging arm muscles. Noticing just how fit Johnson was, Sammi started to realize how attracted she was to him. There was something about his playful smile and caring blue eyes that were enough to make her forget that he was a cop. She suddenly found herself imagining what it would be like to run her fingers through his soft brown, longer-than-police-standard crew cut.

When Johnson finished what he was doing, he turned to face Sammi and opened his mouth to say something, but he saw the way Sammi was looking at him and had to turn away again to hide his smile. After taking a second to clear his own thoughts, shaking his head quickly, he finally walked back over to Sammi. He took her hand and helped her glide over to the bed without putting any weight on her injured leg. "Here, sit up against these pillows," Johnson directed, patting the pillows on his bed.

Sammi obeyed and sat on the bed with her back up against the pillows, pushing one side of the stolen sweatpants down past the gunshot in her thigh. Johnson plopped down on the edge of the bed next to her and rolled the bottom of the NYPD t-shirt up over her thigh. He brushed his thumb over the first wound and then pushed against the skin around it, checking that his stitches would hold. Sammi squeaked once from the pain and pushed his hands away from her leg.

"Sorry!" Johnson chuckled and threw his hands up in forfeit. "I just had to make sure my stitches were secure."

"Okay, they're all good. I can leave now," Sammi said and started to get up. Johnson quickly put a hand on her shoulder and gently pushed her back down against the pillows.

"Nice try. How about I make you a deal? You show me yours and I'll show you mine," Johnson offered and pointed to his shoulder where Sammi had shot him.

"Fine," Sammi sighed and pushed the t-shirt up to uncover the bullet wound on her side.

Sammi couldn't bring herself to look at the still throbbing hole in her side so she watched Johnson instead. He grimaced and she knew it had to be bad. He reached over and grabbed a bottle and a cotton ball out of his nightstand drawer. Then he poured a little bit of his homemade skin-safe antibiotic solution onto the cotton ball and suddenly Sammi felt the coldness on her side. She gasped in pain and squeezed her eyes shut, pushing out a single tear that rolled down her cheek. After a few seconds, she felt Johnson take the bottom of the t-shirt from her grip and roll it back down to cover her wounds.

"I'm done. You can open your eyes," Johnson said, holding back a chuckle.

Sammi opened her eyes and Johnson was standing next to the bed with his shirt off. Her jaw dropped and a crooked little grin appeared on Johnson's face. Part of Sammi's reaction was because of how great he looked, but it was mostly a direct reaction to his own bullet wound. It was much lower than she had originally thought and dangerously close to his heart.

"I'm really sorry that I shot you...and broke your nose," Sammi said, trying to seem innocent as she sat up from the pillows and glanced at his swollen nose.

"I'm sorry as well," Johnson said kindly and sat back down on the edge of the bed.

"So, do you always bring the bad guy home to your place?" Sammi asked, teasing.

"No, you're honestly the first."

"Well, I'm honored, but I should get going. Eli's going to start to worry."

"Eli? I see. Well, look, take my card. Call me if you ever get into serious trouble."

"With all due respect, Lieutenant Johnson, I'm always getting into trouble."

Then Sammi stood up from the bed and fixed her much too baggy clothing that she knew she must've looked absolutely ridiculous in, like a child playing dress up in a parent's wardrobe. She started to leave but as she reached the doorway, she felt a hand wrap around her wrist to stop her. She turned back to look at Johnson and saw concern in his eyes.

"I saw the bruises," Johnson said calmly. Sammi's face fell and angry embers danced in her cold eyes.

"That is none of your business," Sammi hissed and pulled her wrist free from Johnson's grip.

"Samantha, I'm a cop. I've seen how these things end. It's my job to keep you safe."

"So that's why you brought me here? So my boyfriend wouldn't beat me to death?"

"No, but that's why I'm insisting you stay here, at least for the night."

"You're insane."

"Sammi, if you walk through that door, I will personally arrest you and all of your friends from last night before the sun comes up tomorrow."

Sammi stormed out of Johnson's bedroom and slammed the door shut behind her. Instead of heading downstairs to leave, she walked to the end of the hallway where there was a sliding glass door that led to a balcony. Letting herself out onto the small city balcony, she sat down on one of two cushioned chairs and pulled her knees to her chest. She wasn't afraid of being arrested; she knew the consequences of her line of work. But she would protect her friends if she could, no matter what the cost.

*

"I actually thought you had left," Johnson said, appearing next to Sammi on the balcony a few minutes later.

"I'm not afraid of you. But I won't betray my team like that," Sammi responded without even turning to look at him.

"Come have dinner with me and get out of the cold," Johnson replied, offering her his hand. Sammi hadn't even realized how brisk the December air was.

Sammi hesitantly took Johnson's hand and he led her

downstairs to the kitchen. They walked over to the large island and Johnson pulled a stool out for Sammi to sit down before he picked up his cellphone and ordered a pizza. Then he sat next to Sammi to wait for the food in total awkwardness. The two of them were quiet at first, both lost in their own thoughts about the uncomfortable situation they had found themselves in.

"So, who is he?" Johnson finally broke the silence. There was no need to specify who he meant.

"Believe it or not, he's the idiot who shot me instead of you," Sammi told him.

"That's your boyfriend? Do you think maybe he missed me on purpose?"

"Definitely not. He's not dumb enough to kill me. No one else on the team can plan a heist like I can."

"So, you do this type of thing a lot?"

"Like I said, I'm always getting into trouble," Sammi taunted then quickly got up and walked over to the window in the adjoining living room.

Sammi didn't like talking about herself at all, especially with a stranger. It made her uncomfortable and, more than anything, it made her feel weak. As she watched the cars on the street below the apartment, she silently wished for the pizza to get there quickly so Johnson would stop asking her questions.

Johnson hesitated, but he eventually joined Sammi by the window. It was obvious that something had upset her, but he didn't know how to ask. He had never been good with feelings and communication, which he always thought made him a good cop. But it also made him a bad husband.

"You know, I'm really starting to think I should turn you in," Johnson teased, trying to keep the mood light.

"I don't believe you would, not even if I walked out of here right now," Sammi challenged him.

"Oh really? And why is that?"

"Because you didn't notice me at the mall for looking suspicious."

"Touché."

Sammi knew she had made Johnson uncomfortable this time because his voice got quieter and he took a casual step away from her. She wanted to take advantage of his moment of vulnerability, but there was a knock on the door and Johnson hurried over to retrieve the pizza. Sammi slowly returned to the island to join Johnson for a silent meal together.

The awkwardness only continued after dinner as Sammi wasn't sure of Johnson's expectations for the evening and Johnson hadn't thought this far ahead.

"Is there anything else I can get for you?" Johnson asked, still playing the polite host.

"I'm okay. I'd just really like to get this night over with," Sammi told him, trying to make him feel bad about keeping her there.

"Come on, you might as well take my room again," Johnson offered as he got up and headed for the stairs.

*

Back upstairs in Johnson's room, Sammi sat on the bed while Johnson got a few things out of his closet. He was silent so Sammi looked uneasily around the room. Spotting the photo of Johnson and company, Sammi picked it up.

"Who are they?" Sammi asked, holding the frame out to show Johnson.

"That's my son, Luke, my daughter, Julia, and my wife, Lori," Johnson said, sitting next to Sammi and taking the framed photo out of her hand.

"You're married?" Sammi asked, surprised.

"Separated. I haven't signed the final divorce papers yet."

"And she has?"

"Yeah, about a year ago."

"And what are you waiting for?"

"I don't like the idea of failing at a marriage."

"I can respect that. But I think it's a little late for that. You both failed. You need to move on."

"Nobody fucking asked you."

Then Johnson slammed the frame back down on the nightstand and stormed out of the room with his change of clothes. Sammi felt bad for making him so upset, but she was just trying to be honest with him. She couldn't fall asleep because she was worried about how mad she had made Johnson and because she was so out of her comfort zone being away from home. She had never had a home before Eli came along—that was the only reason she stayed with him.

Around three o'clock in the morning, Sammi couldn't take it anymore and decided she had to get out of there. Listening at the door, she didn't hear anything in the hallway, so she made her way to the stairs and stopped at the bottom to listen for any movement. The entire apartment was quiet, so she slipped out the front door, being mindful of the doormat, and figuring Johnson didn't care if she spent the night or not after cursing her out.

Chapter Three
Mr. Sensitive

When Sammi got home to the tiny apartment she shared with Eli, she found her boyfriend passed out in their bed. She kind of laughed to herself as she realized he hadn't worried about her one bit. But the exhaustion from the past forty-eight hours finally overcame her, and she gladly crawled under the blankets and instantly fell asleep next to him.

The next morning, Sammi woke up to the sound of Eli yelling and cursing. She opened her eyes without stirring and saw that he was on the phone, standing next to his side of the bed. Sammi grumbled aloud, knowing that there was no way she was getting back to sleep, and flung the blankets off her body. She shot out of bed and headed out into the kitchen.

After grabbing an energy drink out of the fridge, Sammi sat down at the wobbly little table in the kitchen. Enjoying the peaceful moment to herself, she wondered why Eli hadn't gotten them a bigger or nicer place to live by this point; she knew they could afford it. But as Eli sauntered into the kitchen and leaned against the doorway, Sammi completely forgot what she was thinking about.

Eli was unreasonably attractive, with long chestnut hair

that had grown just past the collar of his shirts. When he looked at Sammi with his sea-green eyes, she always felt like he was looking straight into her soul. He came across as a rugged man with his baggier style and the fact that he was built like a hockey player, but he had the sweetest, softest smile that put Sammi at ease and made her feel safer than she had ever felt in her entire life. It was when that smile faded that he wasn't the man Sammi loved.

"I thought you were arrested," Eli smirked.

"I've never been arrested," Sammi responded, full of sass. "Who was on the phone?"

"Howard. The robbery was covered on the morning news. They only got good descriptions of Shay and Kodi, so they're going to lay low for a while."

"What about the money? I'm assuming Kodi got away with it. Did you guys split it?"

"Yeah, I already put your share in your bank account."

"Awesome. Thanks!"

Happy to have her money and even happier for being able to avoid the topic of her whereabouts for the past twenty-four hours, Sammi got up from the table and grabbed her favorite black travel mug out of the cabinet above the sink. She got some ice out of the freezer and put it in the cup before adding what was left over in her can of Monster Energy Zero Ultra. Lost in her own thoughts of how she wanted to spend some of her latest income, she didn't notice that Eli wasn't moving as he kept his gaze on her.

Travel mug in hand, Sammi was ready to get dressed and start her day. She headed for the bedroom, but Eli intentionally blocked the doorway with his body.

"So, where were you?" Eli asked, burning a hole through her with his eyes.

"The hospital," Sammi lied casually.

"Why didn't Johnson turn you in?"

"How would I know?"

23

"You're wearing his shirt."

Shit! Sammi looked down and her face fell as she realized that she was still wearing the clothes Johnson had given her. She suddenly felt extremely exposed and pushed past Eli, rushing into the bedroom closet to change.

"Answer the question," Eli snarled.

He had followed Sammi and was now standing right outside of the narrow opening to the walk-in closet with his arms crossed in front of his chest. Sammi knew she had screwed up and was beginning to panic over her careless mistake.

"He didn't turn us in because you guys got away with the money," Sammi explained, trying to sound calm as she changed into a pair of jeans and a grey tank top.

"So now you're buddy-buddy with cop boy?"

"No! Look, Eli, he just took me to the hospital because I was shot twice. Once by you, in case you've forgotten."

"That's true. I'm sorry. Can I see it?"

The rage in Eli's eyes had disappeared so Sammi started to relax. She slowly rolled up the bottom of her tank top to reveal the worse of her two bullet wounds. Eli's eyes widened as he stared at the gory injury and approached his girlfriend. He stood next to her on the side of the wound and wrapped one arm around her waist from behind. Resting his head on her shoulder, he gently placed his free hand over her stitches.

Without warning, Eli dug two fingers into the wound and ripped the stitches out all at once. Sammi shrieked in pain and tried to push him away, but his other arm was still hooked around her waist and keeping her in place. Blinded by the unbelievable agony, Sammi fainted and her limp body fell against Eli's chest.

"You didn't go to the fucking hospital," Eli growled in Sammi's ear as she began to come to. Then he dragged her somewhat conscious body out of the closet and tossed her onto the bed.

"Get off of me!" Sammi screamed through the excess saliva in her throat as Eli climbed on top of her.

"Shut up!" Eli hollered and punched her hard in the face, his left fist connecting with her right eye socket.

Dazed, Sammi lay there whimpering, her mind on the now gaping wound on her side. It was wet and sticky with the blood flowing from the torn flesh. Sick from the picture in her imagination and the true pain of it, Sammi rolled over onto her side and vomited onto the comforter.

Eli forced Sammi onto her back again and she could feel his large, rough hands on her side. It took her a minute to realize that he was re-stitching her gunshot wound. She stopped fighting but continued whimpering as tears rolled down her face in rivers.

"Those stitches were done by an amateur. You didn't go to no fucking hospital," Eli grunted as he finished bandaging up the new stitches.

By this point, Sammi knew that nothing she said was going to help her. She rolled over onto her side, away from Eli and away from her puke, but Eli lied down next to her and held her in his arms as her entire body convulsed with her heavy sobs.

"I'm sorry, baby, but you know how jealous I get. Just tell me what happened," Eli said calmly, gently pushing Sammi's hair behind her ear.

Sammi hesitated. She was going to seal her fate no matter what she told him. Growing impatient, Eli gave her hair a quick tug to hurry her up.

"I...I woke up in the cop's apartment, he made sure that my wounds stopped bleeding, and I tried to leave. But he had seen my bruises and made me agree to spend the night away from you," Sammi explained, still choking on tears.

"So, he saw you naked?" Eli asked, his voice deep with anger from already knowing the answer to his question.

"I guess," Sammi whispered, her voice shaking from fear.

Eli's grip tightened on her hair and he yanked her head back, forcing Sammi to look at him. Sammi didn't fight him but tried to hold some composure, telling herself that he wasn't going to kill her.

"Did he touch you?" Eli hissed, his face as close to Sammi's as possible without touching.

"I don't know. I wasn't conscious," Sammi told him through gritted teeth.

Suddenly, Eli's body was vibrating with rage and Sammi couldn't find the man she loved in his own eyes anymore. Before things could escalate, there was a knock on the apartment door. Eli broke free from his fury and shoved Sammi away from him.

"You're pathetic. Go clean yourself up," Eli snapped and went to answer the door.

*

Sammi lay still for a minute, gathering herself, then dragged herself off the bed and stumbled into the bathroom. One look in the mirror and she crumpled to the floor, sobbing. Her face was puffy from crying, which only accentuated her brand new, shiny black eye. Eli had never hit her face before; he knew better. Things had gone too far this time and Sammi finally feared for her life.

When Sammi was able to finally stop crying, she grabbed onto the sink and pulled herself back onto her feet. She turned the shower on as hot as it would go and waited for it to heat up. Before undressing, she spotted her shoes from the previous day out of the corner of her eye. Tucked inside her left boot was the card Mack Johnson had given her with his phone number on it.

Sammi went back into the bedroom, keeping an eye out for Eli, and grabbed her cellphone from the nightstand before locking herself in the bathroom. It took her awhile to be able to dial the number as her hands were shaking so violently.

"This is Lieutenant Johnson," the police officer answered, and was greeted by a sigh of relief.

"Johnson? It's...it's Samantha," Sammi choked out. She hadn't even realized she was crying again.

"Sammi? What's wrong? Are you okay?"

Sammi paused and thought about what she was doing. There was no way this was a good idea. Somebody that she cared about was going to get hurt if Johnson showed up at the apartment.

"Sammi, are you in danger?" Johnson tried again.

"I'm fine. I'm sorry, I shouldn't have called," Sammi told him, trying to make herself sound calm.

"I will be right there," Johnson replied. He spoke slowly so that Sammi would understand, hoping his words eased her fear.

Before Sammi could tell Johnson not to come, he had hung up. Wanting to be ready to run when he arrived, Sammi turned off the shower and then locked herself in the closet to gather a few things. It wasn't even two minutes later before Eli kicked in the closet door.

"Who the fuck were you just talking to?" Eli screamed at the scared girl on the floor of the closet.

"No one!" Sammi yelled back at him and tried darting past him to get herself out of the closet.

But Eli had found Johnson's card on the bathroom sink and was now holding it up for Sammi to look at. She ducked under his raised arm, but he was faster and managed to grab a fistful of her hair. Caught by surprise, Sammi fell backwards and Eli wasn't able to catch her before she hit the floor. Eli knelt on the floor over his girlfriend and wrapped both large hands around her slender neck.

"You think you can just have me arrested and then go live happily ever after with your new cop buddy?" Eli grunted as he started squeezing. "Well, you're wrong! You're mine and you'll die before I ever give you up!"

Spit flew from Eli's lips as he taunted his helpless girlfriend. Sammi made a desperate attempt to pry Eli's hands from her neck but she couldn't even get her own hands around his massive, muscular wrists. Eli continued to tighten his grip even after Sammi stopped struggling, but he hardly noticed when she finally blacked out.

Chapter Four
Home Movies

Four years previously, Sammi had just arrived at an underground bar in New York City with her best friend, Kodi. They had just been evicted from their shithole apartment and were looking to drink their misery away. They sat at the bar and each ordered their drink of choice as every head in the joint turned to look at the stunning blonde with her endlessly long hair tied up in a high, tight ponytail. Her piercing blue eyes shot ice crystals into the heart of every man she caught staring. Kodi, also a blonde, was just as gorgeous as her counterpart, but she wasn't comfortable flaunting it and tended to keep her head down around people she didn't know.

Kodi and Sammi had been friends since grade school, growing up together with limited adult guidance. Sammi's father had left her mother before she was even born, and her mother spent all her time chasing the attention of men. Kodi's mother had died when Kodi was just four years old, and her father had become a full-time alcoholic. The two friends relied on each other for everything, whether it be money for food in order to survive or the support and understanding that they had never received from their parental figures.

Sammi was still sipping on her first drink about twenty minutes later when she saw him walk through the door. He was laughing with a group of friends, but he stopped as soon as his gaze met Sammi's. Unable to look away, he broke free from his herd and made his way directly over to the breathtaking blonde, who smiled as the handsome stranger took a seat next to her.

"Hi, I'm Eli. May I steal your attention for a bit?" Mr. Gorgeous said with the sweetest smile.

"My name's Sammi and I drink tequila," Sammi responded, exuding confidence.

"Fair enough," Eli laughed and ordered two shots of Patrón.

As he talked to Sammi, Eli learned quickly that she was not particularly seeking his attention. She showed just enough interest in him to keep him next to her, but she brushed off all his advances, which was unlike every other girl he had ever met in a bar before. Intrigued, he wanted nothing more than to keep this mythical creature in his life.

An hour later, Kodi was annoyed with her best friend for ignoring her all night and finally pulled Sammi away from her new suitor. She'd only been able to buy one drink and she didn't have attractive men buying shots for her like Sammi did. Although the mechanics of the evening were typical, the guy was not. Most guys who were even brave enough to sit next to Sammi usually burned out with their small talk and walked away within minutes with their tails tucked between their legs. Kodi had never seen anyone even make it to a second round of drinks with Sammi.

The bar was small and crowded so the girls had to elbow their way through people to get to the tiny one-stall bathroom in the back. The stall was occupied so the girls waited for the woman to finish and vacate the room before speaking.

"Who is that guy and when can we leave?" Kodi asked, very aware of how much she sounded like a bratty little kid.

"His name is Eli and he might be the answer to all our problems," Sammi told her best friend with confidence.

"Should I even ask?" Kodi replied with caution.

"He said we could stay with him for a while and he has a way for us to never have to worry about money again," Sammi explained.

"I don't like the sound of this, Sammi. Can't we just get out of here?"

"And go where? We're homeless, remember? We don't really have any other choices right now."

And Sammi was right; they didn't have another choice. So that night, Eli led the two pretty girls to his tiny apartment that he already shared with his sister and her boyfriend. This would be the same apartment where Sammi would suffer this near-death flashback.

*

Kodi had been right to have reservations about Eli, as it only took two weeks for the newly formed group of friends to pull off their first small robbery. Sammi dove right into the new lifestyle and proved to have a skill for planning flawless heists. She enjoyed the feeling of being good at something for once in her life and chose to ignore Kodi's lack of enthusiasm for breaking the law, or maybe it was just a distrust of Eli and his followers.

Unfortunately, Kodi had taken a bit of a backseat to Eli anyway as Sammi and Eli became grossly inseparable. The girls were still best friends and Kodi would never turn her back on Sammi, but Sammi was in love for the first time in her life and Eli was the center of her world. Eventually, the lovebirds wanted their alone time and the team had made enough money for everyone else to move out.

It wasn't until the others had moved out that Eli took Sammi out on a real first date. He took her to a tiny, unassuming Italian restaurant located off the beaten path on the outskirts of New York City. Sammi found Eli's choice of date a little strange because they were the only two customers in the place, and Sammi had never shown a fondness for Italian food.

About halfway through their meal, a single older gentleman arrived and sat at a table behind Sammi and Eli, facing the front window. The rather tall man placed his order in a hushed, impatient tone, keeping his head down but his presence known. Sammi made a joke about him being in the mob, but Eli didn't laugh.

"Come on, I want to introduce you," Eli said, somewhat business-like with a hint of nerves as he stood up from the table after they had finished eating.

Sammi's eyes were unusually wide with confusion as she also stood up and proceeded to take her boyfriend's extended hand. Eli led her over to the only other occupied table and stopped in front of the intimidating man. Sammi clung to her lover's arm, attempting to disappear behind him.

"Mr. Nardino, this is Sammi, the one I've been telling you about," Eli said, trying to bring his girlfriend forward.

"Hello, Sammi, it's nice to meet you," Nardino responded, placing his silverware down on his plate and offering a hand out to Sammi.

Sammi shook the man's hand out of politeness, but she remained silent. Eli had never mentioned this man to her before.

"Sammi, this is Frank Nardino. He has a lot of connections and may be able to benefit our work," Eli finished the introductions.

Sammi still didn't have anything to say. She found it a little forward of Eli to be telling people about their 'work.' And there wasn't a single aspect of Mr. Nardino that screamed 'trustworthy.'

Eli was clearly annoyed at his girlfriend for being rude by

not speaking as he ushered Sammi along and told her to wait outside for him. Sammi started to leave the restaurant but ducked behind a half-wall at the front of the restaurant to hear what other incriminating information Eli was sharing with this man.

"Sorry about that," Eli tried shrugging off his embarrassment, visibly desperate to impress this man.

"No worries. I wouldn't mind a date with that, if you know what I mean," Nardino replied, straight-faced.

Eli nodded with a smirk while Sammi's entire face reddened and burned from within. Before the two men could continue with their crude conversation, a swarm of cops burst through the front door led by their highest ranking. All guns were raised in the direction of Eli and Nardino. Eli put his hands up in surrender, but Nardino sat back in his chair and raised an eyebrow at the head cop.

"Frank Nardino, you are under arrest," the policeman announced as he pushed past Eli and grabbed Nardino up by his arm.

"What are the charges, Sarge?" Nardino spat at him, seemingly familiar with this particular officer.

"Being an all-around scumbag," the Sergeant shot right back at him.

A few cops laughed at their leader's smart-mouth wit as they cleared a path for him to bring their suspect through. The Sergeant recited Nardino's rights and listed his charges of burglary, arson, rape, and murder as he walked him out of the building. As they passed Sammi's hiding place, both men made eye contact with her. She quickly looked away and caught a glimpse of the cop's name badge: Sgt. Johnson.

*

Back at their apartment, Eli sat down in front of the television without a word so Sammi stormed into the bedroom and slammed the door behind her. They hadn't spoken a single word to each other since they left the restaurant and neither understood why the other was mad.

Sammi couldn't let go of the way Nardino had talked about her and how Eli had allowed him. She had never told Eli, but her mom's boyfriends had shown inappropriate interest in her since she had turned thirteen years old up until she ran away at seventeen. Her mother had pretended not to know what was going on in her daughter's bedroom while her boyfriend of the month was supposed to be 'helping Sammi with homework' or 'teaching her how to play guitar.' When Sammi tried to reach out for help, her mother blamed her for being too pretty. Sammi had spent years burying this trauma and refusing to allow a man to have any kind of control over her. Eli was the first man who had been able to break through a layer of her emotionally scarred walls.

Having struggled with these emotions before, Sammi knew just how to block out the images inside her head. She slipped into the shower and let the steaming hot water flow over her trembling body. Without dwelling on it, she took a blade out of Eli's razor and pressed it to her wrist. The sharp edge stung as it bit into her milky pale flesh. She stared absentmindedly at the contrasting dark red sneaking out from under her skin in thick droplets. She kept her unblinking eyes on her wrist as she made another cut, this one just a little deeper.

It was peacefulness that washed over Sammi as she watched her blood mix with the shower water and creep down the drain. She released a heavy sigh, reveling in this feeling of control.

By this point, Eli had entered the bedroom only to hear deep sobs coming from the bathroom. He let himself in, calling out to his girlfriend and asking if she was okay. He could see her outline through the shower curtain, and she seemed to be hunched slightly forward, holding one of her arms with the other. After three attempts to check on her went ignored, he threw back the curtain and froze.

The floor of the shower was covered in blood and there were a few splatters of it up the walls. Eli could see that it was coming from the arm that Sammi was holding, but he couldn't understand why. After a few seconds, the water became clearer and Eli finally saw the razorblade on the shower floor.

Having put the scene together, Eli jumped into action and pulled his girlfriend out of the shower, sitting on the floor with her in his lap. He reached up and grabbed a towel off the rack and wrapped it tightly around Sammi's arm, making sure to apply pressure to the two deep gashes. Sammi still wasn't responding to him and hadn't even looked at him.

Eli, beginning to freak out, stood up with Sammi in his arms and carried her out to the bedroom. He placed her on the bed, keeping her propped up on the pillows, and removed the towel to look at the damage. There were two cuts, one on top of another, horizontal across her wrist. The cut further up her arm was noticeably deeper than the other, but Eli didn't think that either of them needed medical attention, and he knew that there would be a lot of questions asked at the hospital that he wouldn't be able to answer. He quickly grabbed some gauze and medical tape from the bathroom and carefully bandaged the wounds.

Sammi watched Eli's every move from her throne of pillows, hardly blinking, and still not speaking. As she inspected Eli's bandage job, Eli continued to ask her if she was okay. She could hear him, but she couldn't break free from the heavy haze weighing down on her and preventing her from putting words together.

Eli had never seen this side of Sammi and was starting to question their entire relationship. Frustrated, he finally gave up and slapped his girlfriend as hard as he could across her face. Tears welled up in her already puffy eyes from the sting of his hand. But it worked and Sammi finally snapped out of it, throwing her arms around her boyfriend's neck, and crying hysterically as she apologized over and over again. Eli held her while she wept and pet her hair to try to calm her down. But he was secretly reveling in this new feeling of control.

Chapter Five
Goodbye to the Girl

Eli was still choking the life out of his girlfriend when there was a loud pounding on the apartment door. He didn't need to hear the voice calling in to him to know that it was Johnson. If he was going to lose Sammi, he was going to lose her on his own terms. So, he ignored the heavy knocking and continued to squeeze the fragile neck in his hands. Sammi had been unconscious for almost two minutes now and Eli could feel her pulse slowing.

Suddenly there was a loud crashing sound from the front of the apartment: the apartment door hitting the floor. Eli knew Johnson would be on him any second, but he didn't need too much longer. As soon as he felt Sammi's pulse disappear, he released her throat and heard a gun being cocked behind him.

"Police! Freeze!" Mack Johnson yelled with his gun aimed at the back of Eli's head. Eli was laughing as he placed his hands behind his head in surrender.

"Now neither of us can have her." Eli continued laughing. He stood up, hands still behind his head, and turned around to face the arresting officer.

When Johnson let his guard down to look at Sammi's body, Eli dove behind the bed and grabbed his handgun out from under the mattress. He checked the magazine and made sure the Glock 19 was fully loaded. Then he army-crawled under the bed and positioned himself where he could get a clear shot in the direction of the meddlesome detective.

"Give it up, Eli! You're under arrest," Johnson said, his voice shaking with emotion. He held his gun out in front of him as he walked around the bed. Before he could even realize that Eli wasn't there, Eli fired a shot from under the bed.

This time, Eli's aim was spot-on, and Johnson's left kneecap shattered right in front of his eyes. Johnson hollered in pain as he fell forward but was able to get his right knee under himself to catch his weight. Eli rolled out from under the bed and took off running without looking back. Johnson fired several shots after him, but he was gone.

Being an on-duty detective, Johnson was wearing black dress pants and a black blazer with a light blue dress shirt and dark blue tie. His badge and his radio were on his belt along with his empty gun holster. He struggled to get his radio free, fighting against the blinding pain in his left leg. When he finally wrestled the radio free from his belt, he radioed for medical help and reported Eliot Krik as a suspect on the run. Then he dragged himself over to Sammi's unmoving body to check for a pulse. He choked back tears as he examined the extent of her newest injuries. Unable to find a pulse, he began chest compressions on Sammi while waiting for help to arrive.

When medics finally arrived on the scene, two of them rushed over to Sammi while another two tended to the detective. Unable to detect any vital signs on the female victim, they declared a time of death. Then all hands were on Johnson and his gunshot wound, which was bleeding profusely, and fragments of broken bone were exposed through the flesh of his knee. But Johnson was not cooperating, and was instead trying to continue compressions on Sammi.

"Officer! You have to let us help you!" one of the paramedics cried out in frustration.

"It's Lieutenant! And I need you to help her!" Johnson fired back, hysterical.

Upon Johnson's insistence, the EMTs abandoned protocol and treated Sammi's body as critical condition and rushed her to an ambulance. Two of them remained with Lieutenant Johnson and got him into a second ambulance. They were all concerned about the possibility of him losing part of his leg, but no one verbalized it. Johnson's one and only care at the moment was Sammi.

*

On the other side of the city, a disheveled Eli frantically pounded on an apartment door in a dark hallway. It was the middle of the day and Eli had just come from the sunny streets, so the darkness was manipulating. Eli repeatedly looked to either side of him while he kept his gun tucked under his unbuttoned blue flannel shirt. Eventually the door opened, and Eli threw himself into the apartment, quickly closing the door behind him.

"I fucked up," Eli said without prompt, leaning his back against the door as if it were the only thing holding him up. Shay and Howard looked at him in bewilderment. "Sammi's dead."

"What...did you do?" Shay asked, trying to remain calm. She had always known that her brother had a temper, but he had never done anything to hurt anyone he cared about.

"She was going to leave me for that cop from the other night," Eli told her, expecting that brief statement to explain everything.

"How in the hell?" Howard wondered aloud about the entire situation.

"I don't understand. How do they even know each other?"

Shay asked.

"They didn't, not until that night." Eli now had his hands in his hair that fell forward over his face, trying to wrap his own head around how everything had played out.

"Oh, you mean after you shot her and left her to die while you ran away?" Howard finally called him out. That night at the mall had been weighing heavy on him.

"It was an accident! And I didn't see you sticking around to help her!" Eli yelled.

"You shot Sammi?" Shay asked her brother, getting louder to match the men's tones. She was also annoyed that nobody had told her prior to this.

"I was aiming for the fucking cop! And she lived! She was fine!"

"Then why did you just tell us she's dead?" Shay started to get control of the situation again.

"I...I had my hands around her neck and...I just couldn't stop," Eli stuttered through his confession. He slid down the door and sat on the floor with his head in his hands. "I just didn't want to lose her."

While Shay comforted her brother, Howard packed a quick bag with some of his clothes for Eli to take on the run. He was thinner than Eli, so he did his best to gather his baggier items. Then he went into the bottom drawer of his nightstand, grabbed a stack of cash and a fully loaded Berretta pistol, and tucked them carefully into the bag.

"Here, man, this should be enough to get you to the hideout," Howard said, dropping the bag in front of Eli. He was angry that Sammi was dead, but Eli was still a part of their team.

"Call us when you get there," Shay said as she and Eli stood up and stepped back from the door. "We'll figure something out."

Eli tucked his Glock into his waistband, shouldered the duffel bag of getaway gear, and hugged his sister. Then he quietly slipped out of the apartment and disappeared into the crowded city alone.

Chapter Six
Heartbeat

When Sammi woke up, everything was bright. Her throat was burning, and it pained her to swallow, but she was comfortably propped up on pillows in a warm hospital bed. Mack Johnson was standing in the doorway to her room, talking to a doctor. He was on crutches.

Sammi remembered the fear of Eli trying to kill her clear as day. And she remembered calling the detective out of desperation. But she couldn't remember anything after that.

Feeling embarrassed, Sammi didn't want to see or talk to anybody. The doctor and the detective had stepped away from the door so Sammi quietly crept out of bed and slid into the small bathroom, closing the door behind her. She took one look in the mirror and suddenly felt small and helpless. Her face was swollen and bruised, and her neck was completely black and purple. She couldn't bear to look at herself anymore, so she sat on the floor of the bathroom and cried quietly to herself until a doctor came into the room looking for her.

"Miss Reilly?" the young doctor called through the bathroom door.

Unable to speak, Sammi emerged from the bathroom

without a word and let handsome Dr. Sicar help her back into bed. The doctor updated Sammi's chart and made sure she was comfortable before leaving her in peace. Almost as soon as he had left, there was a familiar face in the doorway again.

"Mack?" Sammi questioned quietly. Her throat was dry, and her voice was hoarse.

"Hey, you're awake." Mack smiled as he hobbled over to Sammi's bedside and offered her a cup of water.

"Are you okay?" Sammi asked, keeping her voice faint to avoid straining it anymore as she took the tiny plastic cup from Mack and took one small sip. The intruding liquid set her throat on fire and she shoved the cup back into Mack's hands as tears of pain rolled out of her eyes.

"I'm on my feet, aren't I?" Mack chuckled. "You, on the other hand, almost died. Your throat is severely bruised and swollen so you're going to want to keep this conversation short. But you're safe now."

"I'm so sorry I ever got you involved," Sammi said, still quiet as she looked down and away from Mack. Mack put his hand over Sammi's and gave it a quick squeeze.

"It's my job, remember? Besides, it's just my leg. I'll be fine."

"What happened with...?" Sammi couldn't bring herself to say Eli's name.

"He got away after he shot me. But don't worry, we'll get him."

Sammi nodded and continued to avoid eye contact. She was in too much pain to keep talking and just wanted to rest her eyes. Seeing her eyelids beginning to droop, Mack knew he had to let her sleep.

"I hate to say I told you so, but I told you so," Mack said warmly with a smile. Then he leaned forward and pressed his lips to Sammi's forehead before leaving the room.

*

Sammi was released from the hospital two days later with prescription antibiotics and steroids. It was still difficult for her to swallow but talking was becoming less painful. Mack had hardly left her side, but no one else had come to see her.

Mack had convinced his Captain to hold off on getting Sammi's statement until she was released. He wanted to give her time for her throat to heal and time to sort out her thoughts and feelings before bombarding her with personal questions about her relationship with Eli. Besides, they had more than enough to go off of with Mack's account of what happened, and statements collected from neighbors who had heard the commotion the day Eli had snapped.

As soon as Sammi's discharge papers were signed, Mack rolled her in the obligatory wheelchair outside to where his unmarked squad car was parked. He had been pushing through his physical therapy for his leg and this was his first day without crutches, but he was still wearing a boot all the way up to his thigh to keep his reconstructed knee from moving out of place. He helped Sammi into the passenger seat before getting behind the wheel and driving them to his precinct.

Sammi was silent in the cop car on the drive over. She was nervous about going to a place swarming with cops while having such a strong criminal history. But she looked over at Mack and was somewhat relaxed by his calm, collected composure.

At the precinct, Mack had Sammi wait at his desk while he went to speak with his Captain. Sammi sat in his chair and looked at the cluttered mess on top of his desk. There were empty cigarette cartons and unorganized paperwork scattered everywhere. For a reason that she couldn't explain, this made her feel warmth towards Mack. But then she saw the same framed photograph from his bedroom and was reminded that he was a married man. Suddenly she didn't feel so warm anymore.

Mack returned a few moments later and led Sammi to his Captain's office. Sammi sat across from the Captain at his desk while Mack stood guard by the door behind her. Captain Tyler Hobbs was a tall, lean man in his early fifties. He had golden blonde hair, which was the same color as his unfortunate paint-brush mustache. Sammi couldn't stop staring at the soft bristles on his upper lip as they jumped about when he spoke. He asked her about Eli's abusive behavior, and she told him as much as she remembered from the attempted homicide.

"Thank you, Miss Reilly. I'll get this written up and filed and then a uniform will take you to where you're staying," Hobbs said once he was satisfied with Sammi's statement. "We haven't found Mr. Krik, but we will."

"I don't have anywhere to go," Sammi said quietly to Mack as she squirmed nervously to look at him. Mack shot a pleading look at his boss in a hurry.

"We would actually feel better if you spent the night here tonight. There's a bed in the officer's lounge that we use for situations just like this. We have resources here to help you find a place all your own," Hobbs offered, hinting that he knew a little bit more about Sammi's situation than she had provided. "A uniform will be available in the morning to escort you to your old apartment to collect your things."

"I'm on call tonight," Mack quickly added, "I'll keep you company and help with the apartment search."

Sammi nodded and stood up, leading Captain Hobbs to do the same. Hobbs and Sammi shook hands before Sammi turned and followed Mack out of the office. Mack led the way up a flight of stairs and into the first room on the left where they spent four hours researching dozens of available apartments. As soon as it got dark outside, Sammi couldn't focus on anything other than the insides of her eyelids, so they called it a night and retired to the officer's lounge.

*

The officer's lounge was quite spacious but was hardly being used to its full potential. There was a ratty old couch and an even older television set in the center and a coffee maker and refrigerator along the one wall. And in the far corner was a small cot that looked anything but comfortable.

Mack put a sign on the door that read "OVERNIGHT" and locked the door to keep his coworkers out while Sammi walked over and sat on the bed. She pushed on the thin mattress, wondering how on earth she was going to be able to sleep. But before she could dwell on it for too long, Mack joined her, sitting next to her on the bed.

"Here, you need to take these," Mack said as he pulled two prescription pill bottles out of the pocket of his tan cargo pants. One medication was a steroid for the swelling in her neck and the other was an antibiotic for her now properly treated gunshot wounds.

"Why are you doing this?" Sammi asked, taking the bottles from him.

"Doing what?" Mack turned his back to her as he stood up and went to get her a glass of water.

"Why are you helping me?"

"Honestly, I feel responsible for everything that has happened since I shot you at the mall."

"I'm the only one to blame for my bad decisions. But I appreciate everything you've done for me."

Mack handed Sammi the glass of water without saying anything. Taking her medications, Sammi shifted uncomfortably on the bed. Her thoughts returned to trying to figure out how she was going to fall asleep.

"Come on, let's get you settled," Mack said, beginning to unfold the clean sheets at the foot of the bed. There was no longer any warmth in his tone, and he wouldn't look at Sammi.

"I'm not going to be able to sleep," Sammi replied quietly as she helped him finish making the bed. She suddenly felt like a burden under his cold demeanor and was afraid to upset this man any further.

"Just lie down. One of these is supposed to cause drowsiness," Mack told her and pretended to read the prescription labels on the bottles he had picked up off the floor where Sammi had left them.

Sammi did what was asked of her and got into bed, sliding under the blankets. As soon as her head touched the pillow, she realized her eyelids were heavy. Mack sat on the edge of the bed and turned his body toward her.

"Okay, you win. I'm sleepy," Sammi said, struggling to keep her eyes open. Mack chuckled, warming back up.

"I like you," he said calmly as he reached over and gently pushed a strand of Sammi's golden hair behind her ear.

"Will you be here when I wake up?" Sammi asked through a yawn.

"I'm not going anywhere."

Mack smiled down on the girl that gave him indescribable feelings as she drifted off to sleep. Then he pressed his lips to her forehead before settling in on the couch in front of the television set for a long night of watching over his injured little dove.

*

By the time Sammi woke up the next day, the sun had already come up. She sat up to look around the room for Mack and giggled to herself when she saw him. He was passed out on the couch on his back with one arm hanging over the side and his mouth wide open. A steady snoring could be heard across the room.

Before Sammi could decide whether to wake up Sleeping Beauty or not, there was a knock on the door. Startled, Mack jolted awake and landed on the floor in front of the sofa. Sammi laughed harder as he groaned and picked himself up.

"Stupid couch," Mack grumbled to himself, walking over to open the door.

Mack let Captain Hobbs into the room and Sammi quickly got out of bed, feeling grossly vulnerable. Hobbs explained that a uniformed officer was going to take Sammi to her apartment to get her things and then to either a new apartment or a hotel. Sammi suddenly wished they had tried harder to find her a new apartment the day before.

"Why can't I take her to get her things?" Mack asked his boss.

"The boyfriend could be there, and I can't count on you to act rationally," Hobbs told him.

"Your faith in me is outstanding," Mack replied sarcastically.

"I'll leave you two to plan your inevitable rendezvous," Hobbs said harshly to Mack before turning to Sammi and kindly adding, "Officer Palma is waiting downstairs when you're ready."

After Hobbs exited the room, there was an awkward silence between the two emotionally stunted cohorts. Mack remained by the door and wouldn't look at Sammi while she got herself a glass of water and took her morning medications. The thought of returning to the real world with her hideously discolored neck gave her anxiety, but she didn't want to keep the police officer waiting downstairs. She had just reached the door when Mack stopped her.

"Stay with me," Mack said quickly as he caught Sammi's wrist in his hand.

"What?" Sammi was caught by surprise and wasn't quite sure what he meant.

"I have a spare bedroom. You don't have to go to a hotel," Mack replied, trying to sound casual.

"I don't think your boss likes you hanging out with me."

"He knows about the mall heist and what I did for you."

"What did you do, Johnson?"

"I took your name out of the investigation. Look, I don't want you to feel obligated to stay with me."

"No, I don't. I want to."

"Good. I'll see you in a little bit."

Mack kissed Sammi's forehead and held the door open for her. He pointed out how to get back down to the main lobby then headed in the direction of Hobbs' office. Sammi met up with Officer Palma by the front door of the precinct and he led the way outside to his patrol car.

There was silence in the car on the way to Sammi's old apartment. Officer Palma wasn't entirely familiar with the situation he had been thrown into and Sammi wasn't up for sharing with yet another stranger. She almost wished Hobbs had allowed Mack to bring her to get her things, but she also felt safer being with someone so detached from the storyline.

As Palma parked the patrol car in front of the all-too-familiar apartment building, Sammi became nauseous with anxiety. She almost died in this place and the man responsible could be waiting inside to finish the job. Before she could change her mind about even wanting her belongings, Palma was out of the car and had opened the passenger door for her.

"Don't worry, I'll clear the location before letting you in," Palma said after watching Sammi's hesitation.

"Thanks," Sammi replied quietly with her head down, still uncomfortably aware of how bad her neck looked.

Sammi followed the armed officer up to the fourth floor of the building and waited outside of her own apartment while he went in first to secure the scene. Part of Sammi already knew that Eli wasn't there. She didn't think he'd be stupid enough to go to the hideout, but he would have to be even stupider to stick around the city.

"It's all clear," Palma told Sammi, rejoining her in the hallway a few minutes later. "You can take as long as you need."

"Thanks. I won't be long," Sammi replied, looking at the floor as she let herself into the setting of her second worst nightmare.

The apartment was quieter to Sammi than ever before. Emptiness engulfed her and the feeling that this wasn't her home anymore was overwhelming. She let herself be sad as she filled one storage bin with clothes and a few trinkets. On her way out, she saw her favorite black travel mug on the edge of the kitchen counter where she had left it still holding her favorite energy drink.

In that moment of intense vulnerability, an unexplainable feeling came over Sammi that made her care more about that mug than anything else in the apartment. She gently placed her box of belongings on the kitchen table without even looking away from the mug and quickly crossed the kitchen to it. She picked up the plain and boring object and twisted off the lid. Holding it as if it were the most valuable thing she had ever owned, she poured the stale vice it contained down the drain and scrubbed it clean.

Back in the patrol car, still clutching the black mug, Sammi asked Officer Palma if he had any stickers or tape on hand. Without questioning, he handed her an NYPD logo sticker from the pocket in his car door that they usually handed out to children. Sammi immediately removed the backing and placed it neatly on her travel mug, marking this abrupt shift in her life.

"So where am I taking you?" Palma asked as he started the car.

"Mack Johnson is expecting me," Sammi nervously told him.

"So, you're the reason he spent the night at the precinct?" Palma replied.

"Well, he was already on call anyway."

"No, he wasn't. He's stuck riding the desk until his leg is

fully healed."

Sammi smiled to herself, knowing that Mack had lied to make her feel better. A short while later, Officer Palma parked the patrol car in front of Mack's apartment building and Sammi got out with her one sad, little box of belongings. She took a deep breath and headed for the door.

"Hey!" Officer Palma called through the open window of the passenger door. Sammi stopped and turned to face him. "Johnson is an asshole of a cop, but he is one of the good guys."

After Palma drove off, Sammi headed into the massive building. As soon as she reached the lobby, Mack came out of one of the elevators and they immediately made eye contact. Mack hurried over to Sammi and took the actually-not-so-heavy box from her.

"Perfect timing," Mack said, smiling at Sammi. Overwhelmed, Sammi just nodded and followed Mack back over to the elevators and up to his apartment.

Once in the apartment, Mack showed Sammi to an extra bedroom then gave her some time to make herself feel comfortable while he went downstairs to make dinner. Sammi took a whole four minutes to put her things away and then sat on the bed to finally appreciate some time alone. As her thoughts wandered to what used to be her team, she decided she had to call her best friend, wondering why Kodi hadn't reached out to her first.

Kodi was three bottles of Patrón deep when her phone rang. Too inconsolable to talk to anybody, she threw the phone across the dark bedroom. She cradled the tequila bottle in her lap as she pulled her sweatpants-clad knees to her chest. More tears rolled down her pretty porcelain face.

Earlier that day, Kodi had been visited by Howard who informed her that Eli and Sammi had gotten into a fight and that Sammi had suffered injuries she didn't recover from.

Howard was visibly upset by the incident and let it slip that Shay didn't want Kodi knowing about it. Clearly not accepted by that half of the team, Kodi asked Howard to leave so she could mourn the loss of her best friend and the only person she had had left in the world.

Kodi brought the bottle to her lips for one more swig before the liquor finally took over and helped her drift into unconsciousness. She wasn't aware of this blackout, but she would've opted to remain there if she could.

Hours later, Kodi woke up with the neck of the empty bottle still gripped in her left hand. Sunlight was pouring in through her window, momentarily blinding her and bringing attention to the throbbing pain in her skull. She groaned as she struggled to roll off the bed and immediately vomited on the floor.

Needing water—and ibuprofen, if she could find any—Kodi stumbled toward the door of the bedroom. As she reached the door, she stepped on something with her bare foot. She stopped and looked down to see her cellphone lying there so she picked it up to check her messages while proceeding to the kitchen.

There was only one new message so Kodi placed her phone on speaker and tossed it on to the counter while she got herself a glass of water.

"Hey, Kodi, I'm sorry I didn't call you sooner, but things are just now settling down. If you need me, I'm staying with Detective Johnson. I'll tell you all about *that* when I see you next. Please call me back when you can. I need my oldest friend right now."

Kodi dropped the cup in her hand, causing water, ice, and broken glass to hydroplane across her kitchen floor. She snatched her phone up off the counter and doublechecked the date and time that message came in. Confirming it was less than twelve hours old, she darted back into her bedroom, stepping on shards of glassware with her bare feet. She threw on a sweatshirt over her tank top and stuffed her bleeding feet into a pair of sneakers before rushing out of the apartment.

*

When Kodi didn't answer her call, Sammi calmly placed her phone on the bedside table and leaned back against the pillows on her bed. She wondered what Kodi could be up to and imagined her at a bar talking to her own version of Mack Johnson. Lost in this daydream, Sammi sank deeper into her pillows and her eyelids got heavy. She didn't know she had fallen asleep until Mack was gently shaking her shoulder to wake her up and tell her that dinner was ready.

The two sat at the kitchen island for dinner just as they had only a few nights prior. Sammi was distracted while they ate and kept checking her phone, hoping to at least get a text message back from Kodi. Mack was understanding and offered to take her by Kodi's place the next day if she still hadn't heard from her.

"Why are you so kind to me?" Sammi blurted out after she and Mack had finished eating dinner.

"I already told you. I like you," Mack responded quickly but without looking at her.

"Yeah, but no one has ever genuinely cared like this," Sammi said quietly, looking down at her hands.

"Hey," Mack suddenly changed his tune and turned to face Sammi, "just because Eli was a scumbag doesn't mean you deserved to be treated that way."

An incredible urge came over Sammi. Before she could change her mind, she leaned forward, placed a hand on the side of Mack's face, and softly brought her lips to his. Mack kissed her back without hesitation, but he was the first to pull away.

Mack jumped up from his seat at the island and hurriedly cleared their dirty dishes from the counter. Sammi was still sleepy from her brief nap, but she didn't want to abandon this moment with Mack, especially if it meant leaving things awkward after their first kiss. She feared that they would be right back at square one in the morning if they couldn't get past this discomfort.

"You look exhausted," Mack said in a caring tone after cleaning up. "Ready to take the rest of your meds and go to bed?"

"Do I have to?" Sammi asked.

"You don't have to do anything. Want to watch a movie?"

Sammi nodded and Mack motioned in the direction of the couch where she made herself comfortable while Mack chose a movie. When Mack joined her on the sofa, he sat at the opposite end and Sammi couldn't help but feel disappointed. She had already made a first move but Mack was being so respectful that it was painful.

Twenty minutes into the movie that neither of them were paying attention to, Sammi was struggling to keep her eyes open again. She was half asleep until she heard Mack chuckling and quickly opened her eyes to glare at him. Mack was looking at her with adoration in his eyes and warmth in his smile.

"You should probably go to bed," Mack said with another chuckle.

"But I want to spend time with you," Sammi replied bluntly, through a yawn.

"Then we'll make a deal. If you take your meds, we can go watch TV in my room."

"But I'm going to fall asleep on you."

"That's the point, silly." Mack stood up and kissed Sammi's forehead. "Meet you there in ten minutes."

Sammi followed Mack upstairs and they each went into their separate bedrooms. Thinking only about sleep at that moment, Sammi eagerly changed into a pair of sweatpants, removed her bra, and put on a baggy black t-shirt. These sudden strenuous movements made her realize how sore her side was, so she grabbed her prescription bottles and her travel mug off the nightstand and headed back downstairs. She got some water and sat down at the island, taking her time. After taking her medications, she tucked everything in the back of the counter next to the refrigerator and made her way slowly upstairs.

Mack's bedroom door was open when Sammi made it back upstairs, but she hesitated outside. She could feel the anxiety of the unknown in her chest but couldn't figure out why she cared so much. Her attitude toward men had always been one of disgust and disappointment, she never felt like she had to work to impress a man before Mack.

Taking a deep breath, Sammi entered Mack's room. Mack was standing in front of the large television and playing with the remote to find a movie. He was wearing just a pair of grey sweatpants and Sammi's anxiety tripled at the sight of him and his smooth, shirtless body. Without even turning around, he told her to go ahead and make herself comfortable.

"How does he do that?" Sammi whispered almost inaudibly to herself.

Feeling out of place, Sammi sat on the bed on top of the blankets, closer to the door. Mack finished with the TV and walked over to the same side of the bed. He asked Sammi to scoot over and slid under the blankets next to her. Sammi scooted to the other side of the bed and lay down, pulling the blankets over herself. Mack hooked an arm around her waist, careful not to bump her injury, and pulled her against his warm body. She tucked her head under his chin and rested it on his chest.

"Are you comfortable?" Mack whispered. Sammi only mumbled in response, already more asleep than she was awake.

Chapter Seven
Kiss & Tell

Sammi woke up the next morning to find Mack already awake and quietly watching her sleep. She was still in his arms, so she tilted her head up and kissed the side of his face. Mack smiled and rolled all of his weight to one arm, so he was holding himself up over top of Sammi. Then his lips were on hers as he ran his free hand up her back underneath her shirt. Sammi kissed him back, holding onto his perfectly toned waistline.

The two new lovebirds lost track of time and kissed for nearly an hour before finally making their way downstairs for breakfast. Sammi was late for taking her medications and she could feel the scratchy, burning pain growing in her throat. She quickly swallowed the meds with an entire glass of ice-cold water, hoping the pain would subside by the time Mack finished cooking their omelets.

"So, uh, what do you do for work?" Mack asked cautiously over breakfast.

"You're kidding, right?" Sammi scoffed. "I'm a thief." She put down her fork and turned to look at the cop sitting next to her, challenging him to question her.

"Right..." Mack avoided eye contact by staring intently at his plate of almost untouched omelet.

"Look, I don't need to steal anymore; I'm pretty set on money and could get a little, menial job if it makes you feel better. But I am a thief and if my past bothers you, I can leave. I don't want you to have to live with the guilt of my poor choices."

"I'm sick of being called a hero but never getting what I want. You're the first thing I've wanted in quite some time. I want you to stay." Mack finally looked at Sammi with adoration in his eyes.

"Then I'm all yours," Sammi responded with the warmest smile Mack had ever seen.

Mack leaned in and gently placed his right hand on the side of Sammi's soft face. Sammi flinched and Mack immediately pulled away with a look of confusion mixed with concern upon his face. Before he could ask her what was wrong, her cellphone started ringing and she leapt up out of her seat to answer it.

*

Thirty minutes after rushing out of her apartment on the other side of the city, a mess of a beautiful blonde put all her strength behind her fist as she pounded on an apartment door in an ominously dark hallway. The door flew open and Kodi almost fell forward into the familiar apartment but caught herself on the doorframe.

Howard and Shay stepped back from the door and took in the sight in front of them. Kodi had mascara and eyeliner streaks halfway down her face. Her long blonde hair, which appeared to have once been held up in a bun, hung chaotically from a loose scrunchie on the back of her head. And there was blood seeping slowly through her all-white sneakers.

"Oh, my God, are you okay?" Shay asked, focusing on the

almost unnoticeable bloody shoe prints. But Kodi wasn't acknowledging her and, instead, wouldn't break eye contact with Howard.

"Why did you tell me she was dead?!" Kodi shrieked as she lunged for Howard. She grabbed him by the shirt and clung to him as she put her face directly in front of his.

Shay hurried over and peeled the broken girl off of her boyfriend then stood between them, trying to figure out what was going on. She and Howard had been moments away from leaving to join Eli at their hideout and their packed bags were on the floor behind Howard. And as far as Shay knew, Kodi wasn't supposed to know about any of this.

"What are you talking about?!" Howard yelled back at Kodi, assuming she had gone crazy with grief.

"You came into my home and you told me that my best friend was dead! Why? Were you hoping I would just kill myself so you wouldn't have to deal with me anymore?" Kodi was screaming and still trying to get at Howard but Shay was blocking for him.

"Kodi, I'm sorry, but Sammi is dead. Eli was there and would know better than any of us," Shay remained calm as she attempted to talk Kodi down.

"I don't know what Eli told you, but I do know that you're trying to cover something up for him." Kodi was quieter now, but there was fury in her eyes. Then she saw the luggage on the floor. "You're going to see him, aren't you?"

"I still don't understand. Why would Eli say he killed her if he didn't?" Shay said mostly to herself.

"Eli is not going to get away with this," Kodi hissed and began slowly backing out of the apartment.

Before she could make it to the open door, Shay had grabbed the handgun from Howard's waistband and aimed it at Kodi's face.

"I don't know what you know, but Eli is my brother and I won't let him go to jail."

Shay had become a different person with nothing but darkness in her eyes. She cocked the hammer back on the gun as she gave in to her desperation.

"Shay, no!" someone screamed as the gun went off and Kodi was tackled to the ground at the last second.

Kodi didn't even wait to recover from hitting the hard floor before throwing herself through the open apartment door. Eli picked himself up off the floor and closed the door before Shay could fire the gun again. Then he walked right up to his confused sister, grabbed the gun out of her hands, and shoved it into Howard's chest until he took it from him.

"We're going to need her," Eli said without emotion, "and Sammi."

*

Sammi got off the phone and the look on her face told Mack more than he needed to know. He knew Eli had to be in the area and he wasn't about to let him get away again. He started to head for the stairs to grab a shirt and his pistol, but he stopped himself when he realized the look he had seen on Sammi's face was fear.

"What happened?" Mack asked Sammi, breaking out of cop-mode and wrapping his arms around her, pulling her protectively against his body.

"We have to go get Kodi," Sammi told him, practically mumbling into his bare chest. "Shay just threatened her with a gun and Eli was there."

"It's going to be okay. We'll go get her and she can stay here," Mack replied calmly, still playing the role of the boyfriend, and planted a kiss on Sammi's forehead. "I just gotta run upstairs really quick."

Mack then darted upstairs and returned only a few moments later tucking a handgun into his waistband behind his back. He had put on a snug-fitting black t-shirt and had a grey sweatshirt draped over his right shoulder.

"Here, I grabbed this for you," Mack said and offered the hooded sweatshirt to Sammi. Sammi thanked him and wrestled it on, trying to keep up with Mack as he led the way to his car.

Less than twenty minutes later, Mack pulled the vehicle up to a pay phone six blocks away from where Eli was last seen. Sammi immediately jumped out of the passenger side and pulled her terrified best friend into a protective hug. Kodi had been shaking since she had been shot at, but she didn't start crying until the immense relief of seeing her best friend still alive.

Mack gave the women a few minutes to comfort each other before interrupting. He handed the car keys to Sammi and told her to take Kodi back to his apartment, lock the door behind them, and not leave until he returned. Then he turned and headed in the direction of Shay's and Howard's apartment, but Sammi grabbed his arm and stopped him.

"Where are you going?" Sammi asked, looking Mack directly in the eyes.

"I can't let him get away again," Mack told her with total sincerity, returning her eye contact.

"Mack, he beat you last time. Don't do this. I can't lose you," Sammi pleaded with the man she cared about as she squeezed his arm and pulled him closer toward her.

Mack continued to look into Sammi's sapphire eyes and knew he would do anything she ever asked of him. He sighed in surrender and kissed Sammi on the lips before taking the keys back from her.

"I have to at least call it in," Mack said once everyone was back in the car.

"Please do. I would rather anybody else have to deal with him," Sammi told him.

"I really can't wait to hear this story," Kodi piped up from the back seat, looking back and forth between two people who had been trying to shoot each other the last time she had seen either of them.

*

By the time they had arrived back at Mack's apartment, Kodi had been brought up to speed by Sammi with many interjected anecdotes by Mack—after he got off the radio with his precinct, of course. Kodi remained silent the entire time and just allowed the new couple to tell their story. She had calmed down completely before they were even standing inside Mack's front door.

"Would you be okay bunking with me while she stays with us?" Mack whispered, his lips brushing against the top of Sammi's ear.

"Of course! Let me take her up there awhile and clear my things out of her way," Sammi replied, leaning into Mack so his face was in her soft hair.

"Mhmm..." Mack mumbled as he breathed in her scent. Sammi giggled and kissed his cheek before leading her best friend upstairs to the guest bedroom.

Once the girls were alone, Kodi closed the door to the bedroom, guaranteeing their privacy. Sammi wasn't ignorant to her friend's change in attitude and just sat cross-legged on the bed, prepared to be lectured instead of helping Kodi make herself feel at home.

"Sammi, your neck..." Kodi started, taking a seat on the bed, facing her best friend.

"I know, it's hideous," Sammi replied. "Now let's go, say what you really want to say."

"What are you really doing with this guy, Sammi?" Kodi asked. "He's a cop and you're a criminal!"

"I can't explain it. There's just an indescribable connection between us," Sammi told her.

"Is it because of your past or the fact that you just almost died? Is he the only thing that makes you feel safe?"

"I can't believe you're saying this! He has been nothing but wonderful to either of us!"

"I know. And I'm glad he's good to you. I just don't want you to lose who you are."

Kodi let the conversation end there and didn't mention her doubt again. But that seed of doubt got planted and continued to grow in the back of Sammi's mind.

Chapter Eight
From Here to Zero

Two months passed without a break in the case against Eli Krik. When officers had arrived at the apartment of Shay and Howard, the place had been cleared out and not a person to be found. Kodi remained as a guest staying with Mack and Sammi for safety reasons, but Sammi was grateful for her company once Mack returned to work full-time.

One day, Sammi and Kodi were watching a movie while Mack was at work when the house phone rang. The two girls looked at each other without a word before Sammi picked up the remote to pause the movie.

"I...I didn't even know he had a house phone," Sammi admitted. "Am I supposed to answer it?"

"I don't see why not. You live here, don't you?" Kodi replied.

"Technically, so do you," Sammi said with her trademark sass.

"Fine, don't answer it," Kodi shrugged and the phone stopped ringing.

"Well, that takes care of that," Sammi responded through a smile and resumed playing the movie.

Less than two minutes later, the house phone began ringing again. Sammi groaned, paused the movie again, and got up to find the never-before-seen telephone. The phone ended up being in the kitchen, on the wall between the counter and a hanging cabinet.

"At least it's cordless," Sammi mumbled to herself before picking up the phone. "Hello?"

"Oh, hi... Is Mack there?" It was a female's voice.

"No, he's actually working late tonight. I'm sorry."

"Oh...okay. Uh, are you Samantha?"

"Sammi, yeah. Who is this?"

"It's Lori...the ex."

"Oh!"

"Look, I actually want to thank you. Mack finally signed the divorce papers because of you."

"He told you about me?"

"Yeah, sorry, I'm like one of the only people he has to talk to. He is a piece of work, but he loves you. I wish you two the best of luck."

"Uh, thank you."

After Sammi got off the phone, she returned to the couch and told Kodi all about the uncomfortable conversation she just had with her boyfriend's ex-wife. Kodi agreed that it was strange that Mack had discussed his current relationship with his past partner, especially considering Sammi's history and the fact that he wasn't very open about anything from his own past. He was an expert at shutting down whenever he didn't want to talk about something.

Sammi and Kodi were finally finishing their movie when Mack got home from work later that evening. Mack said a quick hello to the girls then went upstairs to change out of his work clothes. The end credits of the movie started rolling a second later, so Sammi excused herself and hurried after her man.

Mack was wearing only his black dress pants when Sammi

found him in the bedroom. She crossed the room to him and wrapped her arms around him, snuggling into his bare chest. Mack hugged her tightly to his body and kissed the top of her head.

"So, Lori called today," Sammi said, and she could feel Mack's entire body tense up.

"Really? Did you talk to her?" Mack asked cautiously.

"Yeah, she seems nice. She told me about the divorce papers," Sammi told him, planting a few gentle kisses on the soft skin of his upper torso.

"I signed them the day you moved in. It felt like the right thing to do."

"Well, she's grateful."

Unfortunately, the conversation had made Mack uncomfortable and he became almost entirely unresponsive. Sammi squeezed his body to hers once before leaving him to finish getting changed. She headed downstairs to order dinner for everyone and asked Kodi to help her un-spook her boyfriend. But Mack was quiet the rest of the evening and Sammi regretted even mentioning the phone call from earlier.

Later that night, Sammi and Mack lay in bed pretending to sleep after not even saying goodnight. Suddenly, Mack shot up out of bed and turned on the bedroom light. Sammi sat up against the pillows and gave him a confused look, almost too afraid to ask him what was bothering him. Mack began pacing back and forth in front of the bed and Sammi was quickly filled with dread.

"What is happening?" Sammi asked nervously.

"I just...I have so many questions," Mack answered her.

"For who?" Sammi replied, immediately realizing the answer to her question was obvious. "About what?"

"How did you not get caught before me?"

This could have been a romantic conversation had Mack been talking about Sammi's heart. But Sammi had always known her past was going to come back into play. And she was not about to back down if this was going to be thief versus cop.

"Caught?" Sammi scoffed. "I'm sorry, I didn't realize I was a prisoner here."

"You know what I meant," Mack responded. He finally stopped pacing and faced Sammi.

"No, I don't know what you mean," Sammi said angrily as she climbed out of the bed. She walked over and stood by the bedroom door with her arms crossed in front of her chest. "Do you think you bested me that night?"

Mack stood in front of the bed with a bewildered look on his face. He had no idea how the conversation turned down this path and he did not know how to steer it back on track. But there was no going back now.

"Sammi, you were either going to jail that night or you were going to die," Mack spoke softly but seriously. "I provided you with the third, life-saving option."

"Well I lived, I haven't spent a single night in jail, and I got to keep the money. How did I not win that night?"

"You're right, you won...with my help. I guess we make a pretty good team."

Mack had walked over to Sammi by this point, scared that he was pushing her away. He reached out a hand and ran it along one of her arms until she uncrossed them. Then he took her right hand and pulled her over to the bed where he sat on the edge and pulled her onto his lap.

"I thought you didn't want to talk about my poor life choices," Sammi said quietly, looking down at her and Mack's hands.

"Your life choices, good or bad, make you who you are. And I want to know everything," Mack told her. Then he placed his fingers ever so lightly under her chin and gently tilted her face to his for a kiss.

*

After that dramatic evening, there was an undeniable strain on the relationship. Not wanting to give it time to fester, Mack took off work the next day to spend it with Sammi. They spent the afternoon in Times Square and ended the evening with Mack introducing Sammi to Lori and their two children. His family was nice to her, but Sammi couldn't ignore the heavy feeling that she didn't belong amongst them.

The more time Sammi spent with Mack and the better they got to know each other, it became more and more clear to Sammi that she still had some pretty heavy secrets of which Mack was not aware. First, she was having a difficult time mentally adjusting to a life without crime. She seemed totally fine on the outside, but her insides were bursting with desire to get back to the job with so many new ideas. Sammi didn't think this personal battle was anything to concern Mack with because she was doing well enough ignoring it and hoping it would eventually go away.

Sammi's second secret, however, was going to have to come out and it was going to be soon. She and Mack had not been intimate yet and Mack was only going to let it go for so long before he started asking questions. It wasn't that Sammi didn't want to have sex with Mack; she was easily turned on by him. But her past had her seriously screwed up and she had to hope that sex meant something more when it was with someone who truly loved her.

The Friday after Sammi met Mack's family, Sammi and Kodi went out to breakfast after Mack had left for work. When they returned to the apartment, they were surprised to find a gift-wrapped box outside of the apartment door. Looking up and down the hallway, the girls saw no possible suspects. Sammi reached for the package, but Kodi threw her arm in front of her best friend to stop her.

"Sammi! You don't know where that came from!" Kodi scolded.

"Relax," Sammi said with half a laugh, "that's Mack's

handwriting." She pointed to the gift tag emblazoned with her own name.

Once inside the apartment, Sammi put the pretty package on the kitchen counter and undid the large red bow. Inside the thin white box was an elegant blue cocktail dress and a single handwritten note.

"Mack is taking me to dinner tonight," Sammi announced after reading the note.

"Well, he certainly knows your color," Kodi replied, admiring the sapphire blue fabric of the dress.

When Mack got home from work, Sammi was still getting ready in their bathroom so he used the hallway bathroom to shower. He changed into black dress pants and a white collared shirt then headed downstairs to wait in the kitchen for his girlfriend. Sammi descended the stairs only a few minutes later, looking like she had just stepped off a runway. The lovers closed the distance between themselves and met each other with their lips.

Mack had made a reservation at a five-star restaurant and the evening started out beautiful and romantic. But halfway through dinner, the entire mood changed as Mack fell into a habitual shutdown. Nervous, Sammi tried to figure out what caused his switch to flip. They had not been talking about anything even remotely heavy all evening, so she didn't have an answer.

"Are you okay?" Sammi asked after trying to give Mack some time to break out of his almost trance-like state. "You're scaring me."

"I'm sorry, I'm just a little nervous," Mack said quietly, finally blinking.

Before Sammi could question him further, Mack was on the floor in front of her on one knee. He slid his hand into his left pants pocket and pulled out a tiny velvet box. His hands were visibly shaking, but he retained his composure. Sammi watched him with wide eyes, frozen in her chair.

"I know we only met a few months ago, and under very strange circumstances. But I've never been in love with anything as much as I love you. Will you marry me, Samantha?" Mack said from his heart.

Sammi was speechless. Marriage was not something that she ever thought about, not even for as long as she had been with Eli. But she somehow knew that if she was going to spend the rest of her life with any one person, it was going to be Lieutenant Mack Johnson.

After a slight hesitation, Sammi nodded at Mack, agreeing to marry this man. The couple stood up and Mack pulled his bride-to-be into his arms, hugging her tightly. Sammi was so lost in her own thoughts that she didn't even notice as Mack slid the simple, round-cut diamond set in white gold onto her left ring finger.

Back at the apartment, Mack was excited to share their news with Kodi. But Sammi hadn't spoken a word since dinner and headed right for the stairs after mindlessly showing her best friend the ring.

"I love you," Sammi finally spoke once the couple lay in bed together. She snuggled up against his side and held onto his arm that was closer to her, clutching it to her chest. Mack turned his head to smile at her, feeling warm under her touch.

"I am the luckiest man in the world," Mack stated and kissed Sammi goodnight.

*

As weeks passed, Sammi grew more accustomed to the idea of marriage despite still not having had the talk with Mack about her not-so-pretty history. Neither she nor Mack were rushing any wedding planning, which was only letting her get away with keeping her secrets. Kodi did her best to be as supportive as possible, but she couldn't help but feel like Sammi was making a huge mistake and that she was losing her best friend. She knew all about Sammi's traumatic past and she was disappointed in her best friend for not coming clean to the man she intended to marry.

A few weeks after Sammi asked Kodi to be her maid of honor, Kodi took Sammi out for the day to start looking at bridal gowns. Of course, every single dress made Sammi look like a blonde goddess, making dress shopping the hardest part of wedding planning so far. They ended up returning home much later than anticipated and without having decided on a dress. Mack was watching the evening news in the living room when they got home, but he got up as soon as they walked through the door and went upstairs without a word. Sammi shot her friend a confused glance.

"I smell drama," Kodi replied and rolled her eyes.

Sammi didn't know what to expect as she climbed the stairs, leaving Kodi behind. She found Mack in their bedroom, sitting on the bed and cleaning his service revolver. He was facing away from the door and didn't notice Sammi enter the room.

"Is everything okay?" Sammi asked quietly from the door.

"I'm kind of busy," Mack stated coldly without turning to look at her.

"Oh, okay. Well, I looked at wedding dresses today if you want to talk later," Sammi told him, hoping talk of the wedding would brighten his mood.

"Good, something new for you to steal," Mack mumbled as Sammi left the room. But she had heard him and stopped dead in her tracks.

"I'm sorry, do you have something to say to my face?" Sammi asked, regaining her confidence.

Mack was quiet. He didn't see any positive outcome happening from arguing with Sammi. He loved her, but something had happened at work that was making it difficult for him to be understanding of her previous lifestyle.

"Come find me when you're ready to be a man," Sammi

told him and finally exited the room.

She originally wanted to go find Kodi but decided she didn't actually want to talk to anybody and instead went out to the balcony at the end of the hall.

Sammi sat out on the balcony for quite a while, looking out at the night sky. She got lost in her thoughts, trying desperately to think of what she could've done to piss off Mack so badly. As she gave up and got up to head inside, Mack appeared in the doorway.

Without a word, Mack tossed a red folder onto the chair that Sammi had just been sitting in and waited for her to pick it up. As Sammi inspected the contents, she was confused. The folder contained a stack of several different case files, some being robberies of her own design and others seemingly similar but nowhere near as elegant.

"I don't understand," Sammi said innocently as she held the folder out for Mack to take back. "Do you think these were all me?"

"Are they not?" Mack questioned her.

"I mean, some of them are," Sammi admitted, "but some of those more recent ones are an insult to my name. Why anyone would even attempt a heist without hacking into the security system first is beyond me."

"Unless your hacker is dating the sister of the man who tried to kill you."

"Oh, wow, you really do think these were me. Look, you can bet that I miss it; I was so fucking good at it and I miss it every damn day. But I made a promise to you and I don't break my promises."

Feeling hurt and fighting back tears, Sammi pushed past Mack to get back inside and went right for their bedroom. She quickly changed into sleepwear and then found Kodi to ask if she could sleep in her room that night. Feeling guilty, Mack almost tried apologizing, but decided it would be better to give Sammi some space.

*

Mack left for work the next morning without getting a chance to talk to Sammi. When he returned home that night, there was no sign of Sammi or even Kodi. But on his nightstand were Sammi's engagement ring and a note reading, "I guess we're too different people."

Chapter Nine
Life on the Moon

The day after Mack accused Sammi of still being a thief, Sammi and Kodi had a heart-to-heart conversation regarding their future. Sammi wanted to believe that Mack had made an honest mistake, but she couldn't ignore the fact that he didn't trust her. And she missed being a thief just enough that she couldn't guarantee that she was done with it for good.

"I hate to say it, but Mack ruined this by proposing way too soon. You guys don't even know each other," Kodi added her two cents into the debate.

"I know. Believe it or not, we've never even had sex," Sammi told her.

"Oh, I believe it. That guy doesn't have a clue, does he? Have you actually told anyone about your mom's boyfriends?" Kodi questioned her best friend out of concern.

"You mean other than you?" Sammi asked and Kodi rolled her eyes.

While the girls continued their discussion in the living room, Sammi's cellphone rang once. She assumed it was Mack and chose to ignore it. But it rang again so Sammi picked it up off the coffee table and looked at the screen. Her jaw dropped and she showed the screen to Kodi.

"Do not answer that," Kodi hissed. But the phone rang a third time and Sammi couldn't resist.

"What could you possibly want?" Sammi answered the call. Kodi exhaled loudly, and angrily sat back on the couch with her arms crossed.

"I need your help," Eli said on the other end of the call. There were no signs of cockiness nor confidence in his voice.

"Why the hell would I help you?" Sammi scoffed.

"Do you remember Frank Nardino?" Eli asked, ignoring Sammi's question. The name was familiar, but it took Sammi a minute to connect the dots.

"You mean that sleazebag who got arrested during our first date?"

"Yes, but I can't tell you any more over the phone. Sammi, you are the best thief I know, and I really need your help. I will explain everything if you can meet me at the bar where we first met. And bring Kodi if it makes you feel better."

Eli hung up and left Sammi speechless. She put her phone back down on the coffee table while Kodi looked at her in disbelief, awaiting an explanation. Sammi took a minute to collect her thoughts before taking a deep breath and telling Kodi everything that had been said.

Both girls knew that they would be helping Eli before they even began discussing their options. Sammi was dying to get back to the work that she loved and Kodi was desperate to never allow Sammi to be alone with the man who almost killed her. So, an hour later, they came to the agreement that it was the only way out of their current situation and proceeded to pack their bags in a hurry. Sammi knew that no words could justify her decision to Mack, so she wrote a short, vague note to leave on his nightstand with the undeserved ring.

"Let the record show that running away from your problems seems to work for you, Samantha Reilly," Kodi said dramatically as they walked along the sidewalk together, about a block away from the bar.

"When life hands you an easy way out, leap through it," Sammi laughed as they turned the corner to their destination. She held the door to the bar open for Kodi and the two friends crossed the threshold back to their previous life.

*

The tension in the air was undeniable as Sammi and Kodi entered the bar to discover that Eli, Shay, and Howard were the only people there. They sat at a table along the back wall and looked up as the pretty blondes approached them. There were no warm greetings nor talk of any kind as the five thieves traded untrusting glances.

Eli pulled the chair next to him out from the table, offering it to either of the ladies. Both Sammi and Kodi pretended not to notice as they turned around and sat at the bar instead, sitting on the stools so that they faced the rest of the group. They were not a real team anymore and there wasn't any reason to play pretend.

"So, what are we doing here, Eli?" Sammi spoke first, trying to regain her alpha position in the group.

"Nardino thinks that Eli set him up that day in the restaurant," Shay spoke for her brother. "His people hunted Eli down and threatened him."

"What do they want?" Sammi asked aloud as she internally asked herself if she even cared.

Both Shay and Howard looked at Eli, as did Sammi and Kodi. Eli avoided eye contact and stared at a spot in front of him on the table.

"They want you, Sam," Eli said without looking up.

Sammi's eyes widened as she stared blankly in the direction of her former love. Thoughts flooded her head, but first and foremost was that she had made a terrible mistake trusting Eli and showing up there. Upset but not truly panicked, Sammi stood up and walked outside for some fresh air.

Eli waited a beat before chasing after his old girlfriend. He found Sammi outside of the bar, leaning against the front window. Approaching her very slowly, he stood by her side close enough to feel her warmth without actually touching her.

"So, this apology is well overdue, but I didn't know how to say sorry for almost killing you," Eli said quietly, looking down at the ground. "But I really am sorry."

"What do Nardino's guys want with me?" Sammi asked, not wanting to dredge up the past.

"They want you to be a thief," Eli told her, finally looking at her face.

Eli then explained that they had followed him to the team's hideout and demanded that he continue running heists and cutting them in on his earnings. He had planned and poorly executed two or three jobs before having to admit that Sammi was the brains behind the team. Nardino, having known that all along, made Eli a deal that he could walk away unharmed in exchange for Sammi planning and running one major heist for him.

"Well that explains why Mack thought I was still active," Sammi said, shaking her head.

"What does ol' Mack think of you being here?" Eli asked, showing his true colors again.

"He doesn't know," Sammi told him.

"How could he not know? Where does he think you are?"

"He doesn't know because I left him."

Annoyed, Sammi took a step away from Eli and a step away from the building. As she stood by the side of the road facing the bar, she saw Kodi in the open doorway and motioned for her to come outside. Kodi obliged and stood by her friend.

"What's in this for us?" Kodi finally asked the question that had been bothering her since Eli's phone call. She knew the answer, but she wanted Eli to say it to Sammi's face.

"They'll let Sammi live," Eli said, more to his shoes than anybody.

Sammi walked to Eli and slapped him across his face with as much force as she could muster up. Eli brought his hand to his cheek where it stung the worst but still wouldn't look up. Realizing that she had never seen him look so small and helpless, Sammi's anger settled and she backed away from him. She suddenly felt bad for him and remembered that she had once loved him.

She couldn't look at Eli any longer so Sammi turned to the unbusy street and sat on the curb. Burying her face in her hands, she sobbed a couple of times while Kodi stood protectively next to her. There was complete silence other than the city sounds of traffic and sirens in the distance that were easily blocked out by the New York natives.

Eventually, Shay and Howard joined Eli, Kodi, and Sammi outside. Paying customers had begun to arrive at the bar, eliminating the group's privacy. Since the cops had begun staking out outside of Shay's and Howard's apartment, the two of them had been staying in a hotel suite with Eli, which is where they moved the meeting.

The hotel suite had two private bedrooms, one full bathroom, a separate living room, and a kitchenette with a small, round dining table. Kodi and Sammi could have gotten their own room but they didn't want to draw attention to themselves in case Mack decided to look for Sammi. So, Eli offered his bedroom to the two girls and moved his things to the living room area.

"So, does this guy want a specific job done or do we have creative freedom?" Sammi asked as all five of the band of thieves sat around the kitchen table.

"I'm sure he wants a Sammi original," Eli said with a grin.

"Perfect," Sammi replied, returning his smile.

Sammi already knew which job she wanted to run, but there were too many people at the table that she no longer trusted. She decided that she would talk it out and plan the robbery with Kodi and keep the others on need-to-know terms. With nothing else to say to the group, Sammi and Kodi got up from the table and retired to their bedroom.

Around midnight, Kodi was fast asleep but Sammi lay wide awake next to her with every thought she had had in the last twenty-four hours attacking her head at once. Desperate to break free from her worrying mind, Sammi quietly left the room to get a drink of water. All the lights in the suite were shut off as everyone else had also gone to bed. But as Sammi turned to walk away from the kitchen sink, she bumped into somebody in the dark.

"Don't do that," Sammi whispered with a heavy sigh, easily recognizing Eli's body shape.

"I'm sorry," Eli whispered back with the sound of a smile in his voice.

Suddenly Eli's lips were on Sammi's and she shoved him in his chest as hard as she could. He didn't budge even an inch, but he stopped kissing her and turned on the kitchen light. Sammi was watching him with flames of hatred dancing in the skies that were her eyes.

"I won't be that girl again," Sammi said. Her voice was shaking but she meant what she said.

"I wasn't even doing anything," Eli replied with a nervous laugh.

"Please just move out of my way so I can go to bed," Sammi nearly pleaded as Eli took a step toward her, cornering her.

"Are you still afraid of me?" Eli asked, genuinely surprised.

He reached a hand out toward Sammi to touch her arm as she flattened herself against the wall behind her. She trembled at his touch and refused to look him in the eyes as she pulled away from him.

"Don't touch me," Sammi growled under her breath.

But Eli ignored her and carefully pulled her away from the wall and into his arms. Turning around, he placed her where she could easily escape and loosened his arms around her. Sammi regained her balance but didn't run away. She looked into Eli's eyes that were begging for forgiveness and had to sit down on the floor as tears began pouring out of her eyes. Eli was immediately on the floor next to her, holding her as she cried.

"It's okay," Eli whispered over and over again as he rocked her gently in his arms.

Sammi was completely mortified by her display of weakness, but no matter how hard she tried, she couldn't stop crying. After months of her thoughts and her feelings being pulled every which way, she needed this release. Her heart was torn between two entirely different lives and as much as she loved being a thief, she had wanted to love Mack just as much or possibly even more.

As Eli held the beautiful mess in his arms, his legs began to ache underneath him. Wanting to get more comfortable so he could hold Sammi longer, he stood up with her in his arms and carried her out to the living room. He laid down on the couch on his back with Sammi lying on his stomach. The sudden change in location had quieted Sammi's sobs, but she kept her face hidden against Eli's chest. Eli continued to hold her, and he caringly rubbed her back until they were both asleep.

Chapter Ten
Come Back to Me

A week later, the group of thieves was ready to put Sammi's plan into action. There was an intersection just inside the city limits that had a different brand of bank on each corner. What the competing brands didn't realize was that each of their individual security systems were actually all a part of the same larger security firm, which made it that much easier for a hacker to get inside all of their systems at once.

The group waited until closing time on a less busy day, wanting to involve as few bystanders as possible. Howard broke into their systems within five minutes and took control of the automatic locks, the security cameras, and everything in between. He remained inside an unmarked van in one of the parking lots while Eli, Kodi, Sammi, and Shay each walked up to their own corner bank.

Armed with only handguns, the team had to rely on intimidation and communication. Using their earbuds, the thieves let Howard know which doors to unlock and when, until they made it to their assigned bank's vault. Then they loaded duffel bags with cash and waited for Howard to pick them up in the van with their winnings.

With everybody needing to communicate with Howard, the chatter over the earbuds was distracting. Sammi did her best to block it out while she tied up her bank employees at gunpoint and made her way to the vault. But after she had her duffel bags packed and ready to go, she realized Eli was calling for help over the earbuds.

Abandoning her bags, Sammi told Howard to grab them through the earbuds as she ran to Eli's aid. She crossed the street to Eli's designated bank and was alarmed to find the front doors still unlocked. Howard was supposed to lock them once Eli had gotten inside but Sammi didn't have time to worry about the mistake. She ran into the bank and found Eli in the vault. Surprised to see Shay and Howard were also in the vault, Sammi stopped dead right inside the opening. The three people she trusted least in the world were standing around a man they had apparently taken hostage who was on his knees with his hands zip-tied behind his back.

"Shit," Sammi said mostly to herself, starting to realize this may have been a setup after all. Mack Johnson looked up at her from where he sat on his heels as Shay put her gun to his head.

"I should've known you were behind this," Mack said to Sammi, shaking his head in disappointment. He couldn't help but chuckle at how stupid he felt.

"Let him go," Sammi growled at Shay.

"But he's a cop and he saw our faces," Shay argued. "Someone's gotta do something about him always being in the wrong place at the wrong time!"

Sammi was still frozen in the doorway so Eli walked over to her and put a hand on her waist. He tried assuring her that everything was going to work out okay but Sammi couldn't tear her horrified eyes away from Mack. She didn't even notice when Eli planted a kiss on her golden hair.

"Even better," Mack scoffed and continued to shake his head in disbelief.

"No one asked you," Eli snarled and drove his elbow hard into Mack's skull.

The blow knocked Mack onto his side, leaving him unable to get up because his hands were tied behind his back. Suddenly, Eli was on top of him and beating Mack's face with his fists. Mack was spitting out blood as Sammi finally shoved Eli away from him and dropped to her knees next to him.

"You weren't supposed to be a part of this," Sammi spoke quietly to Mack as tears glistened in her blue eyes.

Sammi removed her lightweight blue flannel shirt and used it to wipe the sweat and blood from Mack's face. Then she took her switchblade knife from her right boot with the intention of cutting his hands free, but Shay slapped it out of her hands before making her stand up at gunpoint.

"You're not hurting my brother again," Shay hissed as she backed Sammi into a corner with the gun pointed at her face.

Eli looked terrified of his sister as he very slowly approached her from the side. He made a soft grab for the gun, but Shay wasn't giving it up. Sammi looked back and forth between the two siblings, confused and unsure of who to trust.

"Shay, you're not going to shoot her," Eli said, trying to sound calm. "Put the gun down."

"No! Everything was perfect until she came into our lives!" Shay yelled. "But it's okay, I'm going to fix everything."

Before anyone could ask Shay to elaborate, Frank Nardino had entered the vault flanked on either side by two of his men. With this distraction, Shay walked to Sammi and kicked the backs of her knees until she was sitting in the corner with her butt on the floor and her legs out in front of her. Shay then knelt beside her and wrapped a zip-tie around her elegantly thin wrists, pulling it tight. Once she was sure Sammi was secure, she got back on her feet and stood over Sammi with the gun pointed at her head again.

Meanwhile, Mack had struggled but managed to get back up on his knees. He was facing away from Nardino, but

Nardino would have recognized the pain-in-the-ass detective anywhere.

"Oh, look, it's my favorite cop," Nardino spat as he kicked Mack in the side of the head, knocking him over again.

"I thought I arrested you," Mack muttered, laughing as he inched away from the wannabe supervillain.

Nardino drew his gun and cocked the hammer back in the blink of an eye. There was pure hatred on his face as he put the barrel to the back of Mack's head.

"Leave him alone!" Sammi screamed, leaping forward just to be caught and held back by Shay.

Nardino relaxed and squatted down next to Mack, bringing the gun down to under Mack's chin. He looked between Mack and Sammi, seeing the desperation in Sammi's eyes.

"That gorgeous thief over there seems to care an awful lot about you. But she can't possibly be your girlfriend," Nardino tested Mack.

"Not anymore," Mack grumbled.

Nardino turned his cold grey eyes back to Sammi. Keeping his gun aimed at Mack, he stood up and walked over to the object of his lust that was being held in place by Shay's arm around her stomach. He softly brushed his thumb across Sammi's cheek, and she spit directly in his face. Enraged, Nardino slapped her with the back of his hand. She would have lost her balance had Shay not had ahold of her but her long yellow hair fell over her eyes with the force of the hit.

"Don't fucking touch her!" Mack growled, picking himself up off the floor as the broken zip-tie and Sammi's knife dropped to the floor behind him.

Mack threw himself at Nardino, but Nardino fired his gun and Mack went down. Sammi screamed and desperately tried to free herself from Shay's hold. Throwing her head back as hard as she could, Sammi connected with Shay's skull and Shay finally let go of her, momentarily blinded. Before Sammi could go to Mack, Nardino put his gun directly between Sammi's eyes and she froze.

"I'm not done with you yet," Nardino whispered, wrapping a hand entirely around Sammi's slender neck.

"Mack is going to kill you," Sammi said with certainty.

Ignoring her, Nardino shoved her back into Shay's waiting arms and motioned for Shay to follow him as he started to leave the vault. Howard and Nardino's men followed suit, but Eli hadn't moved nor spoken since Nardino had appeared.

"The cop is all yours, Eli," Nardino said, stopping in the opening of the vault. He waited for Eli to acknowledge him and then continued on his way out of the bank.

*

Kodi hadn't heard anything over the earbuds in almost twenty minutes and had begun to worry. She had been ready with her duffel bags of cash and waiting just inside the front door of her bank for a sight of Howard and the van. When her third call over earbuds was met with complete silence, not even static, she grabbed the largest of her bags and headed outside.

Across the street, Kodi could see the van parked at the bank that Eli had gone into. Kodi waited a minute to see if the van would make it her way next, but instead saw three unfamiliar men followed by Sammi, Shay, and Howard. Shay seemed unusually close to Sammi and Kodi knew something had to be wrong because her best friend did not trust that sociopath enough to let her anywhere near her.

As Howard got behind the wheel of the van while everyone else piled into the back, Kodi knew she had no way of following it. But Kodi was smart and not about to give up. So, she watched the van for as long as she could until it disappeared, noticing that Howard didn't hesitate. He had to be familiar with where he was going, but they wouldn't be going to his nor Eli's apartment where cops would be waiting for them. She had to be hopeful that they were going somewhere close so, taking a chance, Kodi decided the hotel suite they'd been staying in was a good place to start.

Hoping cops would be on their way for the bank robberies, Kodi ran across the street to Eli's bank with her duffel bag. She typed the hotel address and room number into her cellphone and, leaving the screen open, put her phone inside the duffel bag. Then she ran a few blocks deeper into the city to grab a taxi that took her to the hotel.

When she got to the hotel, Kodi headed casually up to the suite. She remained quiet and super aware of her surroundings, not knowing what to expect. Putting her ear to the hotel room door, she could hear voices in close proximity and knew she wasn't going to be able to sneak into the room unnoticed. So, she stayed where she was, listening and watching, waiting for a reason to leap into action.

*

Back at the hotel suite, Shay made Sammi sit in a chair in the center of the living room while Nardino helped himself to a look around the spacious suite. Nardino's men stood guard by the door and Howard stayed uncomfortably out of the way. His girlfriend had always been a little irrational, but he was officially scared of her and for her.

"Did you ever stop to think that Eli and I were never going to work out because he has a fucking psychopath for a sister?" Sammi spat at Shay.

"Shut up!" Shay screamed and smacked Sammi across the face. But Sammi just laughed because Shay was proving her point.

When Sammi didn't stop laughing, Shay drew a knife seemingly from nowhere and put it to Sammi's throat. Sammi finally stopped as she could feel the sharpness of the blade kissing the fair skin of her neck. She leaned back in the chair, away from the pointed weapon, but Shay followed and kept it on her throat.

"If we're talking openly, I never would've guessed that my brother was hurting you, but everyone knew that you were hurting yourself," Shay whispered with her face right up against Sammi's right cheek.

Shay had lowered the knife as she leaned over Sammi, bending her knees to get eye-level with her hostage. Keeping her eyes on Sammi's face, she took ahold of her restrained hands and lifted them out of Sammi's lap. When Shay finally looked down it was to gaze upon the self-harm scars that littered Sammi's exquisitely slim wrists. She smiled to herself as she laid her blade along one of the scars and applied pressure as she slid the knife along the provided line.

It took a second, deeper cut to draw blood from Sammi's arm and tears from her eyes. On impulse, Sammi threw her body forward and headbutted Shay as hard as she could to get her off of her. Shay stumbled backwards, dazed, and Sammi made her run for it only to be met with Nardino's hand around her throat four feet from her exit.

Fed up with Sammi's fighting spirit, Nardino brought his other hand up to her neck and began to squeeze.

*

Left alone with Mack in the bank vault, Eli panicked. He paced back and forth in front of Mack's shot and unconscious body, desperate to come up with a way to fix everything. The only outcome he had desired from this robbery was a chance to get Sammi back and his sister had ruined that by involving Nardino.

As he played back everything that had happened and every possible outcome in his head, he stopped pacing and looked down at his only option. Mack was the answer if the question were how Eli could still win. The goal was still Sammi and he couldn't win her if she was dead or he was in jail. So, he needed Mack to play hero just one more time while he saved his own ass.

Eli squatted down next to Mack's head and shoved him hard in his shoulder. Mack lay on his stomach and Eli could not see the gunshot wound, but he could see that Mack was still breathing. It took a few more even harder shoves before Mack finally started to come around.

Mack coughed as he pulled himself up into a sitting position. He had taken the shot in the chest and the force of the blow to his pectoral muscle had left it difficult for him to breathe. Eli moved directly in front of him and put his hand on Mack's shoulder to help steady him.

"Come on, man, you can still win," Eli said, supporting Mack's weight as he helped him stand up.

"Where's Sammi?" Mack asked and then shook his head, trying to clear up the fuzziness.

Eli told Mack the hotel name and room number, not totally trusting that Mack was aware enough to memorize it. Then he handed him his service revolver that had been confiscated from him upon his capture and sent him on his way.

Once Mack was on his way to save the day, Eli grabbed his own handgun and a duffel bag of cash and ran out of the bank into uncertainty. He had nowhere to go and no one to call, but he had to start with getting out of the city.

*

Mack Johnson dragged himself down the fancy hotel hallway that was carpeted in red and bathed in fluorescent light. He was on his feet, but he was holding onto his chest where he had been shot. His face was drenched in sweat and his clothing splattered in blood. As he approached the correct room, he found a familiar face listening outside the door.

"Mack! What—how did you get here?" Kodi whispered excitedly out of relief.

"Is she in there?" Mack asked with serious pain in his voice.

Kodi was looking at Mack in disbelief as she nodded, wondering what the hell had happened to him.

"Stand back," Mack said as he drew his gun from his waist. "And get out of here."

Mack held his gun in both hands as he threw his back into the door, throwing it open. Nardino's two men immediately went for their own guns but Mack took them out, each with a bullet to the head. Nardino released Sammi who collapsed on the floor desperately trying to catch her breath. Mack shot Nardino before he even had a chance to turn around and his body dropped to the floor right in front of Sammi.

Shay emerged from the living room, pistol raised. Surprised by the sight before her, she hesitated but so did Mack. He knew the files of this entire team by heart and knew that Shay was not a murderer. Unable to take her life, he shot her hand to make her drop the gun. She would live, but she would suffer.

Mack snatched up all the weapons as he quickly cleared the rest of the hotel room. He had expected to come across Howard but discovered an open window in one of the bedrooms and knew the gunshots must have spooked him. He could already hear police sirens in the distance as he let the breeze from the window cool his face for a second.

When Mack returned to the room full of bodies, Shay was writhing in pain on the floor and crying hysterically. Sammi had gotten up and was in the kitchen where Mack found her going through the drawers. Her wrists were still bound so Mack helped her find a knife and cut her loose.

As Mack held Sammi's wrists in his hand, he saw that her skin had been freshly cut and was still bleeding. He led her to the sink and ran the wound under warm water. Sammi was watching his every move but he would not look her in the face.

"I'm sorry," Sammi said quietly, just loud enough for Mack to hear as he shut off the water. He ignored her and grabbed a hand towel to wrap around her wet arm.

Without a word, Mack took the hand of Sammi's good arm and led her toward the door just as cops and EMTs rushed into the room. They were hurried down to the street and separated into different ambulances where they received initial treatment. A medic was examining Sammi's arm when two cops approached the back of the ambulance.

"Samantha Reilly, you are under arrest," the first cop said while the other grabbed her arm and pulled her into the street.

The second cop brought Sammi's hands together behind her back while his partner handed him a set of handcuffs. Mack suddenly appeared and smacked the handcuffs out of their hands.

"She's with me," Mack growled, wincing at the strain he had just put on his muscles.

"Lieutenant, we have to," the first cop argued.

"I said she's with me, rookie!" Mack yelled. "Did I stutter?"

The two cops looked at each other and shrugged their shoulders. They finally walked away, and Mack returned to his ambulance without even a glance in Sammi's direction.

*

Sammi was taken to the hospital per protocol but was released as soon as her slit wrist was cleaned and bandaged. Mack had been taken into surgery to have the bullet removed from his chest so Sammi decided to sit in the waiting room until she received word that he would be okay. She had nowhere to go and nobody to call, but she could at least make sure that the man who saved her life was going to live.

When the surgeon came to tell Sammi that Mack had made it through surgery just fine, he added that she could go see him, even though he might be a little groggy. Sammi just thanked him and sat back down in the plastic chair, knowing she had no right to go see Mack. She sat there, staring at the floor for an hour before getting up and walking aimlessly around the hospital.

Sammi wandered around for no more than twenty minutes before she found herself outside of Mack's hospital room. Without knocking, she slid into the room and stood right by the door. She took a quick look around the room and noticed right away that the hospital bed was empty. Confused, Sammi started to leave the room but was shoved against the wall and held there with her back against it.

Mack held Sammi against the wall by her arms and glared into her fearful eyes. She opened her mouth to say something, but Mack pressed his lips to hers to stop her. His hands moved to her golden hair, gently holding the back of her head as she weakly kissed him back.

"I'm sorry," Sammi mumbled against Mack's lips as tears trickled out of her crystal eyes.

Mack sighed and released her. He walked over to the hospital bed and sat on the edge of it. Sammi remained where she was with her back against the wall.

"Just...stop apologizing," Mack finally growled from across the room.

"Then what am I supposed to do?" Sammi asked, wiping the tears from her face with the back of her hand.

"It's too late for that. You were supposed to not leave me, especially for Eli. You were supposed to not be the reason I got shot in the chest."

"I know! And I understand why you hate me."

"Come here, Sammi."

Mack patted a spot next to him on the bed but Sammi hesitated. After a few seconds, she slowly walked over and sat next to him. He casually wrapped his arm around her waist from behind and pulled her closer to him.

"I can't hate you, Sammi. Trust me, I've been trying. But look at me. I took this beating for you and I'd do it again," Mack said calmly.

"I don't know what to say without apologizing again," Sammi replied quietly, looking down at her hands in her lap. "I never stopped loving you."

Mack leaned forward and tilted his head up, bringing his lips softly to Sammi's. As they kissed, Mack took Sammi's engagement ring from a chain around his neck and slid it onto Sammi's left ring finger.

"This time leave it where it belongs," Mack said softly as he pulled away to allow Sammi to gaze upon her diamond once again.

Part Two

Chapter Eleven
Time Marches On

Sammi sat at an unorganized desk in a room crammed with over a dozen other cluttered desks and threw her head down onto it in exhaustion. There were phones ringing from every direction and people shouting across the room at each other, making it so much harder to focus on anything. Theft had been so much...quieter...

"Sam! Boss is looking for you!" a male voice called from somewhere nearby.

Picking her head up, Sammi waved an arm in acknowledgement. As she stood up, she paused to look at the single framed photo on her desk and smiled at her handsome husband dressed in full formal police uniform gazing adoringly at a particularly dolled-up Sammi in an elegant white dress on their wedding day. It had been two years since they had tied the knot and the rumor around the office was that their marriage was as stale as Lieutenant Johnson's fifteen minutes of *Die-Hard*-style fame.

*

Two floors up, Mack hurriedly grabbed a stack of files off his desk and accidentally knocked over one of the picture frames at the top. He was late for a witness interview, but he stopped and took the time to pick up the frame and put it in its proper place. He smiled at the picture of his young wife from the day she graduated from the police academy a little over a year prior. It was still hard for him to believe that she had gone from breaking the law to being the law.

After a daunting interview, which led to nothing more than another dead end, Mack returned to his desk and took his cellphone out of his jacket pocket. He had two missed calls and a voicemail, all from Sammi. She only ever called him during work hours if she was about to do something dangerous. Afraid of what it could be this time, he nervously listened to her message.

"Hey, babe, Vice is sending me undercover...again. I swear this precinct only hired me because I can pass as a minor and I look good in a short skirt. Anyway, they should've given the details to Hobbs, you know, for when you start to worry. I love you, Mack Johnson, and I'll see you soon."

Mack grumbled under his breath as he put his phone back in his pocket. He had to get Sammi out of that department before they got her killed by a pissed-off pimp in the streets. It wasn't that he didn't trust the Vice squad; it was more about Sammi being too attractive for her own damn good sometimes.

Trying to keep his cool, Mack made an attempt to return some phone calls pertaining to his case for almost twenty minutes before giving up and going into this Captain's office. Hobbs wasn't surprised to see his best but most problematic detective as he sat down on the other side of his desk.

"I'm not telling you where she is," Hobbs said right away. "I know you staked out her location the last three times she was on the street. You're going to blow her cover, Johnson."

"Then just get her out of there already," Mack argued.

"Vice shouldn't be using her as their personal prop."

"Look, Sammi has proven herself to be a pretty great cop and she seems to enjoy being able to help wherever she is needed," Hobbs explained. "You're going to have to loosen your grip if she's going to stay on the force."

"I don't want her on the force if all she's doing is pretending to be a sex worker every day," Mack mumbled as he got up to leave, and Hobbs pretended not to hear him.

Mack went back to his desk and pouted for the rest of his shift. His partner on their current case was Detective Andrew Palma, previously Officer Palma. Palma was all too familiar with Mack's situation and knew better than to get involved. He was the newest detective in the unit and had a ton of respect for Mack but sometimes wished Mack were more open to showing him the ropes of Homicide.

As it reached the end of his shift, Mack still hadn't heard from Sammi nor anything about her. He never left the precinct to go home without her, so he created busy work for himself to give him a reason to be there. Less than an hour later, Sergeant Tanner from downstairs entered the squad room and walked right to Mack's desk.

"I need someone to transport the witness in Interview Room 1A," Tanner directed Mack. "And for God's sake, use discretion, Lieutenant."

Then the Sergeant turned and headed back downstairs. Mack tossed his paperwork into a drawer and rushed down to the ground floor. Interview 1A was closest to the front door of the building, which Mack knew they had done on purpose to keep the "witness" from being seen on their way out. Mack slipped into the room and stood by the door, looking at his lovely wife sitting at the metal table in a tiny purple rave dress and fishnet stockings.

"You ready to go home, party animal?" Mack teased with a warm smile.

Without a word, Sammi stood up from the table and

crossed the room to Mack. She gently pushed him into the walls of the corner and kept her hands on his broad shoulders as she pressed her lips to his. Mack put his hands in her soft, golden hair while he returned her kiss.

"I love you," Sammi breathed against his lips.

"This doesn't make up for you going undercover again," Mack mumbled, moving his face into her hair as he smirked.

"Then take me home, detective," she taunted and kissed the warm, soft skin of his neck.

Mack removed his jacket and placed it over Sammi's shoulders before steering her out of the interview room and out of the building. Anyone who didn't know the couple would easily assume they were just a cop and a civilian.

*

It was a bit of a long drive home to Mack's and Sammi's new place on Long Island. The couple had moved into the adorable little split-level house right before they got married and the peacefulness outside of the city made the hour-long commute more than worth it. They also enjoyed the guaranteed time alone together in the car to talk about their day without distractions.

Sammi knew that Mack didn't really like that she was a cop. He was proud of her, but he worried too much about her on the job. She wasn't totally crazy about it either and would much rather still be stealing money for a living, but this was the only way she knew how to make herself feel worthy of a man like Mack Johnson. She hadn't forgiven herself for leaving him and almost getting him killed three years ago, and probably never would.

When they got home that night, Sammi darted into their bedroom to change out of the obnoxiously tight party dress. Mack leaned against the doorframe and watched her while she dug through a drawer for sweatpants. He had nothing but pure love in his heart for his beautiful wife, but it was sheer lust that Sammi saw in his eyes when she turned around.

"Want to help me out of this?" Sammi asked seductively.

"Leave it on," Mack told her as he removed his shirt and closed in on her.

*

The next day was Saturday and both Sammi and Mack had the weekend off. Sammi always spent her free Saturdays in the city so she woke up after sleeping in a little bit, showered, and put on jeans and t-shirt before kissing her husband goodbye and grabbing her car keys off the kitchen counter. She drove to Mack's old apartment building and headed up to the apartment that was still leased under Mack's name. It took a moment longer than usual after she knocked on the familiar door for it to open, and she was wearing a dramatic frown on her face by the time Kodi greeted her.

"What were you doing?" Sammi asked, judging Kodi as she walked into the clean apartment.

"Sleeping! I wasn't expecting you for another thirty minutes!" Kodi defended herself.

"Oh, sorry." Sammi pouted, sticking out her bottom lip. "I missed you."

"You're hopeless without me," Kodi laughed and stuck her head out into the hallway. "No Romeo today?"

"No, he's spending the day with his kids," Sammi told her.

Kodi closed the apartment door and the friends sat at the kitchen island to discuss how they should spend the day. Neither of them minded when Mack tagged along, but they definitely preferred having some time alone together to talk freely, either about Mack or about their old life. Bringing up their criminal past had become taboo around Mack, but the girls weren't about to forget any of it ever happened.

"Want to do something crazy?" Kodi asked, getting up and

walking to the refrigerator. "Want to go check out the mall where you first met Mack?"

"You mean the mall we robbed where Mack and I literally tried to kill each other?" Sammi replied with a grin. "Sure! Let's go!"

Kodi grabbed two bottles of water out of the fridge and handed one to Sammi before hurrying upstairs to change out of her pajama shorts. She came back downstairs wearing jeans and a cute orange tank top with her blonde hair pulled back in a ponytail. She had begun to come out of her shell and show off her beauty more lately, but no matter what she did, her attempts always fell flat compared to Sammi.

"You look cute! But I think you should wear your hair down," Sammi said, looking her best friend up and down. Kodi scowled but let her hair down anyway.

"I wish the academy had made you shave your head," Kodi hissed, still scowling as she followed Sammi out of the apartment on their way to Sammi's car.

"Bite your tongue!" Sammi cried out after a theatrical gasp, shaking her head to readjust her own golden locks.

The girls laughed as they exited the elevator in the lobby and took a side door into the parking garage. The garage was dark and Sammi noted that it was much quieter than when she had arrived. There was no one around to be seen and no vehicles with engines running to be heard, but Sammi felt someone watching them. About twenty feet from her car, she stopped and took a good look around. She didn't see anybody, not a single soul, but the feeling in the pit of her stomach told her that they weren't alone.

"Get to the car," Sammi ordered strictly but calmly.

Kodi picked up her pace and hurried to the passenger side of Sammi's black Nissan. Sammi continued walking slowly and took in every inch of the parking garage within her sight while keeping her hands at her sides and ready to grab the handgun from her waistband if needed. Even though she didn't enjoy being a cop, she had taken her training seriously and was proud of her ability to protect and serve when necessary. She had actually chosen to not carry her weapon when off-duty for the first year she was on the force, but Mack had talked her into it, at least when he wasn't around.

Sammi made it to the car without seeing anyone and unlocked the vehicle for Kodi. Kodi slid into the passenger seat while Sammi took one last look around the dark garage before finally getting behind the steering wheel. Then she calmly started the engine and drove away.

"What was that about?" Kodi asked, not comfortable with seeing her best friend act like a real cop.

"I think someone was following us," Sammi told her with a relaxed straight face as she kept her eyes on the road.

"Should we be worried?" Kodi replied, immediately thinking about Eli and Shay.

Shay had been arrested on the scene in the hotel room following their final heist but had been released eighteen months later. And Eli had never been caught nor ever heard from again.

"No, relax," Sammi said with a calming smile. "I was just looking for an excuse to go into cop-mode."

"I think a part of you enjoys it," Kodi teased and laughed.

*

When the girls got to the mall, they pretended to shop for a bit but they both knew why they were really there. Without discussing it, they made their way to the spot on the second floor where the shootout with Mack had taken place. Sammi found where she had fallen to the ground after taking the shot to her thigh and stood over it, wanting to feel something from it. The flooring had been replaced at some point over the past few years, and it seemed as though any connection she should've had to the memories there had been removed with the blood-stained tiles.

Instead of the desired connection to the past, Sammi's skin tingled in the present. She froze in the moment, moving only her eyes to look at the people around her. Almost everyone passing by were just regular shoppers carrying bags or chatting lightly with companions. But while Sammi stood by the railing, facing away from Kodi, someone walked by her and casually bumped into her arm. The person wore a hooded sweatshirt that was baggy enough to hide their body type and the hood was up to hide their face. They kept walking and Kodi didn't seem to notice them so Sammi thought it best not to pursue. But she wasn't going to ignore that this stranger and the parking garage stalker were not just a coincidence.

"Do you remember where you took the second shot?" Kodi asked, breaking through Sammi's thoughts.

"Honestly, I don't even know which direction we went from here. I could hardly walk and was in a panic about being arrested," Sammi told her.

"I know I was scared of Mack taking you away from me, but I'm really grateful for him and everything he's done for us," Kodi admitted.

The friends then finally moved on from their historical location and completed their lap around the mall. They shopped a little but mostly talked as best friends tend to do. Sammi kept an eye out for the hooded stranger the entire time but never crossed paths with them again. She never mentioned it to Kodi, even as she dropped her off alone at home.

During her hour-long trip home, Sammi debated whether she was going to tell Mack about the weird occurrences or not. She hadn't told Kodi because she didn't want to make her worry. And she knew Mack would worry and get super overprotective of her. For her own sanity, she decided to keep it to herself unless weird things continued to happen.

By the time Sammi got home, Mack had dinner almost

ready for them. She kissed her husband and asked him how his day was while she filled her NYPD-logo-adorned travel mug with water from the fridge. They talked about Mack's day and about his kids while they ate, and it became somewhat awkward. It always got awkward after Mack saw his kids because he was intentionally keeping Sammi separated from that part of his life. Sammi wasn't totally crazy about kids, but these were her husband's kids and she didn't enjoy feeling like a dark secret.

Feeling put out, Sammi had no more appetite and got up from the table to clean her dish. Then she headed to the bedroom and sat on the edge of the bed to remove her shoes. Mack appeared in the doorway only seconds later and leaned against the doorframe.

"So, what did you do today?" Mack asked.

A wave of déjà vu washed over Sammi as nausea spread from the pit of her stomach. She gripped the comforter beneath her in both fists and hung her head until the feeling passed. Mack, realizing quickly he had unintentionally come across as intimidating to his scarred wife, took a step toward her, wanting to comfort her. But she threw up her hand to keep him at bay and he stopped in his tracks.

"Space," Sammi said quietly without looking up. That was all she had to say, and without a word, Mack grabbed a pair of sweatpants to wear to bed and retired to the guest bedroom for the evening.

Chapter Twelve
Heroes

The next morning Sammi woke up early, feeling bad about banishing Mack to the guestroom. They had this rule in place for a reason, but Sammi never felt good about enforcing it. Deep down she knew that Mack never meant to do or say anything to upset her, but she could only feel free and safe in the relationship if she had this little bit of power over it.

Sammi slipped quietly into the guestroom and found Mack still asleep. She softly climbed onto the queen-sized bed and crawled over top of Mack so she could lightly kiss his nose. Mack scrunched up his handsome face before opening his eyes. Seeing Sammi, he wrapped his arms around her body and held her against him.

"Babe, I am so sorry. I should've paid more attention to how I talked to you," Mack said, hugging Sammi tighter.

"No, you didn't do anything wrong," Sammi told him and kissed him on the mouth. "I just reacted to my past."

"I really did just want to know how your day was," Mack replied, smiling under Sammi's lips.

"And I'd love to tell you. After I make you breakfast!" Sammi jumped off the bed in excitement.

"So, scrambled eggs and toast?" Mack teased, knowing Sammi couldn't cook anything else.

"You'll eat it and you'll love it," Sammi taunted back and stuck her tongue out at her husband before skipping out of the room.

After Sammi left, Mack sunk deeper into the bed with a huge grin on his face. He couldn't think of a time in his life when he was ever happier. He reveled in this joyful feeling for a few minutes before finally dragging himself out of bed and into the shower.

The couple enjoyed their breakfast even though Mack insisted on continuing to tease Sammi about her cooking skills, or lack thereof. Sundays were their usual day to relax and prepare themselves for another week of their stressful jobs.

"You still owe me a story," Mack said kindly and kissed Sammi after clearing the table from breakfast.

"Okay, but don't get mad," Sammi replied innocently as she took Mack's hand and led him over to the couch where they both sat down facing each other. "Kodi and I took a field trip to the place where you and I first met."

"Why did you do that?" Mack asked, sincerely curious.

"I don't know. I thought I would feel something," Sammi told him with a vague shrug of her shoulders.

Mack made a face of confusion and concern as he stared at Sammi. This was the first he was hearing about Sammi lacking feelings and had to wonder if she wasn't as happy as he was in the relationship. And that thought terrified him.

"What...did you want to feel?" Mack asked cautiously.

"Mack," Sammi said sadly, looking down at her hands in her lap, "I miss it. I know it's wrong, but I can't help it."

"Sammi, you're allowed to feel how you feel," Mack replied as he reached over and pulled his wife toward him.

Mack held Sammi in his arms while they sat on the sofa and Sammi snuggled into him. They were both quiet for a bit and enjoyed the comfort of each other. Sammi's mind was racing with thoughts of fear from finally opening up to her husband while Mack's mind was calm because he had always known.

"You are who you are," Mack continued to ease his wife's guilt, "and you are a thief. I'm sorry that I'm not more comfortable with that, but I love you for everything that you are. It might be a longshot, but if you wanted to quit the force, maybe every so often you could get out of town and do what you love to do."

"You would be okay with that?" Sammi asked, surprised, as she tilted her face up to look at Mack's.

"To be completely honest, I think you'd be safer," Mack admitted and kissed the top of her head.

"I guess I have some things to think about."

*

Returning to theft wasn't something Sammi was going to decide overnight, nor did she want to make the decision without discussing it with Kodi first. So, she returned to the precinct with Mack on Monday for another week of being the good guy.

What Mack couldn't seem to understand about the unit Sammi was a part of was that they didn't belong to any specific squad. Their job was to be flexible and comfortable in different units throughout the precinct. Sammi liked working with Vice because she had gotten to know those guys and trusted them. But as she walked through the door on Monday, Sergeant Tanner informed her that she was needed to fill in for a patrol officer for a shift.

Disappointed, Sammi headed into the locker room and changed into her patrol uniform. Sammi was the least experienced officer in the unit when it came to this part of the job because her skills kept her busy in other departments most of the time. And her least favorite part of this gig was getting partnered with a patrol officer she'd never met. These shifts were nothing but awkward and uncomfortable, sitting in the patrol car while her temporary partner issued speeding tickets. If fate had anything to do with it, it was definitely pushing her away from the force and back into the arms of robbery.

Reporting to the front desk in proper uniform and her long, blonde hair tied back in a tight ponytail, Sammi saw the lone patrol officer waiting for his fill-in partner for the day. As soon as he saw Sammi, he didn't have time to hide the disappointment on his face. It was no secret that most patrol officers in the unit preferred male patrol partners and didn't feel nearly as comfortable relying on a female officer. This was precisely why Sammi preferred working with her Vice unit and wasn't feeling so encouraged to stay on the force.

Officer Bryan Mazzeline led Sammi to his patrol car without a single word. He definitely looked like a cop with his lean but muscular build and his blonde crewcut. His eyes were an aquatic blue that certainly stood out on his clean-shaven baby face but were nowhere near as head-turning as Sammi's.

Sammi didn't care enough to start any trouble with Mazzeline so she just got in the passenger side of the patrol car and didn't bother trying to start a conversation. They drove around in silence with minimal action and the day dragged on. Over lunch, Sammi attempted some small talk to try and save the rest of the shift from brutal awkwardness, but Mazzeline just rolled his eyes and gave his full attention to his sandwich.

With two hours left of their shift, a call came over the radio for an armed robbery taking place at a large chain grocery store only a few blocks away. Mazzeline answered the call and sped off in the direction of the store. As soon as they were out of the car, Sammi and Mazzeline could hear gunshots inside the store.

Mazzeline, trying to be the macho man, sent Sammi around back while he went in the front of the building. Sammi had her handgun out of her holster before she even reached the back of the enormous concrete building. The delivery door was unlocked so Sammi let herself into the warehouse with her weapon out in front of her. There was nobody around as she made her way through the stacked crates and boxes toward the front of the building. She heard another gunshot over the low humming of the refrigerators and freezers as she reached the swinging doors that led to the rest of the store.

Peeking through the clouded windows of the flimsy swinging doors, Sammi could see three people hiding behind a row of freezers that held a variety of ice creams and other frozen desserts. Sammi slid silently through the doors and over to the terrified civilians, signaling for them to remain quiet.

"How many shooters?" Sammi whispered, kneeling down by the small group of two store employees and one shopper. There were no signs of injuries among them.

"I only saw one, but I heard a second gun," the teenage male employee informed her, but she knew the second gun was Mazzeline's.

"Where did you last see or hear the shooter?" Sammi asked.

"I think he's a few aisles in," the young adult female employee told her. "He shot a shopper and is holding him hostage."

"Okay. The back delivery door is open and I'm going to cover you guys while you run through those doors that I just came through," Sammi directed the three of them.

Sammi stood up first and the others followed. She waved them behind her and kept her back to them with her gun raised in front of her as they quickly and silently ran for the warehouse. Turning her head only slightly, she made sure they had escaped before looking for the shooter.

Walking down one side of the store, Sammi stopped and looked down each aisle for suspects or any more civilians. She found Officer Mazzeline in the third aisle from the front of the store along with the suspect using a hostage as a human shield. The hostage had already been shot in the shoulder and was bleeding through his t-shirt.

The standoff between Mazzeline and the suspect was going on too long and Sammi could tell right away that the hostage was sweating and fading out. That didn't stop his eyes from widening as they made contact with Sammi's eyes. He knew her and she knew him.

"Is there any way we can end this right now?" Sammi asked the suspect as she took her spot next to Mazzeline with her gun raised.

"I ain't going to jail," the suspect answered. He was an exceptionally large man wearing black pants and a black t-shirt with a long-barreled pistol pointed at the hostage's throat.

"Well, I'm going to need you to let that man go," Sammi said softly and calmly while internally panicking and wondering why Mazzeline wasn't saying anything.

"Oh yeah? You gonna take his place?" the suspect scoffed at Sammi.

Sammi thought about it for a second and decided that was a pretty good idea. She could easily play him with her looks and distract him into letting his guard down. This was clearly going against protocol, but Sammi wasn't interested in trying to keep this job anymore. And it was clear that Mazzeline wasn't going to do anything, so it was up to her.

"Sure, if that's what it takes," Sammi said and lowered her weapon. She removed the rubber band from her hair and let the picture-perfect blonde strands fall around her soft face to increase her appeal.

"I'm not letting him go until you drop the gun," the suspect said, his eyes locked on Sammi.

Sammi squatted down, possibly puffing out her chest for effect, and placed her pistol on the tile floor. She stood up with her hands up in surrender and kicked the gun under the potato chip rack next to her.

"I'm not coming to you until you release that man," Sammi told the suspect.

The suspect turned his gun on Mazzeline to keep him back before shoving his hostage to the floor. The injured man fell toward Mazzeline and Mazzeline yelled at him to stay down. But the man needed medical attention, and the sooner the better.

"Alright, let's go, blondie," the suspect ordered and patted his thigh like he was calling a dog over. He was trying to keep his eyes on Mazzeline so he wouldn't get caught with his guard down.

Sammi began walking slowly to him, swaying her hips as much as possible and drawing his gaze with her hypnotic sapphire eyes. Mazzeline watched the suspect intently and the second he turned his eyes on Sammi, Mazzeline fired one nonlethal shot into the suspect's shoulder. The suspect dropped his pistol, but he didn't go down. Sammi dashed to him, kicked his gun away, and wrenched his arm behind his back, applying pressure to the gunshot wound and causing him to surrender. She kicked the backs of his legs to bring him to his knees as Mazzeline hurried over and cuffed him.

With the suspect in custody and macho man Mazzeline wanting credit for the arrest, Sammi turned her attention to the hostage who was slowly losing consciousness as he bled out on the grocery store floor.

"You're crazy," Howard said through bated breath, forcing a grateful smile as Sammi knelt down next to him.

"That's not the first time you've said that," Sammi replied, returning his smile. "Just hang in there. Paramedics will be here any second."

Sammi stayed with Howard until he was taken away on a

stretcher. By that point, the detectives who had caught this case were waiting impatiently to take her statement. Not having heard Mazzeline's rendition of what happened, Sammi had no choice but to tell the truth and accept the consequences. The detectives didn't question her account so she figured Mazzeline must have been honest in his statement as well, which had her thinking that he cared more about getting her in trouble than getting praise for himself.

When the detectives were satisfied that they had gotten everything they needed from the two patrol officers, they released Mazzeline and Sammi from the scene. Their shift had ended over an hour ago and they still had to get back to their precinct building in the middle of rush hour.

"The overtime will be nice," Sammi mumbled as she scooted forward and leaned back to relax in the passenger seat of the patrol car.

"I'm, uh, I'm really sorry about the way I acted today," Mazzeline said nervously from the driver seat. "You were incredible back there."

"No offense, but I shouldn't have had to prove myself to you," Sammi shot at him. "I'm on the job, just like you, and deserved your respect right out the gate. As do all female cops."

"You're right," Mazzeline admitted. "I'm really sorry and I hope I get the chance to make it up to you."

Sammi still wasn't impressed with Mazzeline's apology and allowed the conversation to drop. She was far too uncomfortable to call Mack with no privacy from her temporary partner, and her anxiety grew as she thought about her husband left waiting and worrying for her back at the station house. Without getting into too much detail, she sent him a text message apologizing and explained that she was on her way back from a crime scene and that she was fine.

*

As soon as they got back to the precinct, Sammi hurried into the locker room to change out of her patrol uniform. She barely had her street clothes on before Mack Johnson burst through the door and hugged her tightly to his body. Sammi let him hold her for as long as he needed before she even tried talking to him.

"I'm sorry I didn't call you," Sammi said softly once Mack loosened his arms around her.

"You're safe and that's all that matters," Mack replied with fear still in his voice.

"No, I acted stupidly, and you have every right to be upset with me," Sammi told him, very aware that he had already heard the entire story of what happened from somebody else.

"What were you thinking? I'm not mad; I just want to understand."

"I honestly wasn't thinking anything, and I wasn't the least bit scared."

"You're crazy and you're going to get yourself killed."

"Not if I get off the job. I just want to finish out the week to get the overtime from today."

"That sounds pretty ideal to me."

Mack kissed his wife's forehead and the two of them left the locker room together. As they got into Mack's vehicle, which was parked behind the station house, Sammi remembered that she wanted to make a pitstop on their way home.

"Do you mind swinging by the hospital quick?" Sammi asked as Mack started the car.

"Why? Are you okay?" Mack replied, immediately concerned.

"I'm fine," Sammi said with a chuckle. "Howard was the injured hostage and I want to check on him."

"Howard, as in...?"

"Yes, and before you say anything, Howard is good people.

He was probably the best person on my team."

Mack gave Sammi an uncertain look and sighed but headed for the hospital anyway. Sammi obviously held Howard in high regards, especially since she had just risked her life for him, so Mack wanted to give him the benefit of the doubt for her sake. He just hoped that Howard wasn't still in contact with Shay because he didn't feel as forgiving towards that crazy woman.

When they got to the hospital, Howard's nurses and doctors somehow knew that Sammi was the cop who saved Howard and insisted on making a big fuss over her heroic actions. Sammi didn't care much for the attention and kept her eyes on Howard in the hospital bed. Howard was already looking and feeling so much better and couldn't hide the gratitude he felt toward Sammi.

"So, you're really a cop, huh?" Howard asked as Sammi stood by his bedside.

"Not for too much longer," Sammi admitted and Mack squeezed her hand, subconsciously showing his support.

"Well, you certainly showed up that jerk of a partner of yours today," Howard stated with a kind smile.

"Dude's not even really my partner," Sammi told him. "I was just filling in for the day."

"I guess fate was on my side today."

Sammi removed her hand from Mack's so she could take Howard's hand in both of hers. She said goodnight to him and promised to visit him after her shift the next day. Then she and Mack finally headed home.

Chapter Thirteen
Firing Squad

Sammi had a hard time waking up the next morning. She was more tired than she usually was, and she had lost the motivation for her job since she had made her decision to part ways with the force. The fear of Sergeant Tanner yelling at her for her actions the previous day wasn't helping her desire to call out of work and was giving her anxiety.

When Mack and Sammi finally got to work, Mack got a phone call before even getting out of the car and sent Sammi on ahead without him. As soon as Sammi walked through the front doors, she saw that the lobby was lined with law enforcement officers who all erupted into cheers at the sight of her. Balloons were released into the air, people were shaking her hand left and right, and Sergeant Tanner waited for her at the back of the lines. Sammi had a look of pure confusion on her face as she walked cluelessly to her boss.

Once Sammi eventually reached Sergeant Tanner, he held out a black leather wallet and flipped it open to reveal a shiny new detective badge. Sammi was speechless as she took the badge from her boss and looked at it with uncertainty.

"I thought I was coming into a suspension today," Sammi

said quietly, not looking away from the badge.

"Although your actions yesterday were not ideal, they were heroic and went above and beyond the call of duty," Sergeant Tanner explained. "You're being assigned to Homicide, and Captain Hobbs is on the third floor waiting to welcome his new detectives."

"Detectives?" Sammi asked, talking more to herself than the Sergeant, but Tanner pointed in the direction of the front door. Sammi turned to look as Officer Mazzeline entered the lobby and received the same celebratory greeting as she just had.

Shit! Sammi didn't want to keep working with Mazzeline and his arrogant attitude, nor did she want this promotion. This had come completely out of left field and was going to make it more difficult for her to quit.

Not in the mood to deal with Mazzeline just yet, Sammi dashed up the stairs ahead of him. She went right to the Captain's office and knocked softly. Hobbs called for her to enter and she let herself into the cramped but comfortable office that she had been in once before.

"Ah, Detective Johnson!" Hobbs said, and Sammi cringed internally. It wasn't often that anyone used Sammi's married name with her and it always caught her by surprise when they did. And she wasn't totally warmed up to this whole detective thing yet either.

"Good morning, Captain," Sammi replied, coming across more shy than normal. She and Hobbs had a good relationship despite Hobbs' knowledge of her not-so-clean past.

"I hate that they decided to promote you without any warning," Hobbs told her. He was always so kind to Sammi and she appreciated him for that. "But once I get a chance to talk to you and Mazzeline, I'm going to send you guys home and give you the day to mentally prepare for this job."

While they waited for Mazzeline, Hobbs and Sammi talked about Mack and the possibility of him taking Hobbs' position when he retired. Hobbs had put in a good word for him, but the entire precinct knew how difficult Mack was to work with and all the problems he had brought to the unit. Of course, only Hobbs and Sammi knew that Sammi was in fact one of those problems.

"I'm really sorry for everything," Sammi said quietly, looking down at the floor.

"Samantha, Mack saw something in you and wanted to give you the opportunity to expose it. And I do not believe that you have let him down," Hobbs replied.

Mazzeline showed up a moment later and Hobbs explained that he and Sammi were going to be partnered with each other in the homicide division of the precinct. They would be able to start catching cases the next day, after taking time to read protocols and standards for their new positions. Then Hobbs took them out into the squad room to introduce them to everybody and show them their desks, which Hobbs had made sure were as far away from Mack's desk as possible.

After they were shown around, Hobbs released Mazzeline and Sammi for the rest of the day. They were still getting paid so Sammi headed downstairs to clear out her old desk and move the necessities up to her new one. While she was setting up the new desk, Mack finally wandered over to see her.

"So, detective, huh?" Mack asked, smiling at his wife from the opposite side of her new desk.

"Did you know about this?" Sammi replied, still wondering and bothered by why this happened so suddenly.

"I wouldn't have talked you into quitting the force if I had known," Mack told her.

"So, let me guess. Now you want me to stay?" she asked, irritated that he was going to change his mind. It wasn't like she needed his permission to quit, but she had liked it when they were on the same page. She wasn't about to feel bad for wanting her husband's support.

"Let's talk about this later," Mack whispered, suddenly

very aware of where they were.

"I'll see you at home," Sammi replied bitterly and slammed a desk drawer before walking away in anger.

Sammi left the station house and walked several blocks to Kodi's apartment building. Kodi wasn't expecting her so she had a look of shock on her face when she opened the door and let Sammi inside. Without speaking, Sammi walked to the kitchen island and sat down with her head down on the counter.

"Why aren't you at work?" Kodi asked, somewhat afraid of the possible answers.

"I got promoted," Sammi mumbled into the countertop.

"That's great!" Kodi said. "Isn't it?"

Sammi sat up and swung around on the stool to face her best friend. Then she took a deep breath and proceeded to tell her about Mack backing her decision to quit the force and become a thief again, her standoff to save Howard's life in a grocery store, and her promotion to Mack's department where Mack had wanted her all along.

"We really need to stay in touch during the week," Kodi stated after having a difficult time keeping up with everything she had missed in just a few short days.

"Do you want to go see Howard with me at the hospital?" Sammi asked, changing the subject to help herself calm down.

"Sure, I'll drive," Kodi offered, "but we're talking about your career dilemma on the way."

Sammi followed Kodi out of the apartment and down to the garage to Kodi's car. She thought about the last time she was in that garage and the feeling of being watched, but she was too distracted and bummed out to be able to sense anything this time. Not that she would've cared if someone was following them again, because she was in a bad enough mood that she was itching for a fight.

On their way over to the hospital, Sammi explained what she had been thinking for getting back into thieving. She

obviously wanted Kodi on her team and she considered it to
be fate that brought Howard back into her life. The three of
them would make just as good of a team as the five of them
had, but without all the drama. She wanted to travel outside
of the state and was willing to spend months at a time
planning and perfecting the heists before pulling them off. The
fewer jobs they did and the further away from each other they
were would make it nearly impossible for anyone to track
them back to Sammi and her friends.

Kodi was onboard with Sammi's ideas, but she only
wanted Howard on the team if Shay was completely out of his
life. She hadn't quite forgiven Shay for trying to shoot her or
wanting to kill Sammi. And she wasn't ever going to.

*

At the hospital, Howard was looking even better than the
night before and was happy to see both Sammi and Kodi. Kodi
told him about Sammi's promotion so Sammi took out her
new detective badge to show him.

"I thought you didn't want to be a cop anymore," Howard
said as he sat up more in the hospital bed to get a better look
at the shiny badge.

"I didn't ask for this," Sammi replied and shrugged. "Hey,
have you been in touch with either of the psycho siblings
lately?"

"Nah," Howard told her. "Shay hunted me down when she
got out of jail, but I closed the door in her face. She always
thought I was a coward anyway."

"You're not a coward," Kodi stepped in, putting her hand
on Howard's shoulder.

"We might be putting a team together again," Sammi told
him, "just the three of us."

"I'd like that," Howard said with a smile.

After Sammi and Kodi left the hospital, they went out for

a late lunch before Kodi drove Sammi all the way home. Mack wasn't going to be home for several hours and Sammi didn't want to make Kodi have to just turn around and drive back to the city, so she invited her inside. They decided to watch a movie, but while Sammi made popcorn, Kodi gathered notebooks, pens, and Sammi's laptop instead of choosing a movie.

"What's all this?" Sammi asked, entering the sunny loft with a large bowl of fresh popcorn.

"You're never going to commit to being a thief again unless someone pushes you," Kodi explained. "So, consider this your push."

Sammi put the popcorn bowl on the coffee table and picked up a notebook before taking a seat next to her best friend on the couch. She and Kodi conspired, planned, and plotted for two hours before Kodi decided to head home. They had made enough progress that Sammi was finally fully confident in her decision to change careers again.

It was still a little while before Mack was expected to get home so Sammi cleaned up the popcorn mess then headed back up to the loft. She began gathering all the heist-planning evidence with the intention of hiding it all from Mack's sight until after they had their inevitable argument. But she heard a car pull into the driveway and, wondering if Kodi had forgotten something or Mack was home early, she left the notebooks on the coffee table to go see who was there.

Taking one step outside the front door, Sammi realized right away that the car in the driveway was neither Kodi's nor Mack's. She had a clear view of the vehicle from the front porch and could see that nobody was in the strange Buick, which made her wonder if it was just somebody visiting one of the neighbors. With a shrug of her shoulders, Sammi headed back inside and closed the front door behind her.

Forgetting about the notebooks, Sammi removed her cellphone from her back pocket as she walked into the master bedroom. She dialed Mack's number, wanting to give him a heads up about the weird car in the driveway, but Mack didn't answer the call. As she brought her phone down in front of her to type out a text message, Sammi saw a shadow in the bedroom doorway and chills shot up her spine.

The little hairs on Sammi's arms stood on end as she remembered the parking garage and the stranger in the mall. She silently rolled off the bed, on the side further from the door, and crouched behind it. Peeking around the corner of the mattress, Sammi watched the shadow move away from the door and listened intently for any noises that would give away the intruder's location before making her next move. Moving slowly so as not the make any noise herself, Sammi turned to the window behind her and, opening it as quietly as she could, used the nightstand below to give her a boost through it.

With a heavy thud, Sammi landed on her back on the ground outside the window. She lay in the grass for a moment, trying to catch her breath from having the wind knocked out of her before jumping up and running around the front of the house to the garage. There was a side door into the garage from the side yard that Sammi was able to slip through without making any sounds. She screamed with joy inside her head seeing that her car key was on the hook by the door that led into the kitchen, where it was supposed to be instead of when she lazily left it in the kitchen, so she dashed over, grabbed it, and let herself into the passenger side of her car. Popping the glove compartment open, she reached in and snatched up her off-duty pistol.

As Sammi backed herself out of the car, she heard the front door open and close. Hoping Mack hadn't just gotten home, she hurried back out the side door and toward the front of the house. She kept her gun in both hands and pointed it at the ground as she snuck around the corner of the house to the driveway.

The intruder had gotten behind the wheel of the Buick and started the engine. Sammi couldn't see their face clearly enough through the slightly tinted windows to recognize them, so she took a step toward the vehicle with her pistol aimed at the closed driver side window.

"Police! Shut the car off!" Sammi yelled, standing her ground.

The driver side window rolled down a few inches and Sammi got a bad feeling in her gut. She darted for cover on the front porch just as she heard gunfire. Landing hard on her back on the cement porch, her gun bounced out of her hands and landed a few feet behind her. Searing pain shot up her left leg and she sat up to see blood flowing out of a hole in the meaty part of her calf.

Before Sammi could even attempt to get to her feet, the intruder was out of the Buick and standing over Sammi with a handgun aimed down at her face. Sammi threw herself backwards, away from the familiar suspect, reaching out desperately behind her for her own gun.

"Why, Shay?" Sammi grunted, struggling to catch her breath as her old teammate kicked her gun away before kicking Sammi hard between her eyes.

Sammi lost consciousness for a second, lying helpless on the cement. Shay put one foot on Sammi's chest and knelt over her to keep her down as she started to come around. She rolled up Sammi's beige dress shirt from the bottom in order to uncover the scar on her side from where Eli had shot her years ago. Getting herself even closer, Shay put the barrel of her gun directly over the gruesome scar.

Going into panic mode, Sammi shoved Shay as hard as she could, throwing her completely off of her. She lunged at the crazy woman, keeping all of her weight on the right side of her body and ignoring the pain in her left leg, and wrestled the gun free from Shay's grasp. Remaining on top of Shay and bearing down all of her weight to keep her still, Sammi removed the magazine from Shay's Glock and emptied it. She tossed the pieces of the gun into the front yard and sighed in relief.

As Sammi took a deep breath, Shay easily threw her off of her and rolled Sammi over onto her back, sitting on her legs as she pulled a second handgun from her waistband. Without giving Sammi a chance to even react, Shay uncovered her side scar once again and fired the weapon as the barrel touched the disfigured skin. Sammi made a strange squeaking noise only once as her body convulsed from the force of the shot.

Shay stood up, gun still in hand, and stood over Sammi. She enjoyed watching as Sammi hopelessly covered the gushing wound with both of her hands, unable to apply enough pressure to make a difference. Once the light in Sammi's eyes started to dim, Shay finally ran to the Buick and sped away from the house.

After Shay had gone, Sammi weakly but desperately patted her pockets, feeling for her cellphone but it wasn't on her. With one last effort, she tried pulling her body to the door with just the use of her arms. But her blood loss had drained her strength and her energy, so she collapsed only inches from where she had been shot.

Having nothing left to fight with, Sammi laid back on the cold cement and let it soothe her sweat-soaked body. She placed her hands over her sticky, blood-soaked side again and just closed her eyes.

Chapter Fourteen
Home Movies (II)

It was two years previously, only weeks before Sammi's and Mack's wedding, and Kodi, Mack, and Sammi had just arrived at a busy bar in the city to celebrate the incarceration of Shay Krik. They had just attended her sentencing hearing and, although displeased with the sentence length, they were glad she'd be off the streets for a little while. No one else was charged in the case of the robbery of the four banks, but Eli was still a wanted man on the run.

As the three roommates got a couple of drinks in them, they finally loosened up and smiled for the first time in months. They hadn't had the easiest time recovering from the traumas of the past year and readjusting to all living together again. But they had made progress and Kodi and Mack had really bonded over their concern of Eli or somebody on Shay's behalf coming after Sammi. Everything regarding the old band of thieves had been left unresolved and it was unnerving that everyone was still out there with their unsettled feelings and their grudges.

Sammi sipped on her third margarita, sitting between Mack and Kodi at the bar. Mack sat on her right with his hand on her bare knee while he chatted over her with Kodi on her left. They were talking about the wedding while Sammi's mind was elsewhere. She was thinking back to when she had first met Shay and wondering how she hadn't seen how unhinged that woman was back then. But then again, she never would've imagined Eli was going to try to kill her when they had first met either.

"You okay?" Mack asked, rubbing Sammi's thigh.

"Yeah, it's just been a weird day," Sammi replied and smiled at her fiancé to reassure him that everything was fine.

"Anything you want to talk about?" Mack continued to question her.

"Not really," Sammi told him. "You just gotta realize it was weird watching someone go to jail who I've broken the law with many times."

Kodi nodded in agreement as her face fell. Both girls knew how unbelievably lucky they were to not be in the same situation as Shay. And they both knew that Mack was the only reason behind their luck. But Mack didn't quite see it that way, though, because he knew they were both good people and they deserved their second chance, regardless of whether Sammi was his bride-to-be or not.

"Sammi, that psychopath wanted to kill you," Mack reminded his fiancée. "Please don't put yourself in the same category as her."

Sammi smiled at the kindness from the man she loved. She put her hand sensually on Mack's leg and looked into his sensitive eyes as happiness and warmth washed over her. Mack leaned forward and brought his hand up to the side of her face to brush her hair away, but she flinched and pulled away.

"I'm so sorry!" Sammi panicked, realizing what she had just done.

"I think we need to talk," Mack replied in total seriousness, trying to hide how upset he was.

The soon-to-be-married couple had yet to be intimate with each other and they were running out of time to address the issue once and for all. Sammi had been doing everything she could to avoid the conversation, but the hurt look on Mack's face told her that it was time to bite the bullet and open up to him. So, she nodded in agreement at his last statement and suggested that they head home.

*

Kodi, Mack, and Sammi all finished their final drinks before Mack paid the tab and they all piled into a taxi. Sammi was being considerate and giving Mack some space after hurting his feelings at the bar. It pained her to be the reason he was upset, and she was scared that their upcoming discussion was going to push him away for good.

At the apartment, Kodi made herself scarce and quickly disappeared into the guest bedroom. Sammi had actually spent more nights sleeping in that room with her best friend than she had spent sharing Mack's bed since the girls had moved back in. They had been more shaken by the events of the past year than they were willing to admit and relied on each other for comfort.

Sammi was practically hiding by the front door to the apartment so Mack walked over and gently took one of her hands in his. He guided her upstairs to his bedroom and calmly closed the door before taking a seat on the edge of the bed. Too nervous to sit down, Sammi remained standing and facing the door, ready to bolt through it at any second.

"So, what's going on with you?" Mack asked with complete sincerity, making eye contact with Sammi to show his concern.

"Look, you know most of the story," Sammi began and started pacing the floor in front of Mack. "You know all about Eli and everything involving the team. But only Kodi knows what I'm about to tell you."

There was fear and sadness in Sammi's eyes as she stopped pacing and looked directly at Mack. Mack swiftly reached out and pulled Sammi to his lap. He wrapped his arms tightly around her body and held her to him, wanting to take her pain away. Sammi let the comfort of his love surround her as she told him about her past with her mother and her mother's much-too-friendly boyfriends.

"Sam, I am so sorry, I had no idea," Mack said quietly as a single tear squeezed out of each of his eyes and he hugged his fiancée tighter.

"I know you didn't because I didn't want you to know," Sammi informed him, seeing the pained look on his face. "I don't want you looking at me any differently."

"And I don't want you to ever feel uncomfortable or in danger ever again," Mack told her. "I will protect you for the rest of my life, but if you ever feel like I'm putting you in a bad spot, please just tell me you need space."

"No, Mack, I know you would never hurt me."

"We both know that, Sammi, but I'm dead serious. There are going to be bad days, just like there are in any marriage, and we're both going to get mad. But I am telling you right now that I can't bear the thought of ever causing you to be afraid. So, whenever you ask me for space, I will drop whatever I am saying or doing with no questions asked."

Mack could feel the tears on Sammi's face as she passionately kissed him. He kissed her back as he slowly brought his hands up to either side of her face and wiped the tears away with his thumbs. Sammi repositioned herself on Mack's lap so her entire body was facing his and wrapped her arms around his neck.

"Are you okay with this?" Mack whispered against Sammi's lips after she pulled his shirt off over his head.

"More than okay," Sammi replied, breathing heavily. "I love you."

*

Two weeks later, the night before their wedding, Mack and Sammi sat down to eat some pizza after a day of unpacking boxes in their new house. Mack had taken the week off from work for the move and the wedding, and the following week as well for their honeymoon. Kodi had assisted them with the move the day before, but she had her own redecorating to do now that she had Mack's big apartment all to herself.

While the happy couple ate their dinner, both of their cellphones began ringing almost simultaneously. As this never happened, Sammi and Mack gave each other surprised looks before looking to see who was calling them. Mack told Sammi his call was from work and went up to the loft to answer it, but Sammi didn't recognize the number on her screen so she was cautious as she answered. By the time Mack came back down to the kitchen, Sammi had already been off the phone for a few minutes.

"Anything important?" Mack asked as he put his phone down on the table.

"I actually have some pretty exciting news," Sammi told him, grinning. "I got accepted into the police academy. I start training when we get back from our honeymoon."

"Wait. You're going to be a cop?" Mack replied, confused and not impressed.

"Yeah, I thought you'd be proud of me. I'll finally be one of the good guys," Sammi explained.

Mack was speechless as he sat down across from his soon-to-be wife, who had never even once mentioned having any desire to be a cop. Sammi watched the torn expression on his face and couldn't believe that he wasn't being more supportive. This moment had played out so much differently in her head and she couldn't help but feel disappointed.

"What did your job want?" Sammi asked, clearly annoyed

and avoiding eye contact.

"They got a call from a unit down in Florida. There has been a string of robberies that they think they can tie to Eli," Mack informed her.

Sammi's eyes widened at the mention of Eli's name. Not a day had gone by that she hadn't wondered what had happened to him. She couldn't bring herself to hate him after their last nights together in that hotel room before their final heist, and she always hoped he was okay wherever he was.

"Did they give you any details?" Sammi tried sounding casual to mask just how interested she was in this conversation.

"Not yet," Mack told her. "Florida is faxing the case files over to the precinct so I'm going to head over early in the morning just to take a quick look and give them my opinion."

"You?" Sammi laughed. "What makes you an expert on Eli or his crime style?"

"Maybe the fact that I'm marrying his ex-girlfriend and ex-teammate," Mack challenged, growing frustrated by Sammi's sudden spark of interest in Eli's situation.

"Why does it sound like you care more about putting my ex behind bars than you do about becoming my husband?"

"How can you say that?"

"You're going to work to read case files on our wedding day!"

"You don't want him to get caught, do you?"

That was the last straw for Sammi. She got up from the table and went into the master bedroom, slamming the door behind her. Mack was right; Sammi didn't want Eli to get caught. But Mack would never be able to understand her reasons for feeling this way.

Sammi wandered into the bathroom and filled the large, round bathtub with hot water as she undressed. She slid into the steamy water and relaxed with her eyes closed. Allowing herself to think about Eli and miss her life as a thief, she began to cry.

Mack, who hadn't given himself enough time to calm down, burst through the bathroom door. Seeing Sammi cry only made him madder and he clenched his fists at his sides.

"Do you actually miss him?" Mack growled as Sammi finally looked at him. Her eyes were drawn directly to his fists and fear flickered in her starry blue eyes.

Sammi reached for a towel hanging on the wall by the tub and wrapped it around herself as she stood up. She backed into the furthest corner of the tub from Mack as she shakily asked him to leave.

"No, Sammi, we have to talk about this," Mack stated. "We're getting married tomorrow."

Mack was standing his ground and Sammi was feeling cornered. Sammi didn't want to fight, she just wanted to go to bed and not wake up until this day was over. Tears began to flow from her eyes again, harder this time, and her head was spinning with emotions until she was dizzy.

"You told me that I could ask for space without the fear of an argument," Sammi said quietly, straining to get the words out. "Please don't take that from me."

Taking a step forward, Mack wasn't ready to back down, but he looked into the emotions of Sammi's eyes and every bad feeling he had was gone. He abruptly stopped his advance and slowly raised his open hands chest-height in surrender. He could see as Sammi's entire body visibly relaxed.

"I'm sorry, Sam. I love you," Mack said innocently, and left his fiancée in peace.

*

Sammi ended up not getting any sleep that night. She lay in bed alone, not even sure where Mack had gone, and wondered how they were possibly going to make a marriage work. No matter how much they loved each other, they were still too different and couldn't seem to figure out how to understand each other's thoughts and feelings. There was no way to change Sammi's past and she didn't think she could handle a lifetime of being made to feel guilty about it.

In the morning, after Sammi was sure Mack had to have left for the city, she strayed out into the kitchen and grabbed an energy drink out of the refrigerator. She sat at the small kitchen table and let the cold, bitter beverage attempt to do its job while she tried to figure out if she was supposed to get ready for a wedding that day or not. As she took out her cellphone to give Mack a call, someone touched her shoulder and she nearly jumped out of her seat. Mack swung around her chair and knelt in front of her.

"Mack! What are you doing here...other than scaring the crap out of me?" Sammi asked, covering her heart with her hand.

"Why wouldn't I be here?" Mack replied sincerely with a look of confusion on his face.

"You were going to look at case files before the wedding today," Sammi reminded him.

"So, there is still a wedding today?" Mack asked, looking at Sammi with hope in his eyes.

"Of course there is, Mack," Sammi said softly and leaned forward in the chair so she could kiss him on the lips. "But why aren't you in the city?"

"Two reasons," Mack told her, putting his hands on her bare knees. "One, I couldn't leave this morning not knowing where we stood as a couple. And two, you didn't want me to go and that should've simply been enough."

"Mack, I do not miss Eli, but I would be happier if we stayed out of his business like he's staying out of ours."

"I think that's fair. He did help me save you from Nardino and his crazy sister."

Mack scooped Sammi into his arms and off the chair. He sat on the floor and held his bride, so relieved that she still wanted to marry him. Sammi tucked her head under Mack's chin and took his hand in one of hers, lacing her fingers through his.

"I love you," Sammi whispered, "and you are the only man I ever want to call my husband."

Chapter Fifteen
Carry You

As the Buick sped through a four-way intersection where Eli was waiting to make a right turn, Eli cursed out the reckless driver and checked his phone again. Two minutes later, he was creeping along the quiet suburban street and looking for the unassuming split-level house. There were no cars in the driveway when he found it and he was going to keep driving, but the body on the front porch made him slam on the brakes. He shut off the car on the side of the road and darted up the front lawn to the porch.

"Sammi! No!" Eli screamed as he realized what he was seeing. He ran to Sammi's almost-lifeless body and dropped to his knees beside her.

Sammi was unresponsive but Eli could feel her pulse. She had lost a lot of blood and it was everywhere, even her golden hair was drenched in it. Eli had forgotten his cellphone in the car, so he picked Sammi's body up in his arms and cradled her as he ran back down the yard to the driver side of his car.

Eli laid Sammi's unmoving body across the backseat of the car, not caring about the inevitability of fabric-ruining bloodstains. Then he jumped behind the wheel and sped off toward the closest hospital. He spoke aloud to Sammi the entire time, begging her not to die.

*

As Eli arrived at the hospital, Mack was finally getting home from work. He had tried to return Sammi's call twice but with no answer. His workday had been long and stressful and made him realize how much he truly appreciated having his wife working in the same building with him every day. As much as he wanted to keep having that in his life, he also knew that he couldn't control Sammi's life and he was going to have to be understanding if he couldn't convince her to stay on the force.

Pulling into the driveway, Mack was hit with an ominous feeling. The house seemed too dark for anybody to be home and Mack wondered if Sammi had actually come home at all that day or not. Stepping out of his car and turning up the front walk, Mack saw the bloody horror scene on his front porch and his heart dropped into the pit of his stomach.

Pulling his cellphone out of his jacket pocket, Mack tried calling Sammi once again as he hurried up to the front door. He stopped with his hand on the doorknob to take a quick, nausea-inducing look around the porch. All the way at the other end of the cement porch was a black pistol and Mack knew it was Sammi's off-duty weapon as soon as he picked it up.

There was still no answer on Sammi's phone, so Mack dialed the local precinct as he finally let himself into the eerily quiet house. He found Sammi's cellphone in their bedroom, but there didn't seem to be any signs of blood anywhere inside the home. The local police hadn't received any calls or complaints for any address on their street. But while Mack was still on the line with them, a call came in from the hospital about a gunshot victim fitting Sammi's description with suspicious circumstances. Mack gave them every bit of information that he could as he ran back outside to his car and broke every speed limit on his way over to the hospital.

*

"Mister, I need to know what happened in order to help her," a nurse argued with Eli outside of the emergency room in the waiting area. They had rushed Sammi into surgery and Eli could tell that they thought he was responsible for her condition.

"I don't know what happened!" Eli yelled at the impatient woman. "I found her like that!"

"But you know who she is?" the nurse asked, challenging him.

"Yes, but like I said, I haven't seen her in three years. What is so hard to understand about that?"

"Sir, we've already alerted the authorities. If you would just tell me what happened to your friend, it could help us save her life."

Eli wasn't surprised that the hospital had reported Sammi's case to law enforcement; she had two unexplained gunshot wounds after all. He wanted to be as helpful as he possibly could and stick around to wait on an update of Sammi's condition, but while he continued to argue with the nurse, he caught sight of Mack Johnson running through the waiting room. That was his cue to excuse himself, at least for a little while.

*

Mack ran up to the reception desk and hurriedly explained who he was looking for. The nurse who had just been talking to Eli overheard him and jumped in to offer the information she had. She explained that Sammi was going to be in surgery for a while yet and guided him to the more secluded waiting room near the operating rooms. After she described Sammi's injuries based on the initial assessment, she described the man who had brought Sammi to the hospital and there wasn't a doubt in Mack's mind that the man she was talking about was Eli Krik.

Not being able to comprehend what had happened, Mack had so many more questions, but cops finally arrived to ask their own questions. They were respectful of Mack and appreciative of Sammi for both also being in law enforcement and took it seriously when Mack told them to investigate Eli Krik as a suspect. Once the detectives had asked all their questions, Mack was left to wait alone for any news about Sammi.

Alone with his thoughts, Mack eventually remembered Kodi and figured he owed her a phone call. He was doubtful that she had any additional information because if she knew anything, she would be there with him in the waiting room. But one could always hope.

"Mack? What's wrong? You never call me," Kodi said, panicking as soon as she answered her phone.

"Sammi was shot. She's in surgery now. It doesn't look good, Kodi," Mack stated simply, only choking up at the end.

"What? No! I was just with her! There has to be a mistake!"

"I came home to a bloodbath on my front porch; there is no mistake. And I think Eli is responsible."

"Seriously? I'm on my way. I'll be right there."

A part of Mack wished Kodi had stayed on the line just so he wouldn't be alone, but the other part of him was glad he didn't have to talk about what happened anymore. It made him feel inadequate to not know what had happened and the fewer questions he could answer, the worse he felt. So, he finally settled into a wide, plastic chair to wait, hoping that every time a door opened, or a person entered the waiting room, that someone would tell him Sammi was alive.

*

After Kodi finally found an open spot in the huge hospital parking lot, she leapt out of her car and hurried towards the building. As she dashed past a second row of cars, she slowed down at the sound of someone calling her name.

"Kodi," the male voice hissed again as Eli came around from the driver side of a parked Honda.

"Eli! What did you do?" Kodi asked angrily, trying to keep quiet so as not to draw attention as she stopped in the middle of the parking lot to face her old comrade.

"Me? I found the girl I love dying on her front porch and rushed her to the hospital," Eli told her. "I'm not responsible for this!"

"Well, Mack thinks you are, so you need to get out of here," Kodi urged him, waving her arms in the direction away from the hospital.

"I will leave when I know Sammi's okay," Eli replied, desperate but standing his ground.

Kodi didn't really care if he stuck around or not. If he did shoot Sammi, he was going to get caught and finally get what was coming to him. And if he wasn't involved, he still really cared about Sammi and Kodi didn't have the heart to take that away from him. After everything, she wanted to believe that deep down he was one of the good guys.

"Fine!" Kodi gave in to him. "Get back in your car and wait there. I will come back out as soon as I get an update on Sammi."

Eli nodded and clasped his hands together out in front of him to motion his thanks. Then he hopped back into the driver seat of his car while Kodi continued on her way into the hospital.

When Kodi found Mack, he was sitting in the waiting room

with his head in his hands. Kodi sat down next to him and put a hand on his back to comfort him, which caused him to pick his head up and look over at her. His eyes were red, and his face was strained with stress. Kodi didn't even need to ask to know that he hadn't received any update on Sammi yet. So, they sat there without speaking, neither of them having any idea what to say. They sat in total silence for at least an hour before a doctor finally came to talk to them.

"Lieutenant Johnson, your wife was brought in with two gunshot injuries," the doctor spoke directly to Mack. "The shot to her leg was a through-and-through—a clean hit through the muscle that isn't causing any concerns. However, the shot to her side was fired at an incredibly close range, creating a more massive area of concern."

"When can I see her?" Mack asked, cutting the doctor off as if he wasn't hearing a word he was saying.

"Lieutenant, she has lost a lot of blood and we have to worry about the likeliness of infection due to the proximity of major internal organs," the doctor explained. "She's not going to wake up for a while yet, if at all."

"So, I can see her now?" Mack repeated himself as the doctor's eyes widened and he silently questioned Mack's mental state.

"What my friend is trying to say," Kodi jumped in to save Mack, "is thank you, doctor. But may we see Sammi anytime soon?"

"I'll send a nurse as soon as her room is ready," the doctor replied, concerned about their lack of understanding regarding Sammi's condition. This wasn't his first time dealing with this level of denial and he knew he'd be having a similar conversation with them again soon.

After the doctor excused himself, Kodi followed suit and hurried out to the parking lot. She easily found Eli's Honda again and Eli was out of the car before Kodi even caught her breath after sprinting the length of the parking lot. Kodi told

Eli everything the doctor had said, word for word, and he was the first person to react appropriately to the update.

*

Eli's head was spinning as Kodi told him what the doctor had said about Sammi. He got so dizzy that he had to sit down and backed up to the curb beside his car and sat on the edge. Feeling like he was going to be sick, he put his head between his knees and focused on his breathing.

"I don't want her to die," Eli said quietly, mostly to himself.

"Says the guy who tried killing her three years ago," Kodi scoffed, feeling angry that he could say such a thing. It was also bothering her that he was acting more upset than she and Mack were combined.

Eli looked up at Kodi with a hurt expression on his face. He couldn't deny the words that just came out of her mouth, but he couldn't believe she would bring it up in that moment. If she hated him that much, it was only a matter of time before she told the police where to find him and then he'd be going to jail for quite some time.

"I'm sorry," Eli whispered, looking down again. "I'll get out of here. Can you just...can you let her know I was here for her?"

"Eli, I'm sorry," Kodi said, taking a seat next to him on the curb. "I'm just a little sensitive right now. But do you mind if I ask you why you were at her house?"

"I was just hoping to catch a glimpse of her, to make sure she's happy," Eli told her.

"Eli...she is happy...with Mack."

Kodi put her arm around Eli's shoulders as he looked at her with tears in his eyes. Eli kept his face composed and let the tears fall silently while Kodi comforted him. But after a few minutes, Kodi told Eli that she had to get back inside before Mack got suspicious and then hurried back into the hospital.

As Eli got back into his car, he realized that he and Kodi hadn't made any plans to follow up or even exchange phone numbers. Frustrated, he drove to the closest motel and got a room for the night. He had already made up his mind that he was going to see Sammi the next day, no matter what.

*

Kodi made it back inside the waiting room just in time as the nurse arrived, who led her and Mack to Sammi's room. Sammi looked unusually small, lying unconscious in the hospital bed, and more pale than she had ever looked in her entire life. Her long, blonde hair, still sticky with blood, was clumped together at the tips and draped over her right shoulder. Appalled at the nurses for allowing her beautiful best friend to look anything but runway-ready, Kodi went into the bathroom and wet a bunch of towels in the sink to scrub the blood out of Sammi's hair.

"Thank you," Mack muttered as Kodi went to work on the already-stained strands of yellow hair. He hadn't gotten within five feet of Sammi and he just stood quietly staring at her.

Kodi just nodded, too upset to talk. She kept herself busy with Sammi's hair for an hour while Mack stayed in the same spot without moving or talking. Eventually the nurse came back to tell them that it was getting late and it would help them feel better to go home and get some sleep. Mack was out of the room before she even finished telling them what time they could return in the morning, so Kodi whispered a quick goodbye to her best friend before hurrying after Mack to make sure he was okay.

"You want to stay at the house?" Mack asked, ignoring Kodi's question of concern for him when she caught up to him in the hallway.

"Your house is a crime scene," Kodi reminded him. "Come

on, I'll treat us to a hotel."

Mack followed Kodi to her car and got into the passenger seat. While Kodi drove them in silence to the nearest hotel, Mack felt something on the floor against his foot and leaned forward to pick up whatever it was. It was dark in the car, but Mack didn't even need the streetlights passing by to know what he was holding.

"She really doesn't want to be a cop anymore, does she?" Mack asked Kodi, holding out Sammi's left-behind detective badge. There was the sound of a smile in his voice even though there were tears in his eyes.

"No. No, she doesn't," Kodi told him quietly and as gently as possible.

"I'm so stupid," Mack said, chuckling as more tears rolled down his squared cheeks. "I just wanted to protect her."

"She knows, Mack. She knows," Kodi reassured him and took her right hand off the steering wheel to hold his left hand in a comforting manner.

Mack took Sammi's detective badge into the hotel with him and wept himself to sleep with it still in his hands that night. Kodi laid awake in the second bed all night, worrying about Sammi and wondering who was to blame for putting her in the hospital. The moment Shay crossed her mind, Kodi couldn't shake the bad feeling that Shay had something to do with it.

In the morning, Mack was awakened by his cellphone ringing. It was Captain Hobbs, who had heard about Sammi and was calling to check in. Hobbs was understanding of the situation and told Mack to take off work for as long as he needed to be by Sammi's side. Normally, Mack couldn't wait to get back to work and threw himself into the job during times of stress, but he was numb and emotionless as he thought about work in that moment.

Since they were both awake, Kodi and Mack headed right back to the hospital. The nurse from the night before ran into them in the hallway and let them know that there had been no changes regarding Sammi's condition. Mack didn't even react as he walked past the nurse and into Sammi's room with his head down. Kodi apologized for him and thanked the nurse before following her emotionally ruined friend.

Someone, Kodi assumed it was the nurse, had brought in two chairs by Sammi's bed for them. Still not getting within five feet of his wife, Mack had pulled one of the chairs back to his spot from the night before and sat, keeping his distance. Kodi shook her head as she walked around Mack and pulled her own chair up to Sammi's bedside and sat down with Sammi's right hand in both of hers.

"There's something seriously wrong with your husband," Kodi joked quietly to Sammi, knowing that Mack could hear her. But Mack wasn't talking.

Kodi spent most of the morning talking to Sammi's comatose body, just doing what she could to try to help. Mack just watched silently from his chair, planning everything he would say to Sammi, if she woke up, in his head. By lunchtime, Dr. Brock made an appearance and suggested that Kodi and Mack go and try to eat something after they realized they hadn't eaten in almost twenty-four hours. They got directions to the hospital cafeteria then Kodi had to steer Mack out of the room to get him moving.

*

When Eli got to the hospital that morning, Kodi and Mack were already sitting in Sammi's room. He knew he couldn't let Mack see him, so he went for a walk around the entire hospital. Checking back in on Sammi's room after his lap, Sammi's visitors were still present. Disappointed, he went out to his car and decided to wait and try again at lunchtime.

Returning to Sammi's room a little after noon, Eli finally found the room empty except for the patient. Eli slipped into the bright, quiet room and closed the door behind him for privacy, knowing he didn't have very long until Mack returned. Then he walked to Sammi's bedside and stood over her, taking her hand in his. She was comfortably warm to the touch and Eli wanted to believe that she could wake up any second.

"Sammi, I know that nothing I can ever say will make up for what I've put you through," Eli spoke softly to his one that got away. "But you gotta pull through this because I know your story's not over yet. And maybe, just maybe, our story isn't over yet either."

Eli then leaned forward, his shaggy hair blocking his face from view, and very carefully touched his lips to Sammi's lips. He had intended for the kiss to be very brief, but as it dawned on him that this could be his last chance to kiss Sammi ever, he couldn't pull away. A single tear escaped his eye and rolled down his nose, landing on Sammi's porcelain face. Embarrassed, Eli quickly wiped it away with his thumb.

"Get away from her," a deep voice growled from behind Eli and he spun around to find himself face-to-face with Sammi's husband.

"Mack, relax, let's talk," Eli spoke gently as he put his hands up in front of him to show that he meant no harm.

Kodi stood next to Mack but didn't look surprised to see Eli. Mack already had his phone out and Eli's eyes popped out of his head in a panic. Torn between the two men who loved her best friend, Kodi acted on impulse and grabbed the phone away from Mack.

"Mack, Eli didn't do this," Kodi said calmly, pocketing the cellphone.

"Who else could it have been?" Mack continued in anger, his eyebrows practically touching in a V-shape on his forehead.

"One word," Kodi stated. "Shay."

"You can't know that for sure!" Mack yelled, suddenly

more upset than mad.

"No, it was Shay," came a small voice from behind Eli.

Chapter Sixteen
Right Here, With You

When Sammi woke up in the hospital, she knew she wasn't alone, but nobody was paying her any mind. She lay still while her friends argued, and tried to remember every detail of her assault from Shay. There was a slight twinge of pain in her super stiff left calf, but her right side was entirely numb. Panicking, she slowly touched her fingertips to the bandaging below her ribcage to make sure her body was still whole.

Sammi's mouth was dry so her first attempt to get Eli's attention went unnoticed. He stood only a foot away from her with his back to her, but her voice was hardly audible. Taking a big breath and swallowing hard, Sammi tried again, this time putting an end to their argument by informing them it was indeed Shay who had shot her. Suddenly, all six eyes were on her.

Kodi was the only one to rush to Sammi, carefully putting her arms around her best friend in a hug. As gentle as Kodi was, she still jostled Sammi enough to cause her discomfort. Sammi grimaced as she weakly put an arm around Kodi to comfort her until Kodi finally released her.

Eli wanted to move closer to Sammi too, but he knew he was already pushing his luck with Mack. So, he stood by the foot of the bed with his hand on Sammi's blanket-covered good leg, trying to watch Sammi's face while also keeping an uneasy eye on Mack.

Mack remained midway between Sammi and the door, trying not to look at Sammi. Being proven wrong about Eli's involvement in the shooting had left an emotionless expression on his face. Kodi walked back over to him and was going to guide him over to his wife, but Dr. Brock entered the room before she had gotten him to budge even a little.

"Okay, first thing's first," the doctor said looking around at everyone in the room, "there's too much going on in here. I need two of you to leave."

Eli, knowing it wasn't his place to stay, made the first move for the door. When he walked past Mack, he was alarmingly aware of Mack's height advantage as Mack glared down at him with unadulterated hatred in his eyes.

"I'll go, too," Kodi offered, snapping Mack out of his stare down.

"No, stay," Mack told her, turning to look her in the eyes. "If you haven't noticed, I haven't been much help."

Kodi opened her mouth to argue, but Mack was already halfway out the door. She wished she could believe he had made this decision for the right reasons, but she knew he only wanted to confront Eli out of Sammi's sight. But they were supposed to be there for Sammi, so she stopped worrying about Eli and Mack and returned to Sammi's side.

"You seem to be pretty popular, Mrs. Johnson," the doctor said while checking Sammi's chart. He was fit and handsome for an older grey-haired man.

"Call me Sammi," Sammi replied after cringing at the use of her married name.

"Okay, Sammi," Dr. Brock replied with a smile. "How are you feeling?"

"Kinda freaking out that my insides are going to fall out of the hole in my side that I can't feel," Sammi told him, returning his smile.

Dr. Brock chuckled and explained that the numbness would wear off soon, then promised he had stitched her up properly. Sammi liked him for keeping things lighthearted with her, which made it easier for her to talk to him.

"So, I'm going to be okay then?" Sammi asked and the doctor's face got serious.

"Sammi, the fact that you are awake and in incredibly high spirits are good signs," Dr. Brock told her. "But I have to let you know that I am worried about infection."

Sammi nodded as her face fell and Kodi squeezed her hand. The doctor clearly felt bad about upsetting his patient and quickly changed the glum look on his face.

"Look, I'm going to keep a close eye on you and make sure the antibiotics are working overtime for you," Dr. Brock added with a comforting smile.

The doctor then promised to check in again after dinner and excused himself from the room. Kodi silently wished that he would hold off on sending the guys back in so she could have a minute to talk to Sammi about her husband acting super distant.

"Did you see if that hot doctor was wearing a ring?" Sammi asked as soon as Dr. Brock was out of the room.

"No!" Kodi replied in complete shock. "But you're wearing one!"

"Not for me," Sammi said with a sigh. "Grey and sophisticated is your type."

"Well, he was right about one thing. You are in a fantastic mood."

*

While the men were banished from the room, Eli had

hurried out to the parking lot. He wasn't intending on leaving, he was just attempting to put space between himself and Mack until Mack had gotten a chance to calm down. They were supposed to be there for Sammi and not their own drama after all.

"Eli!" Mack called after his nemesis just as Eli reached the pavement. Mack had just exited the building and was closing in on him.

When Eli finally stopped and turned around to face Mack, he was immediately knocked to the ground on his back. Mack shook his fist off and rubbed it with his other hand where it hurt from colliding with Eli's skull.

"Do you feel better now?" Eli yelled, angry but not confrontational. He stayed on the ground, not wanting to get hit again.

"No!" Mack yelled back at him. "Why are you even here?!"

"For Sammi," Eli told him. His voice was still loud, but it was calmer now.

"I know why you're at this hospital. But why are you in New York again after almost three years on the run?" Mack reiterated with his arms out at his sides, looking for the truth.

Eli, who had sat up, looked down at the pavement. "For Sammi," he repeated himself, much quieter this time.

Mack's hands balled into fists again as his body shook with rage. He wished Eli would get up off the ground already so he could knock him out.

"You wouldn't hit me if you weren't threatened by me," Eli said with a smug grin on his face, finally finding his confidence. He picked himself up off the ground and put his arms out at his sides as he took a step toward Mack, inviting him to attack again.

"Why would I be threatened by a long-haired punk like you?" Mack asked, laughing and unfurling his fists.

"Because I have history with Sammi and that scares the hell out of you," Eli taunted, knowing Mack wasn't going to hit him.

"And I have a beautiful marriage with her, so you are way out of your league," Mack shot at him.

Believing he had made his point, Mack turned and headed back inside. Eli laughed to himself as he took a seat on the side of the curb outside the hospital. He leaned forward with his head in his left hand and gently rubbed his freshly bruised eye socket.

Eli wasn't going to give up that easily and he believed Mack was a coward for not hitting him again when taunted. As he sat there, giving everybody time to cope with everything, Eli thought about seeing Sammi awake and his desire to talk to her. He knew how lucky she was to be awake so soon and wondered how and why she woke up when she did.

*

Before Mack returned to Sammi's room, Kodi warned Sammi that he seemed a little overwhelmed by his emotions and that she was worried about him. Sammi hadn't noticed anything, but she had only been awake for a few minutes before he had run out of the room.

"I'm sure Eli being here isn't helping," Kodi added, glancing nervously at the open door for either of the guys.

"Yeah, I wanted to ask you about that. Where the hell did Eli come from?" Sammi replied.

"Wait. You didn't know he was back in the city?" Kodi asked, and Sammi shook her head. "He's the one who found you and brought you here."

"I wouldn't be surprised if he and Shay set you up just so Eli could weasel his way back into your life," Mack mumbled as he walked back into the room.

Sammi's eyes lit up upon seeing her husband, but Mack kept his gaze on the floor. Kodi, frowning at Mack's conspiracy theory, looked back and forth between her married friends.

She groaned as Mack sat in his too-far-away chair, then she left the room with an exasperated sigh.

With Kodi out of the room, Mack stared harder at the floor without speaking. Sammi watched him and was torn between wanting to force herself out of that bed to go to him and wanting to cry from frustration. In the end, the crying won out and she pulled her blanket up over her face to hide her tears.

As Sammi cried harder and the sobbing began, she started to feel the stitches tugging at the skin on her side. It was more uncomfortable than painful, but her hand shot up to cover it regardless. She let the blanket slide off her face as she rolled to her left, facing away from Mack.

"Sammi? What's wrong?" Mack asked, finally looking up and filled with concern at the sound of his wife's sobbing.

"You're mad at me for getting hurt and it's all my fault," Sammi told him, sobbing harder and still not facing him.

"Why would you think I'm mad at you?" Mack asked, sincere and confused.

"You won't even get near me," Sammi replied sadly.

Sammi felt the bed shift behind her as Mack sat on the edge of it. He slid his arm under her and carefully lifted her upper body into his lap. With her head propped up against his chest, he brushed her hair away from her face and kissed the top of her head.

"I am so sorry, sweetheart—I love you so much. I just kind of shut down when I thought I was going to lose you," Mack spoke apologetically. "Suddenly I was seeing you as the most fragile thing in the world and I guess I was afraid I would break you."

"Mack, even if your hands could cause my death, I would still want you to hold me," Sammi told him, lacing her fingers with his by her stomach.

"I will remember that," Mack replied, getting serious again. "Now, another question. Why is getting shot your fault?"

Sammi tensed up and looked down at their hands. If Mack wasn't mad before, he was going to be upset with her once he found out she was keeping something from him.

"Because I should've seen it coming," Sammi admitted. "I kind of had a feeling somebody was following me after bumping into them at the mall. Shay was apparently stalking me, and I should've told you."

"Uh, the mall and the parking garage were actually me," Eli shyly said as he quietly slipped back into the room. Kodi was right behind him, wearing an intrigued look on her face.

"Eli, your eye!" Sammi exclaimed as Mack's hands twitched involuntarily, alerting Sammi of his guilt.

"I'm sorry, but did you just admit to stalking my wife?" Mack asked, desperately trying to keep the attention on Eli.

"Yeah, it's not like I could've just looked her up," Eli spoke directly to Mack, tauntingly. "I didn't expect her to be married to her big, brutish cop."

"And I'm supposed to believe you had nothing to do with your sister shooting her?!" Mack yelled and leapt off the bed to confront him.

"Ow, fuck," Sammi gasped in pain. Mack hadn't been careful as he got up from the bed and Sammi hadn't been able to catch herself before her stitched-up side landed with most of her weight on the edge of the mattress of the hospital bed.

Sammi's blood pressure shot up from the jolt of pain, alerting the nurses. The same nurse from the morning ran into the room and helped Sammi get propped back up and comfortable on the pillows. Everybody watched in shock as she rolled the blanket up from the side to reveal a bloody spot on Sammi's hospital gown.

"I'm going to have to uncover the wound, if you all wouldn't mind giving Sammi some privacy," the nurse announced to the room without turning away from Sammi.

Kodi ushered the two boys out into the hallway, not

pleased with either of their behaviors. She felt like a schoolteacher as she directed them to stand against the wall on opposite sides of the hallway while she stayed between them. Eli had his head hung in shame, but Mack couldn't take his glare off of him.

"This has to stop," Kodi hissed, "or you're going to have to take turns visiting her."

"Bullshit. She's my wife. He shouldn't even be here!" Mack cried out.

"I'm not leaving until Sammi asks me to leave," Eli grumbled, eyes still on the floor.

"I'm about to ask all of you to leave!" the nurse announced as she joined them in the hallway. "I want Sammi to have peace and quiet for the rest of the day and I don't care how it happens. Now drop the soap opera drama or go home."

Sammi, with the help of a pain medication, slept for the majority of the rest of the day. Mack sat in a chair by Sammi's side, holding her hand while she slept. Eli, choosing to be respectful but refusing to back down, took Mack's old chair in the middle of the room. Kodi sat on the deep windowsill to oversee the boys, even though everyone was quiet and lost in their own thoughts.

As promised, Dr. Brock checked in around dinnertime. Sammi was fast asleep, rolled ever so slightly to her left toward Mack, who was watching her innocent face as she slept.

"I heard we had a bit of an incident earlier," Dr. Brock spoke quietly so as not to disturb Sammi.

"It was my fault," Mack whispered sadly, not looking away from Sammi's face.

"Let's try to keep that from happening again," Dr. Brock replied, trying his best to be kind. "How is she doing otherwise?"

"She's been kind of out of it all afternoon," Kodi offered from the window.

"That's not unusual," the doctor informed her. "She's on a pretty heavy antibiotic. And she really should keep as calm as possible."

"Dr. Brock," Sammi said with a smile, even though she was still groggy from her sleep.

"Hello, Sammi," the handsome doctor replied, returning her smile. "It's nice to see you again."

Since Sammi was awake, Dr. Brock checked a few things while chatting easily with her. He kept her distracted as he pushed once, gently and precisely, on each of her wounds to gauge an accurate pain reaction. As soon as his hand was even near her side, she shot backwards away from him.

"Did that actually hurt, or do you still think you have a gaping hole in your side?" Dr. Brock asked, raising a curious eyebrow at her.

"Gaping hole," Sammi admitted quietly with a theatrical frown.

The doctor chuckled and shook his head at Sammi. He patted her knee on her uninjured leg before updating her chart and saying goodnight.

"I like him," Sammi said happily after Dr. Brock had left the room, her eyelids still heavy. She turned toward Mack again, holding his hand and pulling his arm toward her to nuzzle against.

"I think he likes you too," Eli replied smartly and smirked at Mack.

"Who wouldn't like Sammi?" Mack shot back at him, petting his wife's hair.

"No fighting," Kodi warned the boys from the windowsill.

Sammi seemed oblivious as she snuggled closer into Mack's arm. Her eyes were getting more and more difficult to keep open and her husband was so warm and comfortable. She wanted nothing more than to be at home in bed with the man she loved holding her. And that's all she thought about as she drifted back to sleep.

Chapter Seventeen
I'm Gonna Love You

The next four days were similar to the first day Sammi woke up in the hospital. Eli, Kodi, and Mack were by her side with Kodi keeping the peace between the testosterone-fueled boys every day. Dr. Brock kept his routine of checking in on Sammi twice a day and was pleased with the decrease in drama in the room. Local detectives came around on the second day to take Sammi's statement, which made Eli visibly uncomfortable and was the only thing that got him out of the room.

On the fifth day, Sammi was finally released and got to go home. She was walking with a bit of a limp until her calf muscle healed, but it was better for her to be taking it easy anyway. Dr. Brock sat down with her before releasing her to go over her restrictions and medications. She wasn't supposed to return to work for two weeks and, even then, she was going to have to be on desk duty until her side was healed almost entirely.

"I want to see you once a week to start out with, just to make sure your side stays on track," Dr. Brock told Sammi after explaining everything.

"That's fine by me. I'm going to miss seeing you every day," Sammi teased, playfully bumping his arm with her shoulder.

"Are you done flirting with the doctor yet?" Mack asked, lighthearted, as he waited by the door for his wife.

Mack had already been by the house to make sure the front porch was free of blood and the house was completely cleaned and fully restocked so that Sammi had nothing to worry about. Kodi was going to stay in the spare bedroom for the two weeks before Sammi went back to work so Mack could return to his job awhile. Nobody knew what Eli's plans were as they all finally left the hospital together and Eli went his separate way.

Sammi had the backseat of Kodi's car to herself but she sat in the middle, popping her head upfront between Kodi in the driver seat and Mack riding shotgun so she wouldn't feel left out. She couldn't believe how great it felt just to be out of that hospital room and back in the real world.

"Here, this is yours," Mack said from the passenger seat and handed the still flawlessly brand-new wallet containing Sammi's detective badge to his wife behind him.

Sammi took the badge from him and sat back in her seat to look at it. The day she had gotten the stupid thing was the day she almost died and that meant something to her. She just didn't know what yet.

When they pulled into the driveway, Sammi held onto the badge as she got out of the car. She knew that Mack had cleaned off the front porch, but she still expected to find something that would spook her as she approached the scene of her attempted homicide. There was nothing to be seen that would even hint that somebody was nearly murdered there, but Sammi still got the chills as she stepped up onto the cement porch. As she stopped to take a look around, her face fell at the absence of her off-duty pistol.

"I guess the detectives have my gun," Sammi pouted and stuck out her bottom lip for dramatic effect.

"We'll get you a better one," Mack offered sincerely as he hooked his arm around her back to guide her inside and away from the bad memories.

Mack steered Sammi into the kitchen where Kodi was already organizing her medications at the counter. Sammi sat down at the kitchen table and placed her badge on the tabletop. The excitement of coming home had drained her of energy and every one of her muscles ached with weakness. Her body slouched forward in the chair and she had to stop herself from resting her head on the table.

"Hey, babe, are you okay?" Mack asked and put his hand on Sammi's shoulder from behind, watching her body language closely.

"I'm just tired," Sammi sighed in reply without turning to look at him, trying to shake him off. She started to yawn but quickly fought it back to hide it from her hovering husband.

"Come on, let's get you to bed," Mack said, wrapping his fingers around her slender arm.

"It's the middle of the afternoon," Sammi argued with a feeble attempt at yanking her arm away from him.

"Sam, I'm exhausted too. I haven't slept much in five days. I know I'd sleep a lot better with you by my side," Mack told her, feigning innocence.

Sammi finally turned toward her husband and glared at him, knowing he would say anything to make her go to bed. But she had been dreaming about sharing a bed with Mack again for five days, so she willingly stood up and followed him into their bedroom. She waited for Mack to lie down first, prepared to continue fighting him if he was just tricking her, then she lay down beside him and snuggled into his solid chest. He was gentle with her, still afraid of breaking her, as he wrapped his arms around her and held her to him. Having been truthful about being tired, Mack was asleep within minutes and his steady breathing lulled Sammi to sleep as well.

*

Mack woke up two hours later, feeling super comfortable and refreshed. Sammi was still sleeping peacefully across his chest so he gently kissed the top of her head before carefully rolling out from under her and off the bed. He made sure he hadn't disturbed Sammi enough to wake her before slipping quietly out of the room.

Kodi was in the kitchen making dinner for everyone and Mack felt bad about disappearing on her the moment they had gotten home. They had talked about her staying there for the two weeks just to keep an eye on Sammi while Mack went back to work, but he hadn't expected her to take care of all of them. He was grateful for her ability to make herself feel at home, though.

"Aren't you tired?" Mack asked Kodi as he took a seat at the kitchen table.

"Yeah, but I'll sleep tonight," Kodi told him. "Is Sammi up too?"

"No, I'm kind of hoping she sleeps through the night," Mack replied, picking up the detective badge on the table and absentmindedly playing with it.

"Well, she's gotta eat, Mack, and take her meds," Kodi reminded him.

"Then you can wake her up," Mack said jokingly, having no intention of waking Sammi up himself.

Kodi finished cooking and serving three dishes of pot pie before realizing Mack really wasn't going to get Sammi. Sticking her tongue out at him, she snatched up Mack's cellphone from the table and used it to dial Sammi's number. They both heard Sammi's Mötley Crüe ringtone in the next room and then it stopped suddenly, followed by a thud as the phone hit the bedroom wall. Kodi quickly put Mack's phone back down in front of him as Sammi emerged groggily from the master bedroom.

"That's how you wake up your injured wife?" Sammi asked, exaggerating a frown as she limped sleepily over to her husband.

"Thanks a lot, Kodi," Mack grumbled as he took Sammi's hand and swept her onto his lap.

Kodi smiled victoriously and slid the third plate of pot pie across the table to Sammi. Sammi tried to eat as much as she could but her appetite hadn't been normal since she'd been shot. Then she took her meds and excused herself to go take a shower, seeming to be in a bit of a hurry to get away from her friends.

While Sammi was in the shower, Kodi and Mack hung out in the loft. Mack was hoping Sammi would be up for a movie, overly eager to spend some quality time with her, so he was flipping through the choices on the television to find a good one. Kodi was pretending to browse the shelves that lined the walls of the loft for something to read, but she was looking for the notebooks that she and Sammi had used to write out their heists. Suddenly they both heard a strange thump that rang throughout the house and caused Kodi and Mack to look at each other.

"Sammi!" Mack and Kodi cried out at the same time as they dropped what they were doing and ran to the master bedroom.

The shower in the master bathroom was still running so Kodi stayed back while Mack entered the bathroom to check on his wife. Sammi was picking herself up off the shower floor and reaching for the foggy glass door as Mack readied a towel for her. As soon as Sammi opened the shower door, all Mack saw was the tiny drop of blood on the corner of Sammi's forehead.

"What happened?" Mack asked more aggressively than he had intended.

"I'm fine!" Sammi replied angrily, ripping the towel out of

Mack's hand.

"No, you're not," Mack told her, softly now, as he wiped the blood off her forehead with his thumb and showed it to her.

"It's not a big deal," Sammi said defensively. "I just underestimated how drowsy my meds make me."

"Oh, Sammi," Mack sighed as he pulled her into a hug and held her for a moment.

Sammi's passing out in the shower made Kodi and Mack worry more about her and want to keep much closer eyes on her. Mack considered delaying his return to work and Kodi supported the idea, but Sammi put her foot down and insisted that they both give her room to breathe and that Mack go back to work already.

*

So the next morning, Sammi slept in while Mack got ready and left for work. Sammi was in such a deep sleep that Mack couldn't have woken her if he wanted to. When Sammi finally did wake up, she was sad that she was alone in bed but happy that Mack had respected her need for space to heal. She loved Mack with everything she had, but his lack of confidence in her, even after the number of times she'd proven her strength, was enough to drive her away.

"Sometimes I like it so much better when it's just you and me," Sammi said casually to Kodi over breakfast later that morning.

"That's because I don't hover over you like Mack does," Kodi told her and Sammi nodded in agreement.

After breakfast, the girls continued their Mack-free day by making themselves comfortable for a movie in the loft. Sammi, who was usually one for a cheap, gruesome horror flick, opted for a mindless comedy that day. She was dozing off before the opening credits had even finished but managed to pull through the sleepy haze with the help of Kodi keeping conversation with her. Once the movie was over, Kodi got up to shut the television off and glanced at the shelves in the cornering wall.

"Hey, Sammi," Kodi said suddenly, still looking at the wall. "What did you do with those notebooks we had up here?"

Sammi's face fell and her body froze on the couch. The notebooks she had wanted to remove from plain sight had been left out in the open when Shay had broken into the house. Sammi tried to remember if she had seen Shay with them or not but she couldn't recall seeing Shay until she was standing over her on the front porch.

"Um, I'm kind of hoping Shay has them," Sammi admitted with a big gulp of guilt. "Because if she doesn't, the police department does."

Suddenly, the doorbell rang and both girls jumped from surprise. Sammi got up to answer it, but Kodi quickly threw her arm out in front of her to stop her. Then she took Sammi's hand and led her into the guest bedroom where there was a window with a view of the driveway. Kodi looked first and breathed a huge sigh of relief.

"It's the lost puppy," Kodi said with a giggle and headed for the front door. Sammi followed her with a look of confusion but she understood when Kodi opened the door and let Eli into the house.

Eli's eyes took in every inch of the house as he entered. He uncomfortably ran his hand through his hair as his gaze landed on Sammi. It was strange for Sammi to see him in her home and she was all of a sudden very aware of how much she had changed in the past two years.

"Sammi, can we talk before I lose my nerve?" Eli asked quietly, his voice shaking with anxiety.

Nodding, Sammi led Eli through the kitchen to the back door. It was nice outside and Sammi had been craving fresh air since her hospital stay, so the former lovers sat on the back porch to talk in privacy.

"You know I've always believed that people design their own future and create their own luck. That's why we're thieves," Eli told Sammi, leaning in towards her and talking nervously with his hands. "But this whole thing has left me feeling like some things do happen for a reason. What are the chances that I showed up in time to save your life? And you're going to think I'm crazy, but I swear that you woke up in the hospital right after I kissed you. I never believed in fate until you came into my life. But you are my fate, Sammi. I know this in my heart."

As Eli finished speaking, he looked deep into Sammi's widened blue eyes. Sammi had not been expecting anything he had just said, and she was too surprised to reply right away. The only part she immediately agreed with was that she thought he was crazy. She took a moment to collect her own feelings and took a deep breath before responding.

"Eli, I will never not want you in my life. We've had a rocky past, but I've seen you grow into a better person," Sammi spoke kindly and softly. "But I am in love with Mack. He is my husband and I adore him and his selflessness. And it would make me incredibly happy if you guys could get along."

"Well, I'm not going anywhere," Eli assured her. "So, Mack is either going to have to accept me or kill me."

Eli smiled, but there was a nervous gleam in his eyes. It wasn't a secret that he believed Sammi to be worth killing for. He just had to hope that Mack didn't feel the same way.

Kodi ended up ordering sandwiches for the three of them for lunch and they all sat around the kitchen table to eat. Eli hung out until after lunch then hugged both of his friends goodbye. After he had gone, Sammi told Kodi about their conversation on the back porch but Kodi didn't look the least bit surprised.

"So, is he on the team again, too?" Kodi asked, sounding annoyed. She and Sammi were still sitting at the kitchen table and Sammi was taken aback by her best friend's sudden attitude.

"I haven't even said anything to him about it," Sammi replied defensively. "It's not like we're stealing anything anytime soon."

"I knew you were going to flake out again," Kodi said, shaking her head in disappointment. "Your indecisiveness is giving me whiplash."

Before Sammi could respond, Kodi stood up and walked into the guestroom. Sammi was aware that she was constantly back and forth with what she wanted to do, but she had other people in her life to consider and was having a hard time trying to make everyone happy. Plus, things kept happening and people kept coming back into her life that were pulling her in all different directions.

Kodi didn't come out of the bedroom so Sammi decided to give her some space. The morning had been eventful enough to leave Sammi feeling sleepy, but she didn't want to seclude herself in the master bedroom in case Kodi wanted to talk. So, she went up to the loft, threw *Die Hard* in the DVD player because she'd seen it a hundred times, and snuggled onto the couch with a heavy blanket. Two minutes later, she was out like a light.

*

Hiding in her room until Mack got home, Kodi eventually felt bad about taking her frustration out on Sammi. It was Sammi who was frustrating her, but she knew she could've handled the situation better and just talked to her best friend instead of getting short with her. She really just wanted Sammi to be happy and she knew all Sammi had to do was rob one place and she would get her spark back. She wasn't so sure about involving Eli, though.

When Mack got home, Kodi met him out in the kitchen. He

had picked up a pizza for dinner and was in a good mood, looking forward to seeing his wife after an exhausting day at work and the lonely drive home. But his entire demeanor changed as Kodi told him about Eli's little visit earlier that day.

"I'm getting really sick of this," Mack growled.

"Don't make a big deal out of it," Kodi calmly requested. "Sammi shot him down and proclaimed her love for you to him."

"Where is Sammi?" Mack asked, suddenly realizing there was no sight nor sound of his wife.

"I haven't seen her in a few hours," Kodi admitted, immediately feeling guilty.

Mack gave her a look to let her know that he was pissed off at her for not keeping an eye on Sammi before darting into the master bedroom to look for her. On a hunch, Kodi ran up to the loft and found Sammi fast asleep on the couch, curled up in a ball with a blanket wrapped around her. Kodi knelt down beside her and gently shook her shoulder to wake her up.

"Hey, bestie, dinner's here," Kodi said quietly as soon as Sammi's eyes opened.

"Kodi, I'm so sorry," Sammi said, sitting up right away. "I don't want to jerk you around anymore. We're going to steal again, I promise. I just need to be a hundred and ten percent before I'm ready."

"No, Sam, I'm sorry," Kodi replied and sat down next to her friend on the couch. "I have no right to rush you after what you've been through. The whole team has to be ready, not just me."

Then the friends went downstairs and joined Mack to eat dinner without any mention of Eli. Mack talked about work and told Sammi that everyone missed her and hoped she'd make a speedy recovery. Sammi hardly believed him and found it difficult to care either way.

Mack finally asked Sammi about Eli as they got ready for

bed a little later that night. Sammi was honest with him about everything Eli said and how she assured him that she was in love with her husband. Hearing these words coming from his wife, Mack couldn't help but smile. He pulled her into his arms and kissed her soft golden hair.

*

The next day, Sammi's and Kodi's friendship was back to normal and they sat down to rework their heist plans that had been stolen. Agreeing that physical copies were too incriminating, they chose to keep everything in a secured folder on Sammi's laptop instead this time. They still planned on it just being the two of them and Howard, partly out of distrust of Eli and partly out of greed with wanting to split everything three ways instead of four.

While the girls took a lunch break and sat in the kitchen, the doorbell rang. Sammi and Kodi looked at each other with much less shock than the day before. Still being cautious, Kodi walked over and looked out the window by the front door, but she didn't recognize the man and had to call Sammi over.

"Ugh, that's Mazzeline," Sammi groaned as she took a peek out the window. "We're supposed to be partners."

Sammi opened the door, not exactly thrilled to see her not-so-likeable coworker. Mazzeline entered the house slowly and handed Sammi a white Styrofoam cup that had a lid and a straw. Looking at the cup suspiciously, Sammi held it out in front of her to inspect it.

"It's a chocolate milkshake," Mazzeline told her reassuringly. "I remember you had one at lunch the one day we got to work together."

"Oh, thank you," Sammi replied awkwardly as Kodi made a weird face out of his view.

Sammi led Mazzeline up to the loft while Kodi made herself scarce. Mazzeline sat on the couch so Sammi sat in the recliner and sucked on the almost-melted milkshake. It was a good milkshake, but an oddly specific thing for Mazzeline to remember about the ten hours they had spent working together.

"I just wanted to stop by to see how you were feeling," Mazzeline finally explained after a bit. "You're clearly tough as nails and I'm really looking forward to working more with you."

"Thanks, I really do appreciate that," Sammi replied. "I'll be back in less than two weeks, but they're gonna keep me on light duty until I'm healed. How do you like being a detective?"

"Last week was great because they paired me with Palma while your husband was out," Mazzeline told her. "But now that he's back, there's not much for me to do."

"Oh, I'm sorry. You should ask Hobbs if you can work with the two of them. You'd learn a lot, especially from Mack."

Mazzeline made a face that made Sammi laugh. It was no secret that Mack didn't have the greatest reputation around the office. He wasn't a total jerk; he was just very serious on the job and didn't care for any tomfoolery while he was on the clock. But most people took that as him being unapproachable.

Sammi and Mazzeline chatted a bit longer and Sammi urged Mazzeline to give Mack a chance. If he could overcome the assumptions, he could really find a great mentor in Mack. Palma had been given that opportunity by being partnered with Mack, but he had allowed his intimidation to keep him from bonding with Mack at all.

After Mazzeline left, Kodi came out of hiding with a lot of questions. She expressed her belief that Mazzeline was infatuated with Sammi as she and Sammi settled back onto the couch to get back to their work. Sammi couldn't deny her suspicions but she assured Kodi that it was a harmless work crush if anything. And she was pretty sure Mazzeline's interest only existed because of her one heroic moment while working with him.

When Mack came home that night, the girls told him about Mazzeline's unexpected visit. Mack laughed as he joined them at the kitchen table and kept laughing harder at their confused looks.

"I sent him," Mack said between chuckles. "He was being annoying, and everyone knows he has a crush on Sammi, so I casually suggested he make the drive out to check on you, just to get him out of the way."

"You're a jerk!" Sammi exclaimed but laughed anyway. "No wonder everyone at work hates you."

"Hey! I am a delight!" Mack argued, still giggling.

"Yep, you're so delightful that you are going to take Mazzeline under your wing and teach him everything you know," Sammi shot at him.

Mack threw his head back and groaned. Sammi got up and stood behind him to lean over and kiss him. He smiled under her lips and she knew Mazzeline had himself a new mentor.

"I'm getting more accomplished at home than I ever did at the precinct," Sammi joked.

"They should make you Captain," Kodi added for a laugh, which earned her a death glare from Mack.

"Nah, my baby's going to be the next Captain," Sammi cooed as she wrapped her arms around Mack's neck from behind. Mack reached around the chair and pulled her into his lap so he could kiss her properly.

Chapter Eighteen
Hard to Believe

The following Monday was Sammi's first checkup with Dr. Brock. Mack had to work, so Kodi happily accompanied her best friend and they decided to make an afternoon of it with a little shopping and grabbing lunch in town. Sammi still had a slight limp due to the soreness of her calf muscle but she hardly noticed it and never made a big deal out of it.

Dr. Brock was pleased with Sammi's progress and lack of infection. He believed her to be out of the woods but wanted her to continue on the antibiotics until she ran out of them, just to be on the safe side. They had already scheduled her following checkups, so he decided to keep those appointments for the time being. As this appointment came to an end, Sammi sent Kodi to pull the car around while she asked the doctor a more personal question about her condition.

"I noticed you're not wearing a ring," Sammi said as soon as Kodi was out of the room. "Are you seeing anyone?"

"Why? Are you newly available?" Dr. Brock asked, only half-kidding. "Because I will buy you anything you want."

"No," Sammi told him, giggling. "What do you think of Kodi?"

"She's cute. And she's obviously a great friend, which tells me more than anything."

"Well, if you are really single, you should come by for dinner tomorrow night."

"I might just take you up on that."

Dr. Brock smiled graciously as Sammi wrote down Kodi's phone number. He already had the address in Sammi's file, so they thanked each other and said goodbye before Sammi hurried to meet up with Kodi. She decided to wait to tell Kodi about her date because she knew Kodi might not appreciate being set up.

When they returned to the house late in the afternoon, Kodi and Sammi were alarmed to find a strange blue Ford sedan parked in front of the house. Neither of them had ever seen the car before, but everything about it screamed undercover police vehicle. Kodi pulled into the driveway and parked before the girls got out of the car, keeping their eyes on the suspicious Ford. As soon as Sammi walked around the back of Kodi's car, a man got out of the driver side of the blue sedan.

"Captain Hobbs!" Sammi cried in relief as she ran awkwardly with her limp down the driveway to her favorite boss. Hobbs chuckled at Sammi's excitement and hugged her with one arm as she reached him.

"How are you, kiddo?" Hobbs asked with a smile.

"Just a little sore," Sammi told him, "but the doc says I'm in the clear."

"That's great. I look forward to having you back at work," Hobbs replied. "Is there, uh, somewhere we could talk?"

The Captain's voice changed with that last question and Sammi knew something had happened. She immediately thought of Mack and her stomach twisted into a knot as she led Hobbs into the house and up to the loft. Hobbs took the recliner so Sammi sat on the couch, leaning forward to ease her nausea.

"Sammi, some evidence has been turned over to me from your case," Hobbs said calmly, bringing a red file folder forward in front of him.

"But I don't have any cases–oh," Sammi replied and froze upon realizing he meant the case against Shay.

Hobbs tossed the thick red folder onto the coffee table between them and it popped open on its own. Right on top was a normal yellow spiral notebook that Sammi recognized immediately as one of the notebooks from the day she and Kodi had planned out a few heists. Sammi didn't move, but her eyes widened as a cold feeling of fear washed over her.

"Now, why would a respected member of the New York Police Department have extensive plans to rob the largest bank vaults in the country?" Hobbs asked. He was playing dumb, which made Sammi feel almost insulted.

"You don't have any proof that they're mine," Sammi finally replied after thinking about it for a second. Her voice shook with nerves, but she was pretty sure she was right.

"Come on, Sammi, you can do better than that," Hobbs said, sounding hurt. "But you're right, technically I cannot prove these are yours at this very second. So, I'm going to keep these, and you are going to return to work as if being a cop is your favorite thing in the world."

"Are you blackmailing me?" Sammi asked with a complete look of shock on her face. This was the last thing she would've expected from her beloved Captain.

"How could I be blackmailing you if these aren't yours?" Hobbs replied coolly. "Seriously, though, it was a pleasure to see you and I look forward to having you back on the job."

Hobbs leaned forward as he stood up and patted Sammi's knee. Then he closed the red folder and scooped it off the coffee table before he turned and left the loft, seeing himself out of the house.

Sammi couldn't move from the couch, she was so in shock from Hobbs threatening her. She was more hurt than anything because she had always liked Hobbs and couldn't believe he would resort to forcing her to do something against her will. Overwhelmed with emotions of anger, fear, and betrayal, she sat there in silence until Kodi came looking for her.

"What happened?" Kodi asked, knowing something was wrong by the pale look on Sammi's face.

"I got busted," Sammi told her. "He had the notebooks."

"So, what now?" Kodi asked, picturing cops swarming the place to arrest Sammi.

"I have to go back to work. I don't have a choice."

Then Sammi told Kodi the entire conversation between her and Captain Hobbs while Kodi listened with a look of disbelief on her face. That disbelief turned to disgust as Sammi got to the part about Hobbs blackmailing her into coming back to work.

"I just don't understand why he cares so much if you're a cop or not," Kodi said as she lounged next to Sammi on the couch.

"I don't think it has anything to do with me being a cop," Sammi told her. "He's just trying to keep me from breaking the law. I'm sure it would be fine if I wanted to sell cars or something."

Both girls giggled at the idea of Sammi being a car salesperson then went back to being quiet. Mack got home a little while later and Sammi had no desire to tell him about the visit from Hobbs. But she did have to tell him about inviting Dr. Brock over for dinner the following evening as they got into bed that night.

*

Sammi ended up telling Kodi about setting her up with Dr. Brock over breakfast in the morning. Kodi made a disgruntled face, but she was eager to talk about something else that had been on her mind overnight and willingly changed the subject without getting upset with her friend.

"This whole Hobbs-blackmail thing bothered me all night and I think I know why," Kodi said, frowning.

"What do you mean?" Sammi asked, still upset about the situation, though she tried to let it go because it felt out of her control.

"I still don't think your Captain would care that much about your career choice," Kodi told her best friend. "But Mack would."

Sammi didn't say anything as her face reddened and her hands balled into fists. Kodi's theory made too much sense that she couldn't believe she hadn't realized it earlier. And she was madder than she'd ever been in her entire life.

Throwing her breakfast dishes into the sink as hard as she could and cracking a plate, Sammi stormed off into the bedroom to sulk. She hid in there, lying on the bed in silence with the shades drawn and hoping to fall asleep, until Kodi asked her if she wanted to tag along to the grocery store to get ingredients for dinner that night. They had plenty of time, so they made a special trip to a cute little boutique in the next town to get a dress for Kodi to wear for Dr. Brock.

That night, Dr. Brock arrived before Mack got home from work. He wore tan khaki pants and a white polo shirt, making him look only slightly younger than he had in his white coat at the hospital. Kodi was still cooking dinner so he immediately went to the kitchen to assist her while Sammi sat quietly at the kitchen table, waiting impatiently for Mack to get home.

Mack was in a great mood when he got home from work and warmly welcomed Dr. Brock into his home. He excused himself into the bedroom to change after saying hello to everyone and Sammi followed him. She waited until he was out of his work clothes before she attacked.

"You couldn't control my life, so you got your boss to do

your dirty work for you?" Sammi asked, getting right up in Mack's face.

"What are you talking about?" Mack replied, a look of confusion on his face as he took a step back from his angry wife.

"You want me to stay on the force so bad that you had Hobbs blackmail me into it!" Sammi yelled.

"Sammi, I seriously have no idea what you're talking about. What would Hobbs even have to use as blackmail?" Mack remained calm as he tried to get Sammi to relax.

Unable to relax but realizing that she may have said too much, Sammi stopped talking. She backed away from her husband and sat down on the edge of the bed, looking at the floor. She wasn't convinced that Mack was innocent, but it was possible that he didn't know about the notebooks.

Mack didn't take his eyes off Sammi as he finished getting dressed for dinner. He wore a pair of black denim jeans with a fitted maroon t-shirt that stretched against his muscles. Then he took a seat next to his wife and cautiously put his hand on her knee.

"What is going on?" Mack asked with uncertainty.

"Nothing. It doesn't matter," Sammi whispered, keeping her head down.

"Sammi, don't shut down on me," Mack replied calmly. "I'm your husband and I have your back...nine times out of ten."

Mack laughed, trying to lighten the atmosphere of the room. But Sammi wasn't in the joking mood and shot her husband a dirty look. Sammi's seriousness only made Mack laugh harder, causing Sammi to groan and throw her body backwards onto the bed. Mack laid back next to her and wrapped his arms around her, pulling her to him even though she tried to resist.

"Please tell me what's going on," Mack begged dramatically, squeezing Sammi tighter and gently rocking her back and forth.

Sammi couldn't hold out against him any longer and giggled at how cute Mack was acting. She snuggled into him and tucked her head under his chin, letting his warmth comfort her. Before Sammi could think of what to say, there was a quiet knock on their bedroom door and Kodi called into the room to let them know that dinner was ready.

"You're not getting off the hook that easily," Mack said as he stood up from the bed and helped his wife up as well. "We will finish this conversation later."

Nodding, Sammi followed her husband out to the kitchen. She had plenty of time to decide what to tell him, whether that was going to be the truth or not.

Dinner went smoothly and Sammi was happy that Dr. Brock, or Anthony, as his new friends could call him, and Kodi seemed to really hit it off. Once everyone had finished eating, the two of them offered to run out and pick up dessert for everyone while the married couple stayed behind to clean up. As soon as they were alone again, Mack wanted answers.

"I'll tell you everything if you clean the kitchen," Sammi offered with a smirk, dropping down into one of the chairs at the table after putting one plate in the sink.

"Deal," Mack said, kissing the top of her head as he reached over her to grab the rest of the plates. "I would've cleaned up anyway since you're injured."

Sammi stuck her tongue out at Mack as she watched him clean the entire kitchen. As soon as he finished, he swooped down to kneel in front of Sammi at the table and looked up into her face with his hands on her legs.

"All right, spill it," Mack said with a pleading look in his face.

"Ugh, you have to promise to still love me if I tell you," Sammi replied quietly.

"Nothing will ever make me stop loving you, sweetheart," Mack assured her.

"The day that Shay tried to kill me, I left some notebooks out in the loft and I guess the police collected them as evidence," Sammi explained. "They had some possibly incriminating details in them and somehow Hobbs ended up with them. He came by yesterday to hold them over my head and demand that I come back to work."

Mack's face fell in complete disappointment as he sat back with his butt on the floor. Sammi knew he was upset and wanted to get up to give him space, but she was afraid to move. She didn't want to upset him any further, so she stayed where she was and waited for him to make the next move.

After a little while, Mack stood up without a word and walked into the bedroom, closing the door behind him. He was more upset than Sammi had initially anticipated and now she was really scared that she had hurt him beyond repair. Before she could think of how to fix anything, Anthony and Kodi returned with ice cream and brought it right into the kitchen. They were laughing as they entered, but one look at Sammi's face told Kodi that something was wrong. Kodi immediately went to her best friend but Sammi didn't want to ruin her date so she abruptly excused herself and went outside to sit on the back porch in the dark. The only other person Sammi could think of to talk to was Eli so she pulled out her phone and dialed her ex-boyfriend's number. Eli could tell right away over the phone how upset Sammi was so he told her he'd swing by to pick her up then hung up before she could argue.

Sammi relocated to the front porch to wait for Eli, but while she waited, Mack came looking for her. He sat next to her on the single cement step and put his arm around her back. She was still too worried to speak, but she didn't want to push him away, so she leaned into him and put her head on his shoulder. He remained silent as well, but he didn't pull away from her. As they sat there peacefully, a car pulled into the driveway and Eli stepped up the front walk.

"You called him?" Mack asked, raising both eyebrows at

Sammi. He sounded amused instead of angry.

"Kodi's busy," Sammi shrugged, defending her actions.

"Go ahead," Mack said and nodded in Eli's direction.

"What?" Sammi asked, confused, and not taking her eyes off her husband.

"Go hang out with your friend. I'm going to go back inside and talk to Dr. Brock about not clearing you for the job," Mack explained calmly as Sammi watched his face for an inkling of whether he was serious or not.

"No, hon, you can't get involved," Sammi told him. "I can't have Hobbs coming after you too. I'll go back to work, at least for a little while."

Mack nodded his understanding as he moved his arm up to Sammi's shoulders and pulled her to him in half a hug. He kissed her then stood up before helping his wife up. They both turned to look at Eli who hadn't said a word the entire time he stood before them.

"Do you want to join us for some dessert?" Mack kindly asked Eli.

Eli just shrugged his shoulders and followed Mack and Sammi through the front door and into the house.

Chapter Nineteen
Better Than Me

Sammi returned to the precinct the following week holding a lot of resentment toward Hobbs. It hurt her more to feel betrayed by him because she had truly liked him as a person and appreciated their ability to be open with each other. Now she had no desire to talk to him at all and was sad about losing an ally.

Being stuck at her desk to make phone calls and take care of paperwork didn't help Sammi's gloomy mood. She got bored quickly with office work and knew with all her heart that she was never meant to spend her life behind a desk. If she had to be a cop, instead of a thief like she wanted to be, she wanted to at least be out doing the job for real instead of playing pretend behind a desk.

On her second day back, Howard surprised his friend by showing up in the squad room to see Sammi. It was about lunchtime and everyone else was out on a case so Sammi knew that nobody would mind if she went out for lunch. She and Howard ended up at a fast food joint in walking distance from the precinct and Sammi shot a quick text message to Mack to let him know where she had gone.

"I came by to see you last week and your Sergeant told me what happened," Howard said as he and Sammi sat down with their terrible meal choices.

"How dramatic was he?" Sammi asked, digging into her French fries as if she hadn't eaten in days.

"Well, it definitely didn't sound like you would be back this soon," Howard told her. "And you're sure it was Shay?"

"Howard, she looked me in the eyes before leaving me to bleed out on my own front porch," Sammi explained, dropping a chicken nugget to get serious. "It was Shay."

"Then how did you survive?"

"Uh, believe it or not, Eli found me."

"Wait. Eli's back?"

"Yeah, but he doesn't know about our plans to put a team together again. He's just a good friend right now."

As the conversation steered toward the team, Sammi vaguely explained her dilemma with leaving her current position. Howard was understanding toward the predicament and admitted he was a little hesitant about breaking the law again. Sammi just smiled at him, glad that he was still the good person she had always known him to be.

Howard and Sammi finished their lunch before Howard walked Sammi back up to the squad room. They exchanged numbers so they could stay in touch more easily, then Howard went on his way and Sammi got back to the work that she hated.

*

Two weeks later, Sammi's wounds were almost healed, but she hadn't been cleared by her doctor yet to return to full duty. She was going stir crazy in the squad room and spending most of her workdays contemplating how to get fired by going around Hobbs. But she knew she would only embarrass Mack if she got fired and she also knew she wasn't physically ready to be reliable enough for a heist.

As Sammi got ready to head home with her husband at the end of the day that Friday, Captain Hobbs came out of his office and approached Sammi's desk. Sammi was already standing, wanting to leave as quickly as possible, but Hobbs motioned for her to sit down as he pulled up a chair to take a seat himself on the opposite side of the desk. Rolling her eyes, Sammi sat in her chair and leaned back in it to casually show her indifference to her boss.

"How much longer until your doctor clears you to get back out there doing your job?" Hobbs asked, straining to sound kind.

"He hasn't said. But he's dating my best friend so I'm sure I could force an all-clear out of him if you wanted to blackmail him too," Sammi shot at Hobbs.

Hobbs looked down at Sammi indignantly. He stood up without another word and disappeared back into his office.

"What was that about?" Mack asked, appearing in front of Sammi's desk and glancing back in the direction Hobbs had gone.

"He was looking for drama, so I gave him some," Sammi told her husband, getting up from behind the desk. "Let's get out of here."

Mack put his arm around Sammi as she came around the desk and they walked out of the building together. Sammi leaned into him, sensing his discomfort about her situation with Hobbs. They hadn't talked too much about it, but Sammi knew that Mack would help her out of this if she would let him, and that was all that mattered to her.

"Hobbs has got to be retiring soon," Mack assured his wife during their long drive home. "And when I'm Captain, I will burn your file myself."

*

By the middle of the following week, Dr. Brock finally cleared Sammi to be on full duty in the Homicide unit. She and Mazzeline caught their very first case together the next morning and headed out to a rundown apartment building to investigate the murder of a twenty-four-year-old male career criminal who had been shot down just inside his apartment door. Sammi, knowing that she was better with people than Mazzeline, sent him to the crime scene while she conducted interviews with potential witnesses.

While Sammi spoke to the owner of the apartment building, she asked if there had been any complaints or disturbances lately. The middle-aged Italian man recalled nothing and admitted that things had been significantly quieter in the building over the past two years since Frank Nardino stopped coming around. Sammi hadn't heard that name in over a year and it immediately piqued her interest, which she mentioned to Mazzeline as they met back up a short while later in front of the building.

"So, wait, who is this Nardino guy?" Mazzeline asked after he and Sammi were in his car and Sammi had told him about her interviews.

"He was like a crime boss or something," Sammi told him. "Mack had to deal with him a lot until he killed him three years ago."

"Well, if he's dead, how is he relevant to our case?" Mazzeline replied, not rudely, but definitely challenging his partner.

"I don't know exactly, but our victim was a criminal and Nardino was a crime boss who frequented his building, so I'd be willing to bet the two knew each other," Sammi defended her suspicions. "I want to question some of Nardino's old so-called business partners."

Back at the squad room, Sammi immediately logged into a computer to begin research on Nardino's old accomplices. She compiled a list of about a dozen names and split them with

Mazzeline so they could each make some phone calls just to see if any of them knew of their victim. Every last one of them confirmed that the victim had worked with Nardino and had unsuccessfully tried to move into Nardino's leadership position upon Nardino's demise.

Mazzeline and Sammi spent the rest of that day and all of the next making phone calls and home visits to confirm alibis for their handful of suspects. Everyone had a solid alibi and no obvious motives, but their strong feelings of dislike toward the victim let the detectives know they were on the right track.

"How are you already better at this than I am?" Mazzeline asked at the end of the second day. Sammi just shrugged her shoulders because she couldn't exactly tell him about her experience on the other side of the law.

Both detectives had the weekend off, so they returned to the case that Monday. By then, their evidence had been processed so they headed to the crime lab to get more information. The only evidence that proved to be any help was the bullet recovered from the victim's body. As soon as they knew it was from a Beretta 92, Sammi didn't need to run it through the database to know it was going to match one of the bullets from her own case.

"Dammit, it's Shay," Sammi mumbled as she and Mazzeline left the lab.

"Who?" Mazzeline asked, seriously confused.

"Uh, Shay Krik is actually who shot me. The bullet from my side is going to match the one from our victim," Sammi explained somewhat nervously.

"If that's true, Hobbs is going to have to take you off this case."

"That's fine. But good luck finding her because my local precinct has been after her for over a month now."

When they got back to the squad room, they referred to the database to get proof that their case was linked to Sammi's case in Long Island. Then the both of them took the connected evidence and went into their Captain's office to reveal their findings. Hobbs took his time looking everything over, expressing his disbelief that the two cases could be tied together.

"Looks like you're riding the desk again," Hobbs said smartly to Sammi once he was satisfied that a mistake had not been made.

"Of course," Sammi grumbled as she let Mazzeline leave the office first so she could slam the door shut behind them.

Sammi walked to her desk in the back corner, not paying attention to where her partner went. She sat down, throwing her arms onto the desk and her head down onto her arms. With a heavy sigh, she made herself comfortable and hoped she could fall asleep before anyone bothered her.

"What's going on?" Mack asked curiously only a second later. Sammi picked her head up to see that Mack had come around her desk and stood next to her.

"Conflict of interest," Sammi stated coldly. "Shay's our main suspect."

"Man, you really can't shake that psycho," Mack said jokingly, trying to get his wife to laugh.

"You should've killed her when you had the chance."

Sammi pushed her chair back and got up without looking at her husband. She walked across the squad room and headed downstairs for the front door. Her thoughts were empty as she exited the building and wandered the streets of New York.

As Sammi walked along with no destination, her cellphone rang several times. She didn't need to look at it to know it was Mack calling her. But he needed to trust her while she took some space from this job that was not working in her favor. She just needed to feel like she could breathe again, free from their controlling boss and free from all the Shay drama.

Sammi ended up on a familiar block and was convinced that the universe brought her there for a reason. She walked up to the sad-looking brick apartment building that looked worse than it had three years ago and let herself into the unsecured lobby. It had been two years so her old apartment had to have new tenants. But as she looked at the wall of mailboxes, the little white card with "Krik" scribbled across it with the heart above the "i" that she had added was still in their slot.

"Samantha?" came a soft male voice from behind Sammi. Sammi jumped a little from fright, not expecting to run into anybody she knew.

"Oh, Mr. Cleary, you startled me," Sammi said, putting her hand over her pounding heart as she turned to face her old landlord.

"My apologies, Miss. It's been a few days since Eli's been by for the mail," Mr. Cleary told her. "Did you need the spare key?"

"Uh, Eli still rents the apartment?" Sammi asked, confused.

"Yeah, he doesn't live here, though. He just sends a check every month and usually collects his mail in a timely manner," the landlord explained.

"Do you mind if I go check out the old place?"

"Sure thing. Follow me and I'll let you in. Your name's still on the lease."

Sammi followed Mr. Cleary up to the fourth-floor apartment where he unlocked the door before leaving her in privacy. He just asked her to let him know when she left so he could lock up after her. Sammi waited until the landlord was out of sight before taking a deep breath and entering the place that she had begun to feel only existed in her memories.

Nothing had changed in the tiny apartment and it looked like just the day before she had been by to collect her things. Sammi opened the refrigerator and cringed at her expired energy drinks and the rotting smell of three-year-old Chinese food leftovers. It took her a second to remember when the leftovers were from, but her heart sank as she realized the whole team had been over for dinner the night before their mall heist. It had been a little tradition of theirs to have Chinese takeout before a robbery and they had all been so happy that particular night. Everything had been going so smoothly back then—life would've been perfect if it hadn't been for Eli's temper. Hell, Mack only got involved in Sammi's life because of Eli's temper.

Sammi closed the fridge as she had to blink back tears. She loved Mack with her entire heart, but she missed this life. She missed the thrill of the job, she missed the closeness with her friends, and she missed the comfort of knowing that she was exactly where she belonged.

Embracing the nostalgia, Sammi walked out of the kitchen and over to the living room where she sat on the old couch. She brushed the dust off of Eli's New York Giants blanket that they had always kept draped over the back of the couch and pulled it down to wrap around herself. Pulling her legs up to her chest, she rested her head on her knees and wondered if she was ever going to get to be a thief again.

"Whoa, talk about a trip down memory lane," Sammi heard from the doorway to the apartment which was behind the couch. There was no mistaking that deep but playful voice for anyone but Eli.

"What are you doing here?" Sammi asked her ex, poking her head over the back of the couch. She wasn't even really that surprised to see Eli.

"I came by to pick up the mail and Cleary told me you were up here," Eli explained as he walked slowly over to the couch.

"Why do you even still have this place?"

"Honestly, just for a permanent address. But what brought you here? Aren't you working?"

"I had to get out of there and I just ended up here."

Sammi made room for Eli on the couch and he took a seat on the side opposite from her. They sat in silence for a bit, letting the memories come to them at an almost overwhelming rate. Before either of them could think of anything to say, Sammi's radio went off on her belt. It was Hobbs calling her back to the station house.

"I really hate him," Sammi grumbled, standing up from the couch with the blanket still draped over her shoulders.

"You know you could use this place if you ever just need to get away," Eli offered, not budging from where he sat.

"Thank you, but I'll be okay," Sammi told him with a smile. Then she took the blanket from her shoulders and wrapped it around Eli before planting a quick kiss on his nose. "Tell Cleary I trusted you to lock up."

Sammi felt better as she left the apartment and didn't feel as suffocated when she thought about returning to work. She was still partly lost in memories and looking at the ground as she walked out the front door of the building and didn't notice the woman standing directly in her path with her back to her.

"Oh, I'm sorry," Sammi apologized, seeing the lady at the last second before bumping into her.

"You have got to be kidding me," the woman replied with attitude as she turned around to face Sammi.

"No," Sammi whispered as her jaw dropped.

"How are you still alive?" Shay asked, drawing her handgun from her waistband, and aiming it at Sammi's face.

"Shay, you have got to stop this!" Eli yelled as he appeared from inside the building. Sammi knew that he was trying to reason with Shay so she wouldn't get shot herself, but Sammi also knew that there was no reasoning with Shay.

Removing her service pistol from her holster, Sammi aimed it directly at Shay's heart. Her head was spinning as she thought about how she was trained to disarm a suspect when possible and to avoid lethal shots at all costs, but also about how this suspect wanted her dead and that taking her out once and for all was the only way to put a stop to this.

"Eli, go back inside. Call nine-one-one and report an officer-involved shooting," Sammi said firmly without taking her eyes off Shay.

"Shay, please!" Eli begged his sister, ignoring Sammi. Sammi could hear the desperation in his voice and as badly as she wanted to be rid of Shay, she didn't want to hurt Eli.

"Listen to the cop, brother," Shay replied with a snarl and a quick side glance at Eli.

That very brief sideways look was long enough for Sammi to lunge forward and tackle Shay down to the sidewalk. Shay had kept ahold of her gun so Sammi grabbed that arm and slammed it into the concrete sidewalk several times until Shay was forced to release the weapon. Then, keeping hold of Shay's arm, Sammi rolled Shay over onto her stomach and patted her down to check for additional weapons.

"Packing light today, huh?" Sammi asked after not finding anything else on the suspect.

"I wasn't expecting to run into you," Shay grunted as Sammi drove her knee into the center of Shay's back to keep her still while she handcuffed her wrists behind her back. Keeping her body weight on top of Shay, Sammi took her radio off her belt to call in the arrest and request backup.

"Why'd you kill that common thug in his apartment?" Sammi asked as she picked Shay up off the ground while waiting for her backup.

"You didn't leave me any other choice," Shay spat at her. "Without the team, I needed to make a living and Nardino's empire was there for the taking."

Sammi shook her head at Shay as a patrol car that had been a few blocks over arrived and took Shay into custody. As soon as Sammi handed her off, she sat down in the middle of the sidewalk to catch her breath and calm her heartrate. She hadn't realized in the midst of everything that she was shaking with anxiety.

"Are you okay?" Eli asked, dropping to his knees in front of Sammi.

"I will be," Sammi told him, still breathing heavily.

"Thank you for not shooting her," Eli said quietly and Sammi looked up at his face to see that he had been crying.

It suddenly crossed Sammi's mind that the only reason Shay would have been at that specific location would be that she knew Eli would be there. And she would only know that if they had been in communication with each other, which would only support Mack's theory that Eli knew Shay was going to come after her.

Spooked, Sammi leapt to her feet and backed away quickly from Eli. Eli looked confused as he also stood up, watching Sammi's face. Before either of them could speak, an unmarked squad car rolled up with the windows down and Mazzeline called out to Sammi that everyone was looking for her. Sammi hurried into the passenger seat without even a look back at Eli.

"Are you okay?" Mazzeline asked as he drove toward the precinct building after glancing over at Sammi and seeing how pale her face was.

"Everyone keeps asking me that. But I could've been shot by the same person for a third time, so forgive me for being a little shaken," Sammi snapped at her partner.

"All right, the Captain can wait for your paperwork," Mazzeline responded as he made an abrupt U-turn and headed in the opposite direction of the station house.

Mazzeline drove to the diner where he and Sammi had lunch together the one day they had worked together on patrol. He got out of the car and waited for Sammi to follow him. They walked inside together and Mazzeline got them a booth where they sat down, and he immediately ordered a chocolate milkshake for Sammi.

"Just relax and enjoy that," Mazzeline said once the milkshake was in front of Sammi.

"Thank you," Sammi said with a smile before taking a sip. She appreciated this moment more than she could put into words.

Mazzeline sat, casual and cool with his arm draped across his side of the booth. His blue eyes met Sammi's for a short second and, in that moment, they finally bonded as partners.

Chapter Twenty
Where Do We Go?

The next six months passed by in a whirlwind. Shay was finally taken off the streets after being served a life sentence and Sammi chose to avoid Eli without telling anyone about her revelation upon Shay's arrest. Everyone knew that she was shaken up after her final battle with Shay, but the proof was in her abrupt dedication to her job and her and Mazzeline's speedy rise to being the top detectives in the unit.

One day, toward the end of six months, Captain Hobbs called Sammi and Mazzeline into his office before assigning new cases for the week. Sammi was still cold towards Hobbs, and his indifference towards her after she arrested Shay had not helped.

"A congratulations are in order for the two of you," Hobbs announced once Sammi and Mazzeline were sitting across from him at his desk. "Both of you are being promoted to Lieutenant, but you each have a decision to make. You can either stay here in the same position, making the same money, and take the Captain's exam with nothing to show for your promotion other than your shiny new badges. Or you can transfer to separate precincts where you'd be top rank in the unit with higher pay."

"Mazzeline is my partner," Sammi stated bluntly, looking directly at Hobbs. "I don't want to work with anyone else."

Sammi could feel Mazzeline looking at her, but she kept her eyes forward. She knew that Mazzeline had every right to leave and take a pay raise elsewhere. But she hoped that he wouldn't. He had proven to her that he had her back and she trusted him as much as she trusted her own husband. The chances of finding a comparable partner were slim.

"You know what? I wouldn't be getting this promotion without Sammi," Mazzeline speculated. "I'm not about to abandon her."

Hobbs nodded and handed his new Lieutenants their new badges. Mazzeline thanked the Captain and stood up to leave the office, waiting for his partner. But Sammi stuck her tongue out at Hobbs so she was asked to stay back.

"Is this ever going to stop?" Hobbs asked after Mazzeline had left the office.

"That depends. Are you ever going to admit that you were wrong to blackmail me?" Sammi replied with sass. "I used to think we were friends."

"Fine. I'm sorry, Sammi, I really am," Hobbs apologized. "I should've talked to you and shown you the proper respect instead of taking away your feeling of freedom. I was wrong."

"Thank you. I wish I could say things can go back to the way they were before, but I'd be lying."

Sammi went back out into the squad room and over to Mack's desk where Mack sat in his chair awaiting a case. Hopping up onto the desk, Sammi sat on the edge of it with her legs crossed toward her husband. She placed her new badge down on the desk in front of Mack and looked at him with a cocky grin on her face. Mack looked between his wife and the badge a handful of times before standing up to passionately kiss Sammi in front of the entire squad room.

"I am so proud of you, baby," Mack whispered against

Sammi's lips.

Feeling indifferent towards her promotion, Sammi just wanted to make out with her husband. She kept her lips pressed to Mack's and kissed him back harder, grabbing his tie to pull him closer to her. The squad room disappeared and all that existed in Sammi's world in that moment was the man she loved.

"All right, lovebirds, that's enough," Sammi heard Hobbs say nonchalantly from behind her. She finally released her man but remained seated on his desk.

"What's up, boss?" Mack asked, sitting back down in his chair and leaning back, clearly feeling pretty good about himself.

"I've got two separate cases," Hobbs told him. "You want to work with your wife on one?"

Sammi and Mack looked at each other and Sammi cracked a smile. She knew that Hobbs was only offering for them to work together to try and make up for blackmailing her while also testing her previous testament of loyalty to Mazzeline.

"Sorry, babe, but I'm a one partner kind of gal," Sammi said to Mack, continuing to smile as she leaned over to plant one more kiss on his lips.

Then Sammi hopped down off Mack's desk and went to sit at her own. Tuning out Hobbs while he explained the two cases, Sammi took her cellphone out of her pocket and sent a text message to Kodi about her promotion. While she still had her phone out, she got an incoming message from Mack telling her to meet him in the elevator while Mazzeline and Palma headed out ahead of them. Sammi looked up to see Mack grinning at her from across the room and couldn't keep from blushing.

After Mack decided which pair of partners got which case, he and his wife sent their separate partners on ahead to pull the cars around. Then the two lovers met in front of the elevator and smirked at each other while waiting for it to reach their floor. Once they were inside the dark, small, rectangular box, Mack pressed the button for the ground floor before wrapping his fingers around Sammi's arms and pushing her up against the wall with his lips immediately on hers. Sammi was able to get her arms out just enough to grab Mack's belt and pull his body to her.

"I love you, Mack Johnson," Sammi breathed into her husband's lips.

Overcome by her words and her passion, Mack moved his left hand up to the right side of her face. He lightly brushed her porcelain cheek with his fingertips and tucked her long hair behind her ear without taking his lips off of her. He kept his hand there, cupping her jawline as she popped up onto the tips of her toes to get a better angle to kiss him with more force. Sammi had Mack's tie undone and completely off his body just as the elevator came to a stop and the door opened.

Mack kept Sammi against the wall of the elevator and ran his fingers down her arm to her hand that held his balled up tie. He made a quick grab for the tie, but Sammi was faster and held the tie above her head.

"I need that back," Mack said, grinning as he pressed his nose to Sammi's. "Otherwise, I might just have to use it on you later."

"Maybe I want you to use it," Sammi teased and kissed him hard, biting his bottom lip as she brought her arm down to hide the tie behind her back.

"You're on, Mrs. Johnson," Mack whispered huskily. Then he pecked her quickly on the lips one time and grinned hugely at her as they exited the elevator together.

Once in their separate squad cars with their separate partners, Mack grabbed a spare tie out of the glove compartment and put it on while Sammi wrapped the tie she took from Mack around her left wrist and tied it off in a bow.

*

A few weeks later, Mack and Sammi spent a Saturday in the city so they could take the Captain's exam with Mazzeline upon Hobbs' request. The three of them knew Hobbs was only humoring Mazzeline and Sammi because he felt guilty about them not getting appropriate pay raises with their rank promotions. Sammi only went along with it because she liked getting to do the same things that Mack was doing, and she felt closer to him than ever.

When they got home in the late afternoon, there was a car in the driveway that wasn't theirs, but they both knew it was Eli's. Sammi groaned and slid down in the passenger seat as Mack parked his car next to Eli's Honda. It had been a good six months since Sammi had talked to Eli, but she had known this day was coming; she couldn't stay in New York and expect to avoid him forever. She was actually somewhat impressed that he had stayed away for this long.

"Want me to send him away?" Mack asked, getting serious but remaining calm.

"No, it's fine," Sammi told him. "Just don't leave me alone with him."

Eli got out of his car as Mack and Sammi got out of theirs. As the married couple walked around the front of the cars toward their front door, Mack kept himself in between Eli and Sammi. He kept a skeptical eye on Eli but did his best to remain neutral so Sammi would feel more comfortable talking to Eli and finally express what had been bothering her for the past six months.

"Sammi, can I talk to you?" Eli asked quietly, taking a step forward.

"Sure," Sammi shot harshly at him. "Let's sit on the front porch where I almost bled to death."

Sammi's sass was a little more brutal than usual and Mack gave Eli a look that told him to run while he still could. But even though Eli felt undeserving of it, he knew Sammi would at least hear him out. So, the three of them walked up the front walk and Sammi sat on the porch step, Eli stood in front of her, and Mack sat behind his wife in one of their new rocking chairs.

"Go ahead," Sammi said impatiently after no one spoke for a minute. Mack snorted, watching in amusement from behind as she tortured her former love.

"I couldn't figure out why you wouldn't talk to me and that day in the old apartment has been haunting me," Eli explained nervously. "It took me until last night to realize that it wasn't anything from the apartment, but what happened when you left."

"Oh, you mean when I ran into Shay outside waiting for you?" Sammi asked smartly.

"She may have been waiting for me, but I didn't know she was there," Eli said, defending himself. "Sammi, I would never set you up to get hurt. I never spoke to Shay, not even once, when I got back to New York."

"Then how did she know you would be at the apartment?"

"The same way you found out; Cleary told her."

Sammi hung her head, feeling bad that she had even thought that Eli could be involved with her getting shot. She was silent as she looked at the ground, so Eli took a seat next to her on the step and put his arm around her back.

"I'm sorry," Sammi whispered without looking up. "You're my friend and I should've talked to you about this way sooner instead of avoiding you."

"No, I'm sorry," Eli told her, squeezing her to him. "Shay's my sister and she was only in your life because of me. I wish I could've protected you from her better."

"Why don't you stay for dinner?" Mack offered, standing up and patting Eli on the shoulder from behind.

Mack then headed into the house and left the door open for the others. Eli got up from the porch step first and offered Sammi his hand to help her up, but Sammi still hadn't picked her head up and didn't seem to notice Eli's outstretched hand. So, Eli reached down to pick up one of Sammi's hands out of her lap and lightly tugged it to get her to follow him. Sammi finally stood up, but she kept her eyes down as she walked into the house with Eli.

Once inside, Sammi walked right to Mack who was going through the refrigerator in the kitchen. She was so quiet that Mack didn't even hear her approach him, so she lightly poked him in his side near his ribcage. Mack flinched at the feeling and turned to look at his wife.

"What's wrong, babe?" Mack asked after seeing the sadness in Sammi's sparkling sapphire eyes.

"Do you mind if I go lie down?" Sammi asked quietly, sounding almost desperate.

"Not at all," Mack told her and kissed her forehead. "I'll chat with Eli and come check on you when dinner's ready."

Sammi gave Mack a halfhearted hug before disappearing into the master bedroom. She lay on the bed and sent a text message to Kodi asking if she was spending time with Anthony that weekend. While waiting for a response, Sammi fell asleep with her phone in her hand.

*

"Is everything okay?" Eli asked as he sat down at the kitchen table.

"Yeah, I think she's just emotionally exhausted," Mack told him, rubbing the back of his own head as he finally closed the fridge. "I really need to go grocery shopping. What do you want from takeout?"

"Chinese," Eli replied with a halfhearted smile as he looked down at his hands.

"Try again," Mack said matter-of-factly. "Sammi won't go for Chinese."

"Since when?" Eli asked, surprised.

"Since coming across three-year-old leftovers in your old apartment. The smell makes her sick."

Eli grimaced, realizing he still hadn't cleaned that fridge out. He told Mack to just go ahead and order whatever Sammi would want. Mack kept it simple and ordered a pizza then invited Eli up to the loft, offering him a beer while they waited.

"Why are you being so nice to me?" Eli asked, clearly suspicious as they sat on opposite sides of the coffee table.

"Sammi missed you," Mack replied, shrugging his shoulders.

"No, she didn't," Eli told him. "She could've reached out."

"I didn't mean this time," Mack explained. "I meant the three years you were M.I.A."

Eli nodded and fell silent. He had nobody to blame but himself for his absence during that time and he regretted every second of it. He still believed that Sammi wouldn't have married Mack if he would have come back sooner.

When the pizza arrived, Mack dropped it on the kitchen counter and told Eli to help himself while he went to get Sammi. He found Sammi fast asleep on their bed and looking incredibly peaceful. Her cellphone lit up in her hand with a message from Kodi, but it was silent and Sammi didn't stir. So, Mack crawled onto the bed and held himself over Sammi's body, kissing her from her belly button up to her lips. Sammi's eyes fluttered open and she giggled from the tickle of her husband's lips.

"Feeling better, princess?" Mack asked, hopping up and off the bed.

"I think so," Sammi said, stretching her arms out as she sat up and smirked at her husband. "Your kisses healed me."

Sammi stuck her tongue out playfully and Mack smiled warmly at her. Checking her phone, Sammi showed her husband the photo of Kodi and Anthony that Kodi had sent her.

"I did a good thing," Sammi said happily, beaming at the

photo on her screen.

"You've done a lot of good things," Mack told her, hooking his arm around her waist. "My favorite is the way you love me."

*

By the end of the following week, Hobbs had gotten the results back that Mack, Mazzeline, and Sammi had all passed their Captain's exams. Although his clear choice for his replacement was still Mack, the department was making him give all three of them an equal opportunity for the position, especially because his two newest Lieutenants still didn't have anything to show for their exceptional work. So, an email was sent out across the precinct asking anyone who had worked closely with any of the three Captain candidates to write a letter of recommendation for their choice. The three candidates also got to have a say, as long as they didn't discuss it with each other and as long as they didn't recommend themselves.

"Can you do me a favor?" Sammi asked Mack in the car on their way home the night the emails had gone out. "Since you can't recommend yourself, can you write a letter for Mazzeline?"

"We're not supposed to discuss it, Sam," Mack replied, only partly serious.

"Mack, literally everyone knows you're going to get the position," Sammi told him. "And I shouldn't even be a candidate because I'm a thief and no one is going to recommend a female Captain anyway. So just help Mazzeline feel like it was a close call between you two."

"Fine, but I don't know the guy like you do so you're going to have to help me write it."

*

Sammi ended up writing Mack's entire letter for him, as well her own recommending Mack for Captain. Although overwhelming, she found that she enjoyed writing about the people she cared about and partly wished that she could show them these letters so they could see just how important they were to her. But she struggled with making Mack's letter sound more like it was actually coming from Mack and worried that the similarities between the two letters would get her in trouble.

With the sudden push to find the Captain's replacement, it was widely assumed that Hobbs was looking to retire. Personally, Sammi was looking forward to the change because with Hobbs out of the picture, she would get her freedom back. She knew she was going to have to ease Mack into the idea of her going back into crime, but she wasn't willing to wait much longer once he got his promotion.

Since Sammi could finally see the light at the end of the tunnel for her police career, she, Howard, and Kodi started meeting up twice a week to go over ideas and work toward getting their connection back as a team. Sammi was the only one to humor the idea of involving Eli, especially when they discussed the possibility of needing some muscle for a job.

"Sammi, you're more than enough muscle," Kodi joked as they all sat around the living room in her apartment one Saturday. Sammi made a face like she'd never been more insulted in her entire life before bursting into laughter.

"I am kind of a badass, huh?" Sammi asked, still laughing as she flexed both of her biceps. She wore a grey tank top, so it was clear as day that she didn't have much muscle to show off.

"Well, you're the scariest one here, that's for sure," Howard teased and Sammi's jaw dropped.

Sammi took the pillow from behind her on Kodi's couch and smacked Howard in the face with it. Howard laughed as he took the pillow from her and weakly tossed it back at her. Both girls giggled at his unfortunate show of strength.

"So, what are you going to tell Doctor Charming when you start disappearing for weeks at a time?" Sammi asked Kodi, leaning back casually on the couch.

"I'll just make stuff up as we go," Kodi told her. "But if he ends up sticking around, I'm going to have to tell him the truth."

"I have a feeling he'll handle it better than Mack," Sammi replied. "And Mack knew I was thief when he met me."

Kodi shrugged, knowing Sammi was probably right. She, Sammi, and Howard spent the rest of the afternoon pretty much just goofing off until Sammi left to make her hour-long drive home.

*

When Mack and Sammi got to work the following Monday, there was a buzz about the entire precinct with rumors that Hobbs would be announcing the new Captain that day. Mack immediately got excited and just a little bit cocky as Sammi held onto his right arm with both of her hands, showing her love and support for her handsome husband. Sammi, other than beaming with pride for the man she had married, suddenly felt like a weight had been lifted and she could breathe so much easier knowing she'd be off the force by the end of the month.

As the couple entered the squad room, Mazzeline exited the Captain's office with Hobbs right behind him. Mazzeline and Sammi made eye contact as Mazzeline crossed the room to his desk, and he shook his head with a disappointed look on his face. Sammi assumed he had just been told he wasn't getting the Captain's position, but she wondered why he would've expected anything different. Hobbs called Sammi into the office next and closed the door behind them.

"Well, this is a tad uncomfortable," Hobbs said, frowning at Sammi as he leaned only slightly against the edge of his desk.

"Aw, no hard feelings, Hobbs," Sammi replied with a smile as she reached over to pat him on the shoulder.

"Sammi, you got the promotion," Hobbs told her sternly.

"I might just miss you after all–wait, what?" Sammi's heart stopped for a second and she had to put her hand on the back of the chair next to her to keep herself standing.

"I pulled every string I could to try and get Mack promoted, but every single letter of recommendation was glowing with support for you, except for your own."

"That can't be true. Mack recommended Mazzeline."

"I don't know what he told you, but his letter was all about how you're a better cop than anyone in the precinct, even when you don't even want to be here."

"I don't want this," Sammi whispered, more to herself than to Hobbs, as she felt all of the color drain out of her face. "Mack is never going to forgive me for this."

The room started spinning as Sammi's strength drained with the rest of her color. Her hand slid off the back of the chair she had been holding onto and she fainted to the floor with a soft thump.

Part Three

Chapter Twenty-One
The Time of My Life

"Sammi, come on, the guys are waiting," Kodi said, poking her head into the motel room.

"I'll be right out," Sammi told her, zipping up her black ankle boots on the edge of her bed. "I still have ten minutes."

Kodi huffed her disapproval before pulling her head out of the room and closing the door. Sammi waited to hear the door latch before snatching her cellphone off her bedside table and dialing Mack's number with a disheartened sigh. Mack didn't answer; Mack hadn't answered once in the two months Sammi had been gone.

"Mack, I'm just going to keep calling until you talk to me," Sammi informed Mack's voicemail. "Whether you like it or not, there is something that we have to talk about."

Sammi ended the call and put the phone back on the nightstand. As she looked down at her beautiful engagement ring and matching wedding band on her left ring finger, she couldn't help but wonder if Mack still wore his own ring back in New York. Just as she placed the tips of her fingers around the rings to slip them off, a car horn echoed from the parking lot blaring through Sammi's thoughts. Leaving her sense of commitment in place on her elegant finger, Sammi sprinted outside and into the backseat of the waiting black Tahoe.

"It's so nice of you to join us," Eli said playfully, turning around to look at Sammi from the front passenger seat.

"Obviously, our mastermind gets to do whatever she wants," Kodi replied smartly from beside her in the backseat. Sammi stuck her tongue out at her while Howard stayed out of it as he drove them a few towns over to the largest bank in Wisconsin.

After clearing a couple hundred thousand dollars out of the bank's vault and loading it into the Tahoe, the team headed back to the motel to grab their things and move on to the next state. They had planned on staying another night, but their adrenaline was still high and they couldn't have slept even if they tried. Once they crossed into Minnesota, Howard pulled the car down a secluded path and Eli hopped out to change the license plates. They were all New York plates and they were all technically legitimate, being that they all belonged to the Tahoe, but Howard had rigged the system to get them multiple plates so they wouldn't be as easy to track from state to state across the country.

When they got to the next motel, which they had already picked out well in advance, the boys and the girls separated into neighboring rooms. Kodi and Sammi took some time to make themselves comfortable in the new room, with Kodi taking the bed closer to the door as she had in every other motel room on this trip. Sammi had assumed she just liked having the bed with the window view and didn't realize that her best friend was subconsciously being overprotective of her after living through almost losing her twice already.

Sammi threw her backpack of clothes and personal items onto the floor beside her bed and dropped her cellphone onto the nightstand. She still hadn't heard from Mack, but she was used to it by now. Her adrenaline had crashed so she slipped her boots off and climbed into bed while Kodi organized their entire bathroom for them, still abuzz with energy.

"Have you heard from Mack?" Kodi suddenly asked as she came out of the bathroom, holding a tube of toothpaste.

"Huh?" Sammi replied groggily, jolting out of her half-sleep.

"What is up with you?" Kodi sounded kind of annoyed. "You've been kind of distant since we left New York."

"You know that I didn't leave on good terms with Mack," Sammi reminded her as she sat up in her bed. "I'm scared he's never going to talk to me again."

"Sammi, you didn't do anything wrong," Kodi told her best friend with sincerity. "It's not like you weaseled your way in to take the Captain promotion from him. If he won't talk to you, that's on him. You deserve better than that."

Nodding silently, Sammi looked down at her rings again. She couldn't understand why she felt so terrible when she knew she hadn't done anything wrong. The only thing she could think of was that she would feel better if Mack knew what it was that she needed to tell him. But he had to talk to her in order for that to happen.

Kodi was still humming with energy so Sammi let her finish what she was doing and settled herself back into bed. Sammi fell asleep listening to Kodi flutter about the room and woke up a few short hours later after Kodi had finally gone to bed herself.

It was early in the morning, just before sunrise, and Sammi wasn't surprised that she woke up feeling nauseous. She turned her bedside lamp on and glanced over at Kodi to make sure she was still asleep before slipping into the bathroom and closing the door. Trying to be as quiet as possible, Sammi knelt in front of the toilet and vomited until she felt better. As she brushed her teeth afterward, thankful that Kodi had set their bathroom up, she remembered she hadn't taken her vitamins the day before.

Exiting the bathroom, Sammi hoped she still had a water

bottle in her backpack. She sat on the edge of her bed, facing the bathroom, and picked her bag up off the floor. After finding a nearly full bottle of water right away, she dug through everything else to find her pill bottle, but it wasn't there.

"Looking for these?" Kodi asked, shaking the pill bottle from her bed behind Sammi.

"What–why are you going through my stuff?!" Sammi replied angrily, turning to face

Kodi after tossing her bag to the floor.

"When were you going to tell me?" Kodi snapped back, matching Sammi's rage.

"Not until I told Mack!" Sammi yelled as she walked around her bed to where Kodi sat and held her hand out for the bottle.

"Mack doesn't know?" Kodi quieted down as she placed the bottle in her friend's hand.

"I knew before I left, but he was too mad," Sammi explained. "And now he won't talk to me."

Sammi turned away from Kodi and walked back over to the other side of her own bed to grab her water bottle and take her prenatal vitamins. Still annoyed with Kodi for going through her belongings, Sammi kept her back to her and sat on the edge of the bed. She tried to calm down as she checked her cellphone, but the lack of messages from Mack only upset her further. After Sammi put her phone down and put everything back in her bag, Kodi came over from the other side of the room and took a seat next to Sammi.

"I'm really sorry, Sam. I shouldn't have snooped," Kodi said quietly, resting her head on Sammi's shoulder to ask for forgiveness.

"I wanted to tell you, Kodi," Sammi replied, calmer now, "but Mack was supposed to be the first to know."

"You know I can't let you go on any more jobs with us now, right?"

"Kode, we'll be finished and in California within two months and I'll hardly even be five months along by then. I will be fine."

Not wanting to argue with her best friend again, Kodi didn't say anything else on the subject. She knew that all she had to do if she wanted to keep Sammi off a job was tell the boys and get them involved. It also crossed her mind to try and reach out to Mack on Sammi's behalf, but nothing had ever felt more like it wasn't her place to tell.

*

Nevada was the team's last stop before ending their forty-eight-state stealing spree across the country in California. The team had been more efficient than they'd planned and had made the rest of the trip in a month and a half as opposed to the intended two months. Sammi still hadn't been able to get in touch with Mack, but Kodi had been able to keep her secret from Eli and Howard.

Eli had surprised everyone on the team by being an incredible friend to Sammi on the trip without trying to make a move on her. He had been nothing but respectful toward her while she pined for her husband. Howard and Kodi had both expected differently and had been almost positive that Eli would have replaced Mack by the end of the trip. In fact, they had even made bets on it.

The plan for Nevada was similar to the team's last forty-six bank robberies, but as they went to check into the Wynn Hotel in Las Vegas to treat themselves, Sammi's brain went wild with ideas. Before Howard made it to the reception counter, Sammi pulled him aside with the others.

"We're robbing this place," Sammi announced in hushed tones as the team of four stood to the side under the trees of the colorful and elegantly ornamental lobby.

"But we've never done a casino," Kodi argued, frustrated

with her best friend.

"I know, but this just came to me," Sammi explained. "Let's grab lunch and talk about it."

"I think we should hear her out," Eli said, to nobody's surprise, as he shrugged his shoulders and followed Sammi out of the lobby. Kodi gave Howard a worried look before the two of them hurried to catch up with the other half of their team.

While the band of thieves sat in the back corner of a well-lit, average chain restaurant, Eli, Howard, and Kodi listened to Sammi's new plan. She wanted Eli and Kodi to pretend to be getting married at the hotel with Kodi acting as a wealthy socialite so the staff would be consumed with keeping her happy. When they decided it was the right time, Kodi would become a total bridezilla and suffer a very public meltdown while Howard helped Sammi hack into the casino's vault. They still needed to do some research on the casino and its security system, and Howard needed time to create aliases for the fake couple.

"I like it," Eli said with a smug grin after Sammi finished sharing her idea.

"Fine," Kodi replied and turned toward Sammi, "but you're playing the socialite. You and Eli are the only two who can pass as a red-carpet couple."

Kodi meant what she said, but she also cared more about keeping Sammi safe by keeping her away from the actual theft. Sammi couldn't argue with her logic so she groaned and agreed to pretend to be Eli's girlfriend once again. Then the team took the next few days to perfect the plan before heading back to the Wynn Hotel.

Eli and Sammi checked into the hotel separately from Howard and Kodi. As the two pairs headed up to their rooms, they kept in character and chatted lightly as if they all hadn't known each other for years. But as they reached their two separate rooms, Kodi looked up and down the hallway to make sure the coast was clear before stopping Eli in his doorway. Sammi had already disappeared into the room, so Kodi grabbed Eli's arm and pulled him down the hallway and into a quiet but echoing stairwell.

"What is wrong?" Eli asked, flustered as he fixed the sleeve of his grey collared shirt.

"I can't protect Sammi on this job, so I need you to step up and do that for me," Kodi explained, looking him directly in the eyes.

"You know I'd kill for that girl," Eli replied with a cocky smirk.

"Eli, I'm serious," Kodi said with a stern look on her face.

"Okay, jeez," Eli responded like a scolded child, shaking his long hair out of his face. "Is there something going on that I don't know about?"

"Yeah. Sammi's pregnant."

As soon as the words left her mouth, Kodi left Eli to suffer in solitude. Eli felt like he had just been shot in the heart as he backed into the wall behind him and slid down it to the floor. He stared at the floor in silence, wishing he really had just been shot so he could die in peace in that empty stairwell.

When Eli had gathered himself and finally met Sammi in their hotel room, he decided to keep Sammi's secret and not let on that he knew about it. He had an opportunity to pretend he was with the woman he loved again, and he intended to enjoy every second of this job. But he remained respectful and gave Sammi her space in the room, making sure she had the bed to herself while he slept on the couch.

It took the team four days to get Kodi into the hotel casino's vault and she and Howard made a run for California. Eli and Sammi laid low for an extra day at the hotel to avoid suspicion before Sammi dramatically called off the wedding, screaming at Eli and crying in front of dozens of staff and guests. Having made off with ten million dollars from the casino, they had gone well above their goal and were in agreement to vacation in California rather than work another job. So Sammi and Eli rented a car and left Vegas to meet up with Kodi and Howard in a five-star hotel in Pasadena.

*

Kodi and Howard were waiting outside in front of the magnificent Langham Hotel as Eli and Sammi pulled up in a rented silver Corvette Stingray. Eli stopped the car in front of the palatial building and got out, handing the key to the valet. Sammi leapt out of the passenger seat and immediately threw her arms around Kodi in a hug.

"Always gotta make a scene," Howard said, laughing as he patted Eli on his shoulder.

"I couldn't show up to a joint like this in something like my Honda," Eli told him, grinning proudly.

The team made their way inside where their two rooms had already been checked into. Kodi led Sammi up to their room so she could drop her bag off before they decided how they wanted to spend their day. Being that they were ahead of schedule and ahead of their income goals, they had about three weeks to just leisure about in California. Sammi had always dreamed of one day seeing the City of Angels for herself and she couldn't wait to get out there and see the sights.

"Ready?" Sammi asked, throwing her backpack on the bed and turning back toward the door.

"Hold on," Kodi said, laughing at her friend's eagerness. "I gotta call Anthony quick."

"Oh, my apologies," Sammi replied and made goofy fake kissing faces.

Kodi laughed again and took her cellphone out onto the balcony to call her boyfriend who was still back in New York. Sammi took a minute to check out the rest of the hotel room and stopped to look in the full-length mirror in the bathroom. Her long, straight hair was just slightly wind-whipped from

Eli driving fast with the windows down in the Corvette. She ran Kodi's brush through the soft, blonde strands until every last one fell into its proper place.

As Sammi reached over to put the hairbrush back on the bathroom counter, her tight baby blue tee lifted up a little on her abdomen and she caught a gasp in her throat. Her perfect flat stomach now had a slight round shape to it, which was easily hidden by her shirt. Sammi suddenly felt dizzy and left the bathroom to sit on the bed and dig her cellphone out of her bag.

Sammi was in a panic and her hands were shaking as she tried to hold her phone and get into the contacts screen. It was all suddenly so real. Before she could scroll down to Mack's name, Kodi came back into the room and headed for the door, asking Sammi if she was ready to go without looking at her. Not wanting to draw attention to her newfound belly, Sammi composed herself while she pocketed her phone and followed Kodi out of the room to meet up with the boys.

The four friends ended up grabbing lunch at the hotel bar before sitting by the pool to discuss everything they wanted to see while they were in California. While they lounged around outside by the pool, Sammi noticed a gorgeous surfer-type guy with shaggy blonde hair staring at her. His hair was slightly shorter than Eli's, but it was wavier. They made eye contact about a dozen times before the shirtless muscular man made his way over to introduce himself.

"I'm sorry, but you are the most incredible-looking Sheila I've eva' seen," the beach boy said directly to Sammi in an unexpected Australian accent. "And now that I see the rings on your finga,' I feel like a fool."

"No, you're fine," Sammi replied kindly, blushing and holding back a giggle. "I'm Sammi, by the way."

"Well, hello, Sammi," the Australian responded with a bright, big-toothed smile. "I'm Christopha.'"

"Maybe I'll see you around, Christopher," Sammi told him,

retuning his smile.

Christopher looked back to smile at Sammi twice as he walked away, blushing slightly himself. As soon as he was out of sight, Sammi burst into laughter while her friends looked at her in shock.

"You're mean!" Eli gasped.

Sammi continued to laugh, feeling better than she had in four months. Flirting with a stranger had taken her mind off Mack and the fact that she was almost five months pregnant. The flattering attention from the attractive Aussie kept her distracted the rest of the day and night, and she forgot all about the need to call her husband.

Chapter Twenty-Two
Laying Me Low

Eli, Howard, Kodi, and Sammi spent the next ten days seeing everything they wanted to see throughout California. They visited the different cities and spent time on the different beaches, taking it all in. Eli had been the only one of them who had ever even left New York and the others were just happy to see that a place existed that wasn't as grey and suffocating as New York was. Sammi was instantly infatuated with Hollywood and Los Angeles, which didn't surprise any of her friends since she'd been talking about those cities since they'd known her.

But by the end of the ten days, the team had seen everything they wanted to see and Sammi's friends were ready to go home. Kodi missed her boyfriend, Howard missed his home, and Eli just hated California because it was too sunny and too pretentious for his taste; he was a New Yorker tried and true. Sammi hadn't said anything, but she was in no hurry to get back to New York.

During the ten days of exploration, Sammi ran into Christopher a few times around the hotel, always in passing. The two of them would always exchange a smile and a wave or even a wink when they were feeling good about themselves. Having gone four months without a word from her husband, Sammi was really enjoying the attention.

When Sammi woke up the morning after their last day of sight-seeing, Kodi was already awake and packing up their stuff from the bathroom. Surprised, Sammi ran over to ask her what she was doing. All that remained unpacked by the sink were Sammi's toothbrush and hairbrush.

"We have to be out of the room before noon," Kodi informed her as she zipped up her own bag.

"What? Why?" Sammi asked, panicked. "I thought we had the room for another week!"

"We all want to go home, Sam," Kodi told her. "There's nothing out here for us."

"Then you guys can go," Sammi said plainly. "I'm not going back to New York."

Sammi then walked out of the bathroom and grabbed her room key and cellphone off the nightstand before storming out of the room. She headed downstairs and quickly realized she was dressed in just her sweatpants and tank top that she had slept in. Feeling discouraged, she just sat down in one of the chairs in the hotel lobby. Holding her phone down in front of her to look busy, she scrolled through her old messages, contemplating reaching out to somebody.

"'Ello, Sammi," came a kind Australian accent from in front of where she sat, causing her to look up.

"Hey, Christopher," Sammi replied, trying to sound cool but she couldn't hide that she was upset.

"What's wrong?" Christopher asked sincerely.

"My friends are ready to go back to New York," Sammi told the stranger, "and I'm not."

"Come on, let's do somethin' fun," Christopher offered as he also offered her his hand.

"Let me go change first," Sammi said, taking his hand and standing up. "Meet you back here in fifteen?"

"You got it, gorgeous."

Sammi dashed back upstairs to her room where Kodi was sitting on the bed with her cellphone in her hand and her luggage beside her. Ignoring her friend, Sammi walked to her own bag and dumped all of its contents onto her side of the king-sized bed. Grabbing a black mini skirt and a blue halter top to match her eyes, she skipped into the bathroom to change.

After Sammi finished getting ready, she exited the bathroom and found Kodi standing in front of the hotel room door. Sammi knew she was blocking her way out on purpose, but Sammi wasn't in the mood to humor her. She avoided looking in Kodi's direction as she walked back over to the bed to get her wallet. Once she had everything she needed, she finally turned her attention on Kodi.

"Well, have a safe trip," Sammi said with a slight shrug of her shoulders, avoiding eye contact.

"Where are you going?" Kodi asked aggressively.

"Christopher and I are going out for the day," Sammi told her and Kodi sighed.

"Sammi, what are you doing? You are married and have a child on the way."

"I'm done, Kode. Mack won and I have nothing to go back to."

Finally saying those words out loud brought tears to Sammi's eyes. She turned back toward the bed and sat on the edge of it with her head down. Kodi dropped her guard by the door and went to comfort her best friend. She sat next to Sammi on the bed and pulled her into a hug, letting her cry on her shoulder.

"Sammi, just call him one more time," Kodi spoke softly as her friend's sobbing quieted. "Just give him one more chance."

Sammi nodded and forced herself to be composed as she opened the screen on her cellphone. Taking deep breaths, she scrolled down to Mack's name and pressed on it to make the call. It rang all the way through to voicemail just like it had every other time over the past four months.

"Mack," Sammi spoke quietly to her husband's voicemail, still holding back tears, "I'm guessing you don't want me to come home and I'm trying to be okay with that. But, uh, I can't just stay in California without telling you what I've needed to tell you for four months now. Mack, I...I'm pregnant. Please...please just call me back."

With a disheartened sigh, Sammi hung up the phone. Kodi felt sad for her best friend, but she was also realizing how furious she was with Mack for acting as childish as he was. As badly as she wanted to go home to Anthony, she couldn't make Sammi go with them and she couldn't leave her in California on her own.

"I'll talk to the guys," Kodi said, almost whispering as she rubbed Sammi's back to comfort her. "Maybe we can stay a bit longer."

"You guys don't have to stay. I'll be fine," Sammi told her, hopping off the bed and fixing her skirt.

"If you must hang out with that gorgeous Australian, just don't do anything you might regret," Kodi replied with a distrusting look. "Stay out of trouble."

Sammi giggled as she crossed the room to the door. She stopped with her hand on the door handle to look back at her best friend.

"But I'm always getting into trouble," Sammi said with a wink before disappearing into the hallway.

*

Back in New York, Mack had consumed himself with the job. Captain Hobbs had been convinced by the department to keep his position after Sammi turned it down and abandoned the precinct. And Mack's already difficult attitude had only gotten worse, making him impossible to work with and forcing Palma and Mazzeline to pair up without him.

Without a partner, Mack was practically working seven days a week and either sleeping at the station house or driving home to Long Island only to turn right back around and return to work without any sleep. He wouldn't admit it, but he hated being in that house without Sammi and he was avoiding it every way he could. Mazzeline and Palma were too afraid to try to talk to him, but Hobbs had tried, only to discover that Mack partly blamed him for chasing Sammi away.

"Have you even talked to her?" Hobbs asked, trying to ignore Mack's accusation.

"There's nothing left to say," Mack replied coldly, sitting casually in front of his Captain's desk.

"You are acting like a child, Johnson!" Hobbs yelled and slammed his fist down on his desk. "Your wife didn't ask for the promotion she was offered and refused. She was the only damn colleague who was rooting for you! I obviously wasn't the biggest fan of your relationship, but she loved you, you jackass."

"If she loved me, she wouldn't have left," Mack replied, trying to hide the pain in his voice. Then he got up and walked out of the Captain's office.

Mack knew that Sammi had never wanted the Captain's promotion, but he couldn't let it go. He resented her for being a thief—for stealing his heart and stealing his job. Every time his phone rang and it was Sammi, his heart ached as he was torn about wanting to answer it. But every scenario he played out in his head ended with him asking her to come home and her demanding her space to complete her trip of thievery. And he just couldn't handle that rejection.

Even though Mack acted like Sammi had just up and left him, Sammi had actually left him a schedule of where she would be and when. The itinerary ended with the date she was expected to return home and Mack hoped that day would come but he couldn't be so sure anymore. He realized that his refusal to talk to her wasn't helping his chances, but he wanted to see her, not just hear her over the phone. And he would learn to be okay when she didn't come home.

The last voicemail from Sammi came while Mack was passed out on the cot in the officer's lounge where Sammi had spent the night after getting out of the hospital after Eli tried to kill her. He thought about that night every time he slept in the lounge and how it was where he first told Sammi that he liked her. It had bothered him that it didn't faze her because she was so used to guys falling all over themselves for her. But then he'd think about how she married him instead of any of those other guys and he'd start missing her like crazy. It wasn't much that he had to offer her, but it had been enough.

When Mack woke up and found the missed call from Sammi and the accompanying voicemail on his phone, his heart sank. It had been weeks since her last call and he had gotten comfortable with the silence. Staring at his wedding band on his left ring finger, he put the phone to his ear to listen to his wife's message just as Captain Hobbs burst into the room.

"Mazzeline's been shot!" Hobbs announced in a frenzied panic. "Palma's gonna need your help on this one."

"Is he okay?" Mack asked as he jumped up and pocketed his phone with the unheard message.

"He's being taken to the hospital as we speak," Hobbs told him. "He and Palma were at a crime scene and the suspect was still in the building."

"Sammi's going to be really upset if he dies," Mack muttered more to himself as he walked past Hobbs and out of the room to get the address of the crime scene.

*

As Sammi entered the lobby to meet Christopher, Christopher took one look at her and a clownish grin spread across his face. Sammi blushed as she smiled at the floor before greeting Christopher with a quick hug. Christopher then led her outside to where the valet already had his bright yellow Jeep Wrangler waiting and opened the passenger door for her.

While Christopher drove them into Los Angeles for the day, they chatted in the car and took turns playing music. During a break in conversation, Sammi looked down at her hands with her eyes drawn to her wedding rings. She checked her phone, giving Mack one last chance to have come through for her, and saw that he had not. So, she slid the two symbols of her marriage off of her still slender finger and tucked them securely into a pocket of her wallet.

Christopher and Sammi had fun in the city, but it was obvious right away that Christopher was younger by his lack of life experience. Sammi was attracted to him, but his lack of depth made her miss Mack more than she ever had. She missed her life in New York for the first time since leaving and even surprised herself by talking fondly of her time on the force as they discussed what they did for a living.

"Wait, I didn't think cops made a lot of money," Christopher speculated as they sat across from each other over dinner. "How can you afford the Langham for such a long stay?"

"Says the guys who runs a surf shop!" Sammi scoffed at his rude assumption.

"Yeah, but my parents are loaded," Christopher told her. "Is your police officer husband kind of like that Will Smith movie where he's just a cop to be cool even though he's got so much money he's ruining Ferraris without thinking twice?"

"First of all, he's a detective," Sammi corrected him. "And he's more like the Bruce Willis sequel where he's a cop with a little bit of fame, but definitely still has to work for a living."

"So, come on, how can you afford the Langham?" Christopher pushed the issue.

"Prove to me that I can trust you," Sammi offered in a flirting manner.

"Fine. We don't just have surfboards at my surf shop," Christopher told her.

"Snorkels?" Sammi asked and giggled at her own smartass response.

"No," Christopher said, getting serious and starting to whisper, "try cocaine and ecstasy."

"Oh, so you're a real gangster," Sammi replied with a mocking tone, rolling her eyes at him.

"What would you know?" Christopher asked, visibly offended.

"I'm a thief," Sammi stated with a slight shrug of one of her shoulders.

"Shut up, you are not. You're way too hot to have to steal anythin.' You can't tell me any man has eva' denied you anythin' you've asked for."

Sammi didn't owe this guy an explanation so she changed the subject and never mentioned her career again. After dinner, she and Christopher walked the city streets in the warm night air. She didn't fall in love with another man that night, but she did fall in love with another city. She fell in love with the lights that shined brighter than the ones in New York, she fell in love with the warm breezes that refused to cool off even after the sun went down, and she fell in love with the person she could be in California.

After such a long day, both Sammi and Christopher were quieter as Christopher drove them back to the hotel. Sammi put her Cavo playlist on the radio and sank into the passenger seat of the Jeep to daydream about starting a new life in Los Angeles.

Back at the hotel, Christopher and Sammi said goodnight in the lobby. As Sammi moved in for a hug, Christopher quickly tilted his head and bent his knees to catch Sammi's lips with his own. Sammi froze in a sudden wave of panic, not having expected this guy to make a move on a married woman. But it was a fantastic kiss, so passionate and so forceful that Sammi chose to go with it. She angled her face up to meet his and buried her hands in his glorious sandy blonde hair.

"I'll see ya tomorrow," Christopher whispered, pressing his forehead to Sammi's and looking down into her crystal blue eyes with a genuinely happy smile on his face.

"Sleep well, Christopher," Sammi replied quietly and rubbed his arm before letting him walk off first.

Sammi wasn't smiling like Christopher was. She knew that her only attraction to Christopher was a physical one and she felt guilty for leading him on and guilty for kissing another man behind her husband's back. And that kiss, as great as it was, wasn't the kiss she wanted. It wasn't Mack's kiss.

Knowing Kodi was up in the hotel room, Sammi wasn't in a hurry to return. She wasn't ready for the conversation about Christopher and she definitely wasn't ready to tell her best friend that she was staying in California. Turning slowly toward the elevators, she finally looked up, and her eyes met those of a tortured Eli.

Chapter Twenty-Three
Avalanche

The hurt look on Eli's face was like a kick in the teeth to Sammi. She couldn't think of a word to say before Eli hung his shoulders in defeat and retreated into an elevator. As badly as Sammi wanted to chase after him, she knew he needed space before he'd be ready to talk to her, so she headed slowly for her hotel room, feeling like the cruelest human on the planet.

"I got the guys to agree to another week," Kodi said as soon as Sammi entered the hotel room.

"No, you guys should go," Sammi said quietly and rolled onto her side of the bed with her back to her best friend.

"What's wrong?" Kodi asked, walking around the bed so she could see Sammi's face.

"Eli saw me kiss Christopher," Sammi told her, her voice filled with guilt. "I think he finally hates me."

"Why were you kissing the Australian?!"

"Not the point, Kodi!"

Sammi leapt off the bed and walked into the bathroom. She slammed the door shut with as much force as she could and slid down the length of it so that she was sitting with her back against it. Knowing she was about to have an emotional meltdown, she had one last thing to say.

"I'm not going back to New York," Sammi called through the door, hardly even raising her voice.

Having said what she needed to say, Sammi buried her face in her hands and allowed herself to break down. At first, she was crying over Eli and how she had probably just lost one of the best friends she had ever had. But there was a deeper reason for her breakdown, a more distant cause of pain. Sammi never would have imagined that this would be the way she and Mack ended. Even when she knew that he didn't support her career choice, she always thought they'd be able to talk about it. After everything they had been through, Mack had always at least talked sooner or later. But now even the life growing inside of her that they had created together couldn't break his silence.

Kodi could hear Sammi crying and sobbing on the other side of the bathroom door, but she believed that Sammi needed this release. She waited about half an hour until it got a little quieter before she let herself into the bathroom and found Sammi curled up in a ball on the tile floor. Sammi was still sobbing lightly, but her tears had run dry, leaving behind red eyes and smeared eyeliner.

Kneeling down where Sammi could see her, Kodi patted her friend's shoulder to try and comfort her. Sammi immediately pulled herself together and sat up, hugging her knees to her chest and resting her head on them.

"I cannot imagine what you are feeling," Kodi spoke very softly, "and I'm not going to try to convince you that you have to go back home. But I sincerely hope you will change your own mind because New York won't be the same without you."

"Don't worry," Sammi said, finally smiling and putting her legs down to place her hands on her little baby bump. "I'm sure two days after this little nugget is born, I'm going to be begging for your help."

Kodi's eyes widened, seeing proof of the baby for the first

time. She slid across the tile floor to sit next to Sammi and added a hand to the slightly bulbous tummy.

"Can we schedule you a checkup before I leave?" Kodi asked, unable to hide her excitement.

"Of course," Sammi said, smiling bigger at the thought of her first ultrasound.

Thinking about her baby and the excitement of its future possibilities, Sammi realized that everything was going to be okay. She didn't need Mack, she didn't need Eli, and she didn't need to even see Christopher ever again. All she needed and all she wanted was a happy, healthy life for the little being growing inside of her.

*

When Sammi woke up the next morning, she was feeling so much better and made her first priority to make amends with Eli. Not wanting to wake him up, she showered first and waited a bit longer before having Kodi text Eli just to see if he responded. He wrote back right away so Sammi dashed out of the room and knocked on the door across the hall. Howard opened the door and gave her a look of disappointment.

"Where is he?" Sammi asked, getting right to the point.

"Bathroom," Howard replied, moving out of the way to let her into the room but still shaking his head disapprovingly at her.

Sammi entered the room and crossed to the bathroom. The door was closed so Sammi leaned against the wall outside of it to wait for Eli. Howard shook his head one more time before leaving to give them privacy.

Eli came out of the bathroom with just a towel wrapped around his waist and using another towel to dry his shoulder-length hair that looked almost black when wet. He didn't notice Sammi as he crossed the room to the couch to dig clothes out of a gym bag. After finding what he wanted to wear, he finally looked up and dropped his handful of clothing to the floor at the sight of his ex-girlfriend.

"Nice pecs," Sammi said, staring directly at Eli's chest.

"What do you want, Sammi?" Eli asked coldly, tossing the towel for his hair to the couch and putting on a grey t-shirt.

"I don't want you to hate me," Sammi told him, trying to sound innocent as she looked at the floor.

"I don't hate you," Eli replied, "but I don't want to talk to you right now."

"Was kissing that guy really the worst thing I could've done?" Sammi asked with pain in her voice.

"Do you even know why it upset me?" Eli asked with his arms slouched forward, giving in to this conversation.

"Because I cheated on Mack?"

Eli laughed to himself as he threw his gym bag on the floor and plopped down on the couch with his head down, avoiding eye contact at all costs. Sammi stayed where she was and wondered what Eli thought was so funny.

"No, believe it or not, I don't actually give a damn about Mack," Eli growled, finally expressing his anger.

"Then why do you care who I kiss?" Sammi asked with growing frustration.

"Seriously, Sammi?!" Eli roared, aggressively pushing his own hair out of his face. "Are you so full of yourself that you don't know how I feel about you?! That I would give my life for you and that everything I have done since making the biggest mistake of my life has been for you?! And I really believed that if you left Mack for anybody that it would be for me."

Eli put his head in his hands, desperate to force back his tears. He could feel the couch shift as Sammi sat beside him and put her hand on his back, but his body tensed up and his hands curled into fists against his face.

"Eli, I'm so sorry," Sammi spoke softly.

"Get out," Eli continued to growl, knowing he couldn't

hold his tears back much longer, which was only making him angrier.

When Sammi didn't move, Eli dropped his fists and looked at her with rage in his eyes. They both knew he wouldn't hurt her, not after everything they'd been through. A brief glimpse of fear flashed across Sammi's face, but it quickly changed back to sadness.

"Get out!" Eli screamed and punched the arm of the couch, trying harder to scare Sammi away.

But Sammi doubled down and rested her head on Eli's shoulder, wrapping her arms around his left arm to hold him. Eli melted under her touch and could no longer hold back his breakdown. As he began sobbing, Sammi pulled him to her and wrapped both her arms around his body. She held him as he cried and combed her fingers through his wet hair to provide comfort. Her heart cried for Eli and she knew that she would always love him, but she owed it to both of them to properly say goodbye to Mack before even thinking about being with Eli again.

"I'm not going to see Christopher again," Sammi said quietly as Eli's sobbing started to calm down.

Eli finally freed himself from Sammi's hold and sat up on the couch. He lifted the bottom of his t-shirt up to wipe off his face before turning his content gaze on Sammi. Forcing a smile, he swiftly scooped an arm around Sammi's waist and pulled her into his lap. He kept his hands gently on her hips as he looked deeply into her sparkling eyes.

"You are everything to me, Samantha," Eli whispered with his face as close to hers as possible without touching. "And I can't wait to meet your little mini-me."

Sammi's face lit up at the mention of her child and that glow of joy made Eli fall in love with her all over again. But it was the fact that she had stayed by his side and didn't run away in fear of him when he tried to push her away that let him know that she loved him too. She trusted him again and that was all he needed to know to be okay.

"Kodi told you, huh?" Sammi asked, still smiling and keeping her face close to Eli's.

"Yeah, and it nearly killed me," Eli told her with a nervous laugh.

He wanted to ask if Mack knew and he wanted to confess his eternal support for her and her child. But he was distracted by the overwhelming desire to kiss her and it took all of his strength to fight it. It wasn't the right time and that was okay with him because he truly believed that the right time would come.

Still in Eli's lap, Sammi wrapped her arms around him and snuggled into his chest with her head tucked under his chin. He squeezed her tighter to him and they held each other in silence, letting the quiet heal their hearts.

*

Back in New York, two days after Mazzeline had been shot, Sammi's old partner pulled through. Mack, who had been working around the clock with Palma to find the shooter, was relieved because he had not been looking forward to the potential heartbreaking phone call to Sammi. But the idea of having a real reason to call Sammi had been somewhat appealing.

"You could always ask Mazzeline to call her," Palma offered during a previously quiet ride back to the station house after a ten-hour stakeout throughout the entire night. Nobody had to talk for Palma to know what was on Mack's mind and the squad had only been able to put his situation with Sammi together through Mack's behavior.

"That's what I need," Mack scoffed, "someone else that Sammi likes more than me to remind her that she's right and I'm wrong."

Palma immediately stopped trying and stopped talking.

Mack spent the rest of the ride back to the precinct thinking about all the messages Sammi had left him over the past few months and how he had never thought of anything he could possibly say back to her. As Palma pulled the squad car into the lot behind their building, Mack suddenly remembered the message he never listened to.

Mack removed his cellphone from his jacket pocket as he followed Palma into the building and had to go through several screens to find his voicemail. He put the phone to his ear after touching the little cassette-tape icon on the screen just as they reached the stairs leading up to their floor. Seconds later, he turned around to sit on the step he was on as his jaw dropped and he lowered his phone.

"Dude, you okay?" Palma asked when he realized his partner wasn't behind him anymore. He had walked back down the stairs until he was in front of Mack.

Mack didn't know what to say. He could feel the color drain from his face as his surroundings began to spin around him. Nausea overcame him and he knew he was going to be sick, so he jumped up and dashed up the stairs and into the bathroom. Sitting in a dimly lit stall, he rocked back and forth while awaiting the inevitable vomit and trying to force it up by thinking about how badly he had screwed up.

While Mack cradled himself on the bathroom floor, he heard the door that led to the squad room open and close. He remained in his stall and tried to keep quiet so whoever it was wouldn't know he was in there.

"Johnson?" Captain Hobbs asked and Mack immediately knew Palma had told him something was wrong.

Mack forced himself to relax as he stood up and straightened his clothes. He exited the stall and was face-to-face with his boss, who was wearing a look of concern. Hobbs stood there and stared at him, waiting for him to speak.

"She's pregnant," Mack said, swallowing hard as he threw up his arms in surrender. "She's been trying to tell me for months and I ignored every one of her calls."

Tears were brimming in the corners of Mack's eyes as he spoke the words aloud. He had never felt worse about himself or more hopeless in his entire life. Hobbs looked at him with pity as he put a hand on Mack's shoulder.

"It's not too late," Hobbs told him, trying to sound reassuring. "You can still try to fix this."

"I gotta go," Mack replied, suddenly in a hurry as he pushed past his Captain for the bathroom door.

"Good luck!" Hobbs called after him, not sounding entirely hopeful.

Mack needed time to think about what he could possibly say to his wife before committing to calling her. He rushed out of the building to his car and took the hour-long drive home to collect his thoughts. Once in the growingly unfamiliar home, he sat on the cool, undisturbed bed and called Sammi.

*

The day after Sammi's and Eli's heart-to-heart, Sammi waited out front of the hotel with Eli and Kodi while Howard collected the Tahoe from the valet. Eli had returned the Corvette to the rental company days ago in preparation for their trip home, so they were down to one car between the four of them again.

"All three of you don't have to go to my doctor appointment," Sammi grumbled as the four friends piled into the Tahoe with Howard behind the wheel, Kodi riding shotgun, and Eli in the back with his favorite person in the world.

"We wouldn't miss this for the world," Kodi told her from the front seat, turning around to smile with excitement at her best friend.

"Yeah, you've got the fifth member of our team growing in there," Howard chimed in, winking at Sammi in the rearview mirror.

"Our newest ride or die," Eli added, taking Sammi's hand and giving it a good squeeze.

"I love you guys," Sammi said with a smile, feeling happier than she had in months. Her friends were more support than she could ever ask for, and the only family she needed.

As Howard pulled up to the stop sign to leave the hotel parking lot, Sammi looked down just in time to catch her phone screen light up with a call from Mack. She had her phone set to silent so nobody else knew that her heart just sank into the pit of her stomach. The only call that she had wanted in the past four months was the call she had given up hope for two days ago. Of course he would wait until she was finally okay without him to reach out and make her need him again.

"Do you guys hear that?" Howard asked, still with his foot on the brake at the traffic sign.

The car fell silent as everyone listened intently for what Howard could be hearing. There was a very faint beeping coming from the front of the Tahoe and it soon became apparent that it was the sound of a timer. Eli, Howard, Kodi, and Sammi all exchanged a mixture of looks of confusion and worry.

"Bomb!" Eli screamed as he threw himself across Sammi's lap to throw her door open and pushed Sammi out of the vehicle. Her body was hardly out of the SUV before it blew and the explosion forced her hard into the blacktop, where everything went dark.

Chapter Twenty-Four
Home Movies (III)

After Sammi fainted in Captain Hobbs' office, Hobbs had insisted that she stop by the hospital to get her head checked out. He wasn't surprised that Sammi was freaking out over the promotion and he couldn't blame her for worrying about having to tell Mack. But fainting was just enough out of character for her for Hobbs to be concerned that something else was going on.

Sammi felt fine, other than the emotional distress, but a trip to the hospital got her out of work and could possibly get her some pity from Mack. She was prepared to walk the several blocks to the hospital, but Hobbs wrangled a rookie patrol officer to escort her before she had even made it down the stairs to the lobby. She and the rookie were quiet in the patrol car because Sammi had nothing left to say to anyone in the precinct. She wasn't taking the Captain's position and she was done with law enforcement altogether.

Mack, who had seen Sammi leave the building in a hurry, quickly sent his wife a text message asking her if she was okay. She let him know that she was getting checked out after a brief fainting spell, but he never replied and she could only presume it was because he had found out that he was not the precinct's new Captain.

At the hospital, a receptionist had Sammi fill out an intake questionnaire before a nurse took her back to collect more information and run a few tests. Sammi couldn't help but notice that the nurse seemed to be extra cautious with the way she asked Sammi questions and it bothered her not knowing if that was just her temperament or if there was a reason behind it. She had to assume that the nurse already looked up her health records and Sammi worried that she suspected a complication from her previous shooting.

"I'm sorry," Sammi finally spoke up, "but you are really freaking me out. Is something wrong?"

"Oh, no, no, no," the nurse said with a tsk, suddenly making Sammi feel like a kindergartener. "Your fainting was brought on by extreme mental stress so I'm just keeping everything light and fluffy."

The nurse smiled so theatrically and spoke with such fake sweetness that it made Sammi nauseous. But she was too distracted by the needle in the nurse's hand to focus on the sick feeling in her stomach.

"What is that?" Sammi asked harshly, not taking her eyes off the terrifyingly sharp point.

"I have to take some blood, sweetie," the nurse told her. "Don't tell me a cop such as yourself who has survived multiple gunshots is afraid of a little needle!"

Sammi despised the woman and wished she would've gone home to Long Island to see Dr. Brock instead. The nurse told Sammi to relax, but she couldn't. She would seriously rather have a gun aimed at her than that needle.

"Honey, you are too tense," the nurse said after putting her fingers to Sammi's wrist to gauge her heartrate.

"I thought you were keeping things light and fluffy?" Sammi snapped at her.

"On your intake, you mentioned that you fainted after

receiving a promotion. Why don't you explain that?" the nurse replied, visibly frustrated.

Sammi didn't think it was important, but she dove into the story anyway and told her about the promotion belonging to her husband and how even her Captain didn't want her to have it. The more involved in the story she became, the more worked up Sammi got until she got to the end and sighed heavily. As Sammi exhaled deeply, the nurse stuck the needle in a vein in her arm.

"Ow! You tricked me!" Sammi cried in disbelief as she tried not to look at the gross intrusion in her arm.

"Works every time," the nurse laughed. "But I usually only have to do it with children."

Sammi rolled her eyes, disliking this nurse more and more. The nurse finished taking the blood sample then disappeared briefly to take it to the lab herself. Sammi checked her phone while she was gone because it had been two hours since she'd been at the hospital and she was disappointed but not surprised that Mack hadn't reached out again. When the nurse came back, her attitude had somewhat changed as she was more genuinely kind this time.

"Detective Johnson, I don't want to put any ideas in your head," the nurse said, getting serious, "but I spoke with a doctor before I came back, and she supports my suspicions. I want to wait on the test results, but you *should* be prepared to start discussing the possibility of being pregnant."

Sammi's face fell as she tried to comprehend what she had just heard. She and Mack hadn't felt the need to rely on birth control because after everything Sammi's body had been through, doctors were pretty pessimistic toward the idea of her being able to conceive. And that had been okay with them because Mack already had children and Sammi had never been burdened with the desire to procreate.

"I...I don't understand," Sammi finally spoke, looking straight ahead but not actually seeing any of her surroundings.

"Like I said, I don't want to get your hopes up or anything," the nurse told her. "But I also don't want you to get a surprise phone call with the test results and black out again. It seems that limiting stress is going to play a big role in your ability to carry a baby to full term."

"But...this...I have to go," Sammi stuttered then grabbed her jacket and sprinted out of the room and out of the hospital.

Even with Sammi's dramatic history, this was the weirdest day of her life. Stealing Mack's promotion out from under him was enough to deal with without also trying to explain being pregnant. Sammi wasn't even sure how Mack would feel about the idea because they'd never really had to discuss it. He had seemed okay with her not wanting to be a mother, but that was when they didn't know there was a possibility.

Sammi wanted to go home but Mack had to use the car for work, so she called Kodi. Kodi picked her up a block from the hospital and Sammi told her about the promotion and the fainting but not about the possible baby. She was pale and visibly shaken so Kodi didn't push her to talk more than she willingly offered. But she did insist on staying with Sammi until Mack got home instead of leaving her alone. They didn't speak much once they were at the house on Long Island and Sammi disappeared to take a phone call as Mack pulled into the driveway.

The phone call was the one Sammi had been told to expect and it confirmed the nurse's suspicions. Sammi was pregnant and she was feeling nauseous all over again.

*

Mack walked in the front door and was immediately greeted by Kodi, who expressed her concern regarding Sammi. But Mack was even less interested in talking than Sammi had been and Kodi began to worry all over again. She left to give the husband and wife some privacy, but she went to see Anthony so that she had an excuse to stay in the area in case Sammi needed her.

Once Kodi left, Mack went into the bedroom to change out of his work clothes. He had hardly spoken at all since Hobbs told him about Sammi getting his promotion and he couldn't shake the cloud he was under. He was angry; so angry that his vision was blurred, and his entire body was tensed up. If there was a way for him to let it go, he didn't know what it was.

While Mack changed, he didn't even know where Sammi was until she came out of their bathroom. She stopped and stood in front of him, looking him in the face. Mack could see that she had no color in her own face and there was a strange glimmer in her seemingly distant blue eyes. He wanted to ask her if she was okay, but his anger wouldn't allow him.

*

As Sammi stood there and looked into her husband's eyes, all she saw was indifference. He wasn't speaking so Sammi walked out of their bedroom and sat on the couch in the living room. Her mind was racing, wondering how she was supposed to tell Mack the biggest news of their lives together when he wouldn't even talk to her. She wanted this to be good news, she wanted to be excited about this, but it didn't seem like Mack was going to let that be the case.

When Mack finally came out of the bedroom, he walked over to the couch where Sammi sat and stood beside his wife. Sammi wouldn't look at him, but she could feel his eyes burning into her shoulder closest to him. She could sense her own emotional meltdown coming and didn't want to express that kind of display of vulnerability in front of her husband when he was like this.

"You're not taking the promotion, right?" Mack finally spoke. There was no kindness in his voice.

"No, Mack, I'm not going to be your new Captain," Sammi

shot coldly back at him.

"You just couldn't stay out of it, could you?" Mack asked gruffly, growing angrier.

"Stay out of what?" Sammi yelled, jumping up from the couch to face her husband. "Once again, I didn't ask for this!"

"You have taken everything from me!" Mack screamed, only a foot apart from Sammi. "You weaseled your way into my life with those bullshit blue eyes and became my reason for existence. The only thing I had left of myself was my job, but you had to go and take that too!"

Those words hurt worse than a punch to the gut and tears began to flow freely down Sammi's ghost-white cheeks. Her stomach was knotted and heavy with queasiness. Her head was light enough to make her question her ability to remain standing and her legs weakened under her.

The next thing Sammi knew, Mack was walking away from her while shaking his head. Sammi hit her knees as her tears came twice as heavily and the uncontrollable sobbing began. She couldn't believe Mack was acting this way and she really didn't understand what she had done wrong.

Sammi cried as she fumbled her phone out of her pocket and called Kodi. Kodi couldn't understand anything that Sammi was trying to tell her, but she knew her friend needed her.

"Please, Sammi, calm down," Kodi said calmly as her best friend continued hyperventilating. "Go pack a bag and I'll be right there to pick you up. We can leave in the morning for our crime tour."

Sammi forced herself to calm down enough to tell Kodi she would be ready in half an hour. She was still crying as she got off the phone and returned to the bedroom to pack a few bags. Mack wasn't in the room, so she took a minute to write out the team's already planned-out schedule of theft across the country.

"What are you doing?" Mack asked, appearing in the

doorway, and staring at Sammi's luggage on the bed.

"Letting you have your life back," Sammi mumbled with her back to her husband as she slid the schedule onto the nightstand.

"You have got to be kidding me!" Mack shouted and tossed her luggage to the floor in a blind rage before cornering her on the side of the bed.

"Space," Sammi whispered, backing away from him with fear in her eyes. It wasn't like him to raise his voice like this.

"Take your damn space," Mack growled, taking a step closer to his terrified wife. "Run away like you always do."

Mack then turned his back on Sammi and walked out of the room. Sammi started crying again as she picked her luggage up off the floor. She checked the time to see how much longer she had to wait for Kodi, desperate to get out of there, and was relieved to find she only had a few minutes to wait before she could expect her friend. Collecting her things, she headed out to the front porch to await her getaway car.

Kodi picked up her best friend and drove them to her apartment in the city while Sammi told her everything that had happened with Mack. Being Sammi's best friend, Kodi was going to take her side anyway, but she was sincerely upset with Mack's actions and wasn't holding back sharing her opinion of disapproval with Sammi. They agreed that Mack couldn't separate work from his personal life which explained why he was taking his disappointment out on Sammi.

Sammi was quiet all evening, even though Kodi kept trying to cheer her up. She told Kodi she'd sleep on the couch because she needed the television on to keep her mind off everything, but she didn't sleep that night. It was making her sick to her stomach leaving things the way she had with Mack and it was taking all of her inner strength to keep herself from reaching out to him.

In the morning, Howard met the girls out front of the apartment building with the black Tahoe from the old days with the original five-person team. Being a gentleman, Howard loaded their luggage into the back of the SUV while Kodi and Sammi stood on the sidewalk and chatted.

"Got room for one more?" came a voice from their right and everyone turned to see Eli coming down the sidewalk with luggage of his own.

"Eli! What are you doing here?" Sammi cried out as she ran to hug him.

"Kodi called me," Eli told her. "She said you might appreciate the extra company."

Sammi hugged Eli, appreciating him so much in that moment. Even though they weren't together, Sammi loved Eli and was more comfortable around him than she was around most other people. And he was especially good to have around when breaking the law.

While the guys finished getting everything into the Tahoe, Sammi pulled Kodi aside and they walked down the sidewalk until they were out of earshot of the guys. Sammi was smiling for the first time in no less than twenty-four hours.

"Thank you," Sammi said, looking directly into Kodi's eyes so she would know she was sincere.

"You were right," Kodi told her. "We need the muscle. And I figured you could use another friend."

"Did you tell either of them about Mack?" Sammi asked, quiet from shame.

"No, but they're going to be able to put it together. They're not stupid," Kodi replied.

Before Sammi could respond, Eli had approached the girls to let them know they were ready to head out. Kodi walked toward the Tahoe first, leaving Eli and Sammi to walk together. Eli smiled warmly at Sammi as he opened the back door of the Tahoe for her. Kodi had already claimed the front passenger seat so Eli climbed in next to Sammi in the back.

"Are we ready for this?" Howard asked from the driver seat as he started the car.

"I live for this," Sammi replied confidently, buzzing with excitement for the first time in years and wearing a huge smile on her face.

As the four friends made their way out of New York, Sammi was quiet. She felt guilty about how happy she was to be a thief again and about walking out on Mack the way she had. But she was surrounded by three people who she loved and who loved her back, and who felt more like a family to Sammi than anyone else ever had.

Chapter Twenty-Five
Light On

Sammi jerked awake in a complete panic, gasping for air, her ears ringing violently. She coughed several times out of desperation to clear the pressure in her chest, but her lungs remained heavy and she quickly realized she had oxygen tubes going into her nose. It was hard to turn her head because she was wearing a neck brace and when she tried reaching for it, she discovered that her right arm was in a sling.

As her panic grew from her inability to move freely, the spike in her heartrate alerted a nurse who came running into the room. The nurse tried to get Sammi to calm down and explained that she had smoke in her lungs from the explosion and needed to relax in order to breathe properly. But Sammi was way past the possibility of relaxing and the nurse had no choice but to increase her morphine and get her to go back to sleep.

*

When Sammi woke up again, she had no idea how much time had passed. But the morphine was doing its job this time around and Sammi remained calm as she stared at the ceiling, feeling as if she were under a heavy cloud. She couldn't stop the tears from falling as she thought about her friends still being in the car when it exploded.

"Samantha?" someone asked as they stood over Sammi's hospital bed and looked down at her.

Sammi used her left hand to wipe the tears from her eyes as she looked into the face of the lovely brown-haired doctor beside her bed. She was scared to try to talk so she just nodded to let the doctor know that they had indeed identified her correctly.

"My name is Doctor Gloria. I'm really sorry about your friends," the doctor said calmly, resting her hand on Sammi's injured shoulder.

"Are they...?" Sammi choked out, already knowing the answer. The doctor sadly nodded and Sammi completely broke down, thrashing her head back and forth with tears pouring down her cheeks and onto her pillow. She was inconsolable so Dr. Gloria had no choice but to help her sleep with more medication.

*

The next time Sammi woke up, her neck brace had been removed and she tried to keep her mind blank with her head turned to the side to watch out the window. There was nothing she could do trapped in that hospital, but she was glad she was alone because she deserved to be alone. She knew her friends were dead because of her and she found peace in daydreaming about joining them. Nothing, not a single thing about her, made her deserve to live any longer than they had, and she couldn't help but feel somewhat angry at Eli for pushing her out of death's grasp.

Some time passed before a police detective showed up to speak with Sammi and collect her statement about the car bomb. Wanting to be held accountable, Sammi kind of brushed over the car explosion and focused more on telling him that she was a thief and had millions in stolen cash in her hotel room. The detective wore skepticism on his face the entire time she told her story but assured her that he'd look into her confession. But he was too kind about it and Sammi knew he only pitied her.

The pretty doctor had been standing in wait by the door for the detective to leave and immediately replaced him by Sammi's bedside. Dr. Gloria was quiet and her actions were careful and cautious as she looked down upon Sammi. Sammi avoided meeting her eyes, not wanting to see more pity in them.

"Samantha," Dr. Gloria spoke softly, "is there anyone I can call for you?"

Sammi shook her head, forcing herself to hold back tears as her thoughts turned to Mack. She couldn't stand the idea of Mack seeing her like this or knowing that she got everyone killed and looking at her with pity like everyone else was. That was even assuming Mack would want to see her. But as she thought about her husband, her mind finally allowed her to remember the fifth person in the exploding SUV and her left hand flew to her stomach.

The blanket covering Sammi was thick and didn't help her find her baby bump. Sammi looked pleadingly at the doctor for answers and the woman hung her head as she shook it slowly. Every muscle in Sammi's body fell weak as a dark cloud engulfed her. The heavy fog inside her head blurred her vision and she didn't even see Dr. Gloria reach over to administer another dose of morphine.

*

When Sammi woke up the next time, she called for a nurse and asked them to send Dr. Gloria in. Heavy grief continued to weigh down on her, but her thoughts were finally clear, and she needed to get out of that hospital. But she needed the doctor to stop babying her to make that happen.

"Please, no more morphine," Sammi begged when the doctor arrived.

"Are you sure?" Dr. Gloria asked. "I just want you to be comfortable."

"I don't deserve to be comfortable," Sammi mumbled, unintentionally loud enough for the doctor to hear.

"Alright, don't start talking like that," Dr. Gloria told her. "Don't make me keep you here longer on suicide watch."

"If I'm good, when do I get to leave?"

"Honestly, I'd feel a lot better if I knew you had somebody to help you when you leave here."

Sammi suddenly sat up in the bed, using her left arm as leverage to prop herself up. She began tugging at the tube going into her nose until the doctor jumped in to help her remove it. Getting serious, Sammi straightened her back and looked Dr. Gloria directly in the eyes.

"I don't need anybody," Sammi said sternly.

Before the doctor could argue with Sammi, there was a soft knock on the open hospital room door and the detective from before let himself into the room. He was carrying a folder and Sammi's eyes lit up at the prospect of being busted. Dr. Gloria excused herself so Sammi and the detective could have some privacy.

"Do you know this man?" the Hobbs-aged detective asked, opening the folder, and showing Sammi a mugshot of a very familiar face.

"That's Christopher," Sammi told him nonchalantly. "He was staying in the same hotel."

"His name is actually Logan Paulson and we believe he is responsible for planting that bomb in your vehicle," the detective explained.

"That wannabe thug? But why?" Sammi questioned,

finding that highly implausible. Christopher had hardly seemed intelligent enough to pull off something as big as killing three skilled thieves.

"Your two hotel rooms were completely cleaned out. I'm guessing you had something that he wanted."

"The duffel bags, there was millions in them."

"Yeah, I looked into your story and I could only find Eliot Krik in the system. Nothing else checked out."

"I'm not in the system because my husband's a New York detective! I promise you that I am a thief! Arrest me, dammit!" Sammi nearly threw herself out of the hospital bed as she yelled at the detective.

"As appealing as it sounds to arrest a fellow officer's wife with absolutely no proof of any crime committed, I'm going to have to pass. Go home, Miss."

"Call Captain Hobbs in the New York Police Department," Sammi growled through gritted teeth. "He will verify everything."

"You don't mean Tyler Hobbs of the Homicide unit, do you?"

"Yes! He has an entire file on me! Call him!"

Exclaiming that he went through the Academy with Hobbs, the detective finally took his cellphone out. He dialed a number and asked for Captain Tyler Hobbs.

*

Captain Hobbs had Mack Johnson in his office when his phone rang. Mack had just told him about calling Sammi and never hearing back from her and asking his boss for advice. When the phone rang, Hobbs put a finger up to ask Mack to wait a minute while he answered the call.

"This is Hobbs... Randy! How's Cali?... You what–oh, yes, I know Sammi... A thief? Ha ha, no, she was actually an incredible detective in my unit just a few months ago... I'm sorry, I don't know why she would say something like that... Oh, wow, is she okay?... Wow, yeah, I'll tell him. Thank you, Randy. I'll talk to you soon."

Mack watched and listened to the one side of the conversation with a look of concern on his face. His boss was obviously talking to someone about his wife and he had a bad feeling in his gut that something had happened. The longer Hobbs was on the phone, the sicker Mack's stomach felt.

"She's all right," Hobbs said as soon as he hung up the phone, seeing the look on Mack's face.

"What happened?" Mack asked seriously, wanting the most direct answer.

"There was a bomb in their car, and she was the only survivor," Hobbs told him bluntly.

"Oh...no," Mack felt dizzy with panic. "She must feel totally alone. I...I gotta go."

Mack stood up, but it was clear that he couldn't focus as he couldn't remember where the door was. He stumbled to his left then stumbled to his right before swaying where he stood. Hobbs hopped up and hurried around his desk, putting his hands on Mack's shoulders to steady him.

"You have to breathe, Mack," Hobbs told him. "It's going to be okay."

"Wait, you lied for her," Mack replied, furrowing his brow inquisitively as he suddenly remembered that part of his boss' conversation.

"I was always going to protect her, Mack. Go get your wife; bring Sammi home."

Mack walked out of his Captain's office in a haze, still needing a minute to catch his breath. He sat at his desk with his head in his hands and tried to clear his mind so he could calm down. But all he had to do was picture Sammi all alone in the hospital and he rushed out of the precinct building. This couldn't wait.

*

When the detective got off the phone, he looked at Sammi with even more pity as he shook his head in disappointment. Sammi had been able to decipher that Hobbs had lied and she was furious. After everything he had put her through, and he couldn't even take the perfect opportunity to out her to another detective.

"Hobbs says you're a good detective," the officer told her with a raised eyebrow. "You looking for a job out here?"

"Bite me," Sammi snapped at him and sunk down in the bed to signal that she was done talking to him.

The detective saw himself out of the room and Sammi returned to feeling sorry for herself. She knew she wanted to get out of the hospital, but she had no idea what she was going to do when she finally did. Trying to pass the time, she daydreamed about seeking revenge on Christopher for taking her loved ones away from her.

Sammi spent another twenty-four hours in the hospital before the doctor was ready to release her. Her right arm was still in the sling from being broken under the pressure of the explosion and all of her bodyweight landing on top of it, but she was healthy otherwise. Dr. Gloria went over aftercare for her arm as Sammi finished her paperwork then handed her a list of therapists for her to talk to back in New York.

"Like I said, I don't need help," Sammi scolded the doctor. "And I'm not going back to New York."

"Please?" came a voice from the doorway. Sammi looked up and saw her husband leaning against the doorframe with his arms crossed in front of his chest.

Sammi froze in shock. She could see the pain and torture in Mack's eyes, but she wasn't prepared for this and she didn't know how she wanted to react. She looked to Dr. Gloria for help with desperation in her eyes, but the doctor just signed off on her paperwork, rubbed Sammi's shoulder, and smiled kindly at Mack on her way out of the room. Feeling cornered, Sammi sat on the edge of the hospital bed, hoping she could wait out Mack and he would just leave. She hadn't seen him in four months, and it killed her to see him now, so she just stared at the floor in silence.

It took a little while, but Mack eventually worked his way into the room and took a seat next to Sammi on the bed. He left a good distance between them and Sammi could sense how uncomfortable he was. But she was just as uncomfortable, and he was the intruder in this situation. She hadn't asked him to come and she didn't want him there.

"Sammi," Mack said quietly, stealing a glance in his wife's direction.

"Just go home, Mack," Sammi replied with a sigh as she hopped down off the bed.

With Mack out of the doorway, Sammi had an opening to leave and she intended to take it. Before she was even within five feet of the open entryway, Mack leapt up and grabbed her left hand to stop her. That was Sammi's only good arm so she couldn't exactly fight him off; she turned to face him with fury in her ice-cold eyes.

"Sammi, I'm sorry," Mack whispered, keeping ahold of his wife's hand so she couldn't run away. He could feel that her ring finger was void of any jewelry and tried to convince himself that the hospital had removed her wedding rings for safety reasons.

Fighting back tears, Sammi just shook her head at Mack, wanting him to just stop talking and go away. She couldn't handle these emotions after everything that had just happened, and she didn't believe she owed Mack that explanation. With a desperate plea in her eyes, she made an attempt to tug her hand free from Mack's, but he held on and pulled her closer.

"Please, just talk to me," Mack begged.

"I tried talking to you for months!" Sammi yelled at him,

unable to hold it in any longer. "You cut me out, not the other way around!"

"I was wrong and I'm sorry," Mack told her calmly. "Not getting that promotion destroyed me because I thought that my job was all that I am. But you make me who I am, Sammi. You brought me to life four years ago and I'm nothing but an empty shell without you."

"You told me I took your life from you," Sammi replied quietly with hurt in her voice.

Remembering that fight, Sammi couldn't hold back her tears any longer and the harder she cried, the less she could see in front of her. Her muscles felt tingly as her crying and sobbing drained her energy and her head spun with dizziness. She swayed once where she stood, and Mack immediately scooped her up and placed her back on the edge of the hospital bed.

"I am so sorry that I hurt you, Sammi," Mack said, kneeling in front of her with his hands on her knees. "My world had just crumbled around me and because you're my world, you were the easy choice to blame. But I never should have said the things I said to you. My words came from a place of anger and you didn't deserve that. You deserve so much better."

"What do you want me to say to that?" Sammi asked through heavy sobs.

"Say you don't hate me. Say you'll come home with me," Mack pleaded.

Sammi shook her head as she continued to cry. She wanted to forgive Mack, but she knew things could never go back to the way they were before. Mack had allowed her to suffer for far too long without a word and now she didn't have anyone to lean on. As far as she was concerned, her life was over.

Mack's face twisted in torture as he watched Sammi grow more upset by the second. He finally got up and sat on the bed so he could pull his distraught wife into his lap and held her while she cried. She didn't fight him and turned her head to cry into his white t-shirt. They remained like that for nearly ten minutes until Sammi was able to pull herself together and dried her tears.

"Come on," Mack said once he could feel Sammi's body relax in his arms, "let me take my wife home so I can start making up the worst four months of my life to her."

Sammi nodded her head against Mack's chest and allowed him to help her stand. She was still wobbly on her feet after crying so hard and Mack kept an arm around her to steady her. He didn't say anything, but it showed on his face that Mack was unreasonably content over this small victory.

Chapter Twenty-Six
Wait for Me

Sammi was quiet during the entire trip back home to New York so Mack let her be, hoping she would talk when she was ready. He had a lot of questions about her four months away from him and it was difficult for him to be patient. But he knew pushing her was not the way to go and would only make things worse.

Having already taken time off to go to California and retrieve his wife, Mack wasn't expected back at the precinct right away. He and Sammi got home in the middle of the day on a Friday and Sammi vocalized wanting to go right to bed, but as soon as she walked into the house, she became spooked and ran back outside. Not realizing right away that she was gone, it took Mack a second before chasing after her and finding her at the end of the driveway crying by the mailbox.

"Hey, are you okay?" Mack asked, putting his hand on Sammi's back to try and comfort her. Sammi pulled away from him.

"I'm sorry, but this is happening too fast," Sammi told him, her voice shaking. "I can't just go back to being your wife, in our home, as if nothing happened."

Mack's face looked like Sammi had just slapped him. He had known things wouldn't be perfect right away, but he hadn't expected Sammi to be so resistant. It was starting to feel like she didn't want to be married anymore and that terrified him.

"What can I do to help you feel safe in the house?" Mack asked quietly, struggling to find what to say.

"Let me work up to it at my own pace," Sammi told him.

Another emotional slap to the face and Mack took a step backwards. He watched Sammi for a minute or two, trying to catch her eye so he could read her face. But she wouldn't even glance in his direction and he felt stupid just standing there, openly unwanted, so he went back into the house without his wife.

Looking out the windows every couple of minutes to check on her, Mack watched as realization crossed Sammi's face that she couldn't stand down by the road for no apparent reason all day, no matter how badly she wanted to stand her ground. Sammi finally looked up at the house, causing Mack to duck, and frowned at the adorable little home that she and Mack had made together. It suddenly dawned on Mack that it wasn't just him keeping her from entering the house. Kodi and Eli had also made their own marks on the home and now they were gone forever.

As Mack reached the front door with the intention of trying to talk to Sammi once more and acknowledge her grief, Sammi entered the house. She was moving cautiously and looking in every direction around her as if the ghosts of her friends could jump out at any second. There was fear in her eyes and that upset Mack more than anything because he had once made a promise to protect her from anything like this.

Respecting Sammi's wishes to go at her own pace, Mack took a step back to leave her be. He chose to sit in the kitchen, which was sort of like the center of the house, so he could be out of the way but still in Sammi's sight in case she decided she needed him. Keeping his head down and pretending to look at something on his cellphone, he watched as Sammi made her way through the house and into the master bedroom.

Since Sammi was silent, Mack gave her a little while to settle by herself. After a bit, he got up and walked to the bedroom door to listen for any noise his wife might be making to give him an idea of what was going on. He could hear her crying and, figuring he had a duty to check on her, he let himself into the room.

Curled into a ball under the blankets in the center of the huge bed, Sammi was sobbing lightly and staring at the wall. She didn't even blink as Mack entered the room, but Mack still tried to be as quiet as possible. He stayed against the wall and sat on the floor in Sammi's line of sight.

"I'm just checking in on you," Mack spoke quietly but directly to his wife. "Is there anything I can get for you?"

"No. Thank you," Sammi said coldly, looking at Mack but not really seeing him. "I just need to rest."

"I understand. I'm going to sleep in the other room tonight to give you some space. But please don't hesitate to come get me if you need anything," Mack told her.

"Thank you," Sammi sputtered out, emotionless again.

"I love you, Sammi," Mack whispered as he stood up and brushed her hair behind her ear before leaving the room. She still didn't budge.

Mack was exhausted but he lay awake in the guest bed all night, worrying about Sammi. It was taking all of his strength to give her space when all he wanted was to be in their bed holding her tight. He wanted to cry with her about the loss of their child, but that wasn't his job right now. His job was to get Sammi through this grieving process in one piece.

When Sammi didn't get out of bed the next day, Mack tried not to worry too much but it was hard. He checked in on her a handful of times, struggling to not be overbearing. The only relief he had was that Sammi seemed more present than she had been the night before, changing positions in the bed and not just staring at the wall. But she wasn't eating and by seven o'clock that night, Mack had made the decision that he couldn't go to work the next day and went out on the back porch to call his boss.

"How's she doing?" Hobbs asked when he answered Mack's call.

"Not great," Mack told him with sadness in his voice. "I'm worried about her, Cap."

"I'm not a psychologist or anything, but I think she just needs time. She needs to come to terms with everything that happened," Hobbs replied, trying to sound reassuring.

"I understand that she needs space, but I can't leave her alone all day. Not yet," Mack explained.

"It's okay, Mack, take care of your wife. We'll see you when you're ready to come back."

"Thanks, Captain."

As Mack got off the phone, it suddenly crossed his mind that if he had actually gotten the Captain's promotion, he wouldn't be able to take time off like this. He wouldn't be able to take care of his wife the way she needed, and he was suddenly grateful that he wasn't the Captain. And that thought made him feel terrible because he had chased Sammi away over a position that he didn't even want anymore. Sitting on the back-porch step, Mack rubbed his head and allowed himself to feel as awful as he felt he deserved.

When Mack checked on Sammi one more time before retiring to the guestroom again for the night, she was fast asleep and snoring ever so slightly, which had probably been brought on by hours of crying. It was the most peaceful she had looked in days and Mack's heart beat a little faster in his chest, reminding him that there wasn't anything he wouldn't do for that girl. He took a risk and leaned over her to kiss her soft hair before leaving her alone in the dark, quiet room.

Still unable to sleep, Mack lay awake in the guest bed wondering how different things could be if he had been able to keep his head right about the Captain situation. His imagination only hurt him, laying the guilt on thick, and he considered going out to the kitchen to grab a few beers to help him sleep. Before he could act on that thought, he heard a lot of movement in the other bedroom and he jumped out of bed.

Mack walked quietly into the master bedroom and found the lights on with Sammi throwing every last article of her clothing into open luggage carriers on the floor. His heart dropped into his stomach and he stopped breathing for a moment at the fear of Sammi leaving again.

"What...what is going on?" Mack asked, struggling to catch his breath. The room was spinning around him.

"I can't heal with you hovering," Sammi told him in a huff, not even turning to look at him. "I'll be at my old apartment in the city."

Mack was confused. He had intentionally kept his distance all day to avoid exactly what Sammi was accusing him of. He was doing everything right.

"Sammi, please don't do this," Mack pleaded as he approached his wife and tried to take her hand in his, but she pulled away. "I know I didn't stop you last time, but I'm asking you this time. Please don't leave me."

"I need to do this on my own if I'm going to have any chance of ever being okay again," Sammi replied, finally turning towards him but keeping her eyes down to avoid his gaze.

"We can do this together, Sammi. I lost a child too."

And Mack immediately knew that had been the wrong thing to say. Sammi finally made eye contact, glaring at him with fire burning in her sharp eyes. Her breathing got heavy with anger and she was either going to scream or cry. It was the first time Mack acknowledged that he knew about their baby and she clearly hadn't been prepared for that.

Zipping up her luggage, Sammi turned her back on Mack again to hide her tears. She struggled with the zipper on the second bag, fighting against it with only one usable hand and she broke down crying on top of it. Mack picked her up and placed her on the bed so he could close the zipper for her then he picked up both bags and carried them out to her car while Sammi continued sobbing on the bed.

"You're all set," Mack whispered, sitting next to her on the bed and dangling her car key from his finger in front of her face.

Sammi wiped the tears from her face before taking the key. She and Mack stood up at the same time and Mack followed her out to the garage to see her off. He was the furthest thing from okay with this, but he couldn't force her to stay. He didn't have any other choice than to be strong for her.

"Please drive safe and promise you'll pull over if you're crying," Mack said from the doorway as Sammi opened the driver side door of her Nissan that she hadn't even seen in four months.

Sammi nodded, looking Mack in the eye to let him know he could trust her. They gazed at each other across the garage with goodbye in their eyes and uncertainty on their faces. As he watched Sammi get behind the wheel of her car, he hated himself for not forbidding her to go, knowing there was no guarantee he'd ever see her again.

"I love you," Mack said, even though Sammi couldn't hear him as she backed out of the garage, onto the street, and out of his life.

*

Sammi grew more and more upset as she drove into the city, but not enough to make her feel like she couldn't drive safely. She knew seeing the apartment was going to be worse than anything else she'd endured over the past few days, so she was harboring her emotions until that traumatic punch to the gut. Her friends had been taken from her so suddenly that she hadn't had the opportunity to really say goodbye to them and surrounding herself with their memories seemed to be the only way she could think of to force herself to face this loss.

The old apartment was just how she and Eli left it: disgusting. Sammi smiled at the thought of the day she found out that Eli still rented this place and ran into him all in the same day. Maybe there had been more fate to their relationship than she had been willing to admit. But thinking about that day reminded her of Shay and how relieved she had been that she didn't end up shooting Eli's sister in front of him. She wondered if Shay had received the news in prison of Eli's passing and realized that Shay would have a whole new reason to want her dead.

Reliving these memories made Sammi feel good about her decision to stay in the apartment and she spent the rest of that night and all of the next day cleaning the forsaken place. She went out and bought a new bed set, but she washed Eli's Giants blanket and put it right back on the couch where it belonged. The fridge was gross beyond rescue and had to be replaced, but everything else stayed.

It wasn't until the distraction of cleaning went away that the gravity of the situation sank in for Sammi. What had felt like cleaning the apartment for her friends to come home to suddenly turned into a spotless but lonely home for one. Now that everything was done for the apartment, she didn't know what she was supposed to do about her grief, a job, or even about her marriage.

Cleaning had at least earned her some time to rest, so Sammi curled up on the couch and pulled the Giants blanket down over top of her. She found episodes of her team's old favorite show saved on the television, wondering why Eli had also continued to pay for cable if he didn't live there, and allowed herself to enjoy something that had once brought her and her friends joy and laughter. Halfway into the first episode, Sammi was already yawning and she drifted slowly off to sleep while telling herself that this was exactly what she had needed.

But the memories couldn't do good forever and Sammi quickly learned that over the next few days as every corner of every room was haunted by invisible images of her friends. It had been soothing at first, having their memories keep her company. But days later, they were weighing heavy and all but consuming her as she never left the apartment. And her not talking to anybody, anybody at all, was not helping.

*

When Mack showed up for work on Monday after Hobbs had given him time off, everyone was surprised and confused to see him since his name had been taken off the case board for the week. Hobbs immediately called him into his office and Mack knew that he wasn't going to trust him to be level-headed out on the streets. But Mack hadn't known what else to do when he woke up in the morning.

"What happened?" Hobbs asked out of true concern as Mack sat across from him at his desk.

"She's gone," Mack told him with a shrug. "She told me she has to figure this out for herself and she left me."

"Do you at least know where she is?" Hobbs questioned him.

"She said she'd be staying in the old apartment she had shared with Eli. But I really wouldn't be surprised if she lied." Mack shrugged again. There was no hope anywhere in his voice.

"I think I have that address in a case file somewhere, and I'm pretty sure Mazzeline is home from the hospital. Would you mind if I sent him over there?" Hobbs offered.

"If you want to risk his life like that," Mack said, finally cracking a smile.

"I'll tell him to go armed," Hobbs added with a chuckle.

Hobbs told Mack that he could work with Palma for the week, but Palma was to take the lead on any of their cases. Mack didn't argue because he knew he wouldn't be at the top of his game. And he knew he was lucky that Hobbs was even letting him on a case.

Mack was very docile working with Palma that day, and Palma was alarmed by the out-of-character behavior. Mack was obviously distracted, and he wasn't exactly helpful while talking to any witnesses or suspects, so Palma ended up doing most of the work. But Palma didn't mind covering for Mack because he felt for the guy and what he was going through. He also felt like he owed him for everything Mack had done for him when he first got his shield, and now he finally got the chance to pay him back for it all.

*

Sammi was half asleep on the couch in the apartment when there was a knock on the door. Assuming it was Mack, which annoyed her because he wasn't respecting her need for space, she ignored it. She hadn't talked to anybody else since being back in New York so nobody else should know that she was even there.

"You in there, Sammi?" the visitor called through the door after knocking again. "It's Mazzeline!"

Surprised, Sammi rolled off the couch and hurried over to the door to let her former job partner into the apartment. Mazzeline was dressed in black jogging pants and a white t-shirt with his right arm in a sling, matching Sammi's own. He handed her a chocolate milkshake as she let him inside and led him over to the couch.

"What happened to your arm?" Sammi asked as she and Mazzeline sat next to each other on the sofa.

"Shot in the shoulder," Mazzeline told her nonchalantly. "Hobbs told me about your friends...and, you know..."

"Hobbs needs to stay out of my life," Sammi grumbled, more to herself than to Mazzeline.

"You do know that we all care about you, right?" Mazzeline asked sternly to get his point across, his eyebrows narrowing.

"And you get that I don't want anyone to worry about me, right?" Sammi responded, making herself sound just a little bit more serious than he had.

"Sammi, I have always admired how tough you are. But you can be strong without pushing everyone out of your life. It's often harder to let others help you than to cut them out completely."

"I don't want help. I don't want Hobbs sending his little pets to lecture me. And I don't want Mack to wait for me to feel better."

As soon as the words left her mouth, it felt like a large rock crash-landed on her chest and rolled down into her stomach. She regretted even thinking that way about Mack and she felt sick about it.

"I didn't mean that," Sammi whispered, guilt written all over her face.

"I know you didn't," Mazzeline told her. "I know you don't believe me, but Mack has been a mess without you. The two of you have something special and I'd hate for you to throw that away."

"I'm not trying to hurt him," Sammi replied quietly, hanging her head.

"He probably knows that. Just try to take it easy on him."

Sammi nodded and Mazzeline tried changing the subject by offering to take her out for lunch. But she hadn't even taken a sip of the milkshake and it was no surprise that she had nothing even resembling an appetite. So, he forced another few minutes of conversation before hugging her goodbye and letting her be alone again.

Mazzeline's visit actually helped Sammi feel a little bit better. She was grateful to have him in her life and for helping her realize she didn't want to lose Mack. She wasn't ready to go after her husband just yet, but she vowed to never treat him as coldly again as she had that weekend.

Chapter Twenty-Seven
Fade into Me

A week passed with Sammi not leaving the apartment and not speaking to anyone else since Mazzeline's visit. She slept most of the time, always on the couch and never in the bedroom. The bedroom had the hardest memories to face and Sammi didn't like the way they hovered over her like a heavy cloud when she was just passing through to the bathroom or the closet.

By the end of that week, though, Sammi had no choice but to finally leave her hiding place and go grocery shopping. It was late in the afternoon when she left the apartment and chose to walk the six blocks to the store that she and Eli had always gone to for their groceries. Much to her surprise, the ghost of Eli's memory seemed to tag along to remind her of how obnoxious but adorable they had been as a couple. They had always made out on street corners and chased each other down grocery aisles. People always stared, but they had always liked to think it was out of jealousy.

Of course, Sammi hadn't been prepared for these thoughts and they were more than she had bargained for. Not only did they remind her that Eli was never coming back, but they also made her miss Mack more than ever. As she entered the supermarket, she completely forgot why she was there and ended up aimlessly wandering the aisles.

Forty-five minutes later, Sammi left the store empty-handed. Clouds had moved in to hide the sun as it had begun raining, but Sammi didn't mind or even seem to notice. She took her time walking back to her apartment building and didn't do anything to shield herself from the cold raindrops falling on her exposed, vulnerable skin. Cars honked as they splashed through puddles beside her, trying to give her a fair warning, but she never once looked up.

Approaching her building, Sammi noticed someone standing just outside with an umbrella. The way the man held himself and the shape of his body was very familiar to Sammi but the rain pelting her face made it difficult to see. It wasn't until she was within a few feet of him that she realized it was Anthony, and her heart hit the wet ground. As badly as she didn't want to face him, she knew he was there to see her, and it was too late to avoid being spotted. So, she stood in front of him, soaking wet, and looked up into his face, wearing nothing but self-pity on her own.

Anthony looked at Sammi with coldness in his eyes. It was such a change from the usual fondness he'd always shown her, and it frightened her. She waited for him to speak first, unsure of the purpose for this visit.

"You just couldn't stop until you drained every last bit of Kodi's soul from her, could you?" Anthony snapped at Sammi, rage flashing across his face.

"What—what are you talking about?" Sammi asked, her voice shaking with fear as she took a step back from him.

"She wanted to come home and you wouldn't let her," Anthony explained, drawing a handful of loose papers from inside his long black coat. "She wanted to come home and start a life with me but now she's dead because she had to put YOU first!"

"I told her to come home to you!" Sammi cried out as tears came to her eyes. "Nobody could ever tell her what to do! You should know that!"

"And you shouldn't have taken her from me!"

"I didn't!"

"YOU killed her!"

Anthony raised his arm as if to swing at Sammi's face, but Sammi ducked, closing her eyes and squeezing out more tears.

"Hey!" someone yelled, coming up the sidewalk. "Leave her alone!"

Anthony tossed the letters from Kodi at Sammi, who was still squatting in the rain. They landed in puddles on the sidewalk around her and the rain washed away Kodi's words. Then Anthony turned and walked away, still as dry as could be under the protection of his umbrella.

Sammi finally dropped all the way down to her knees and held her head while she let go entirely, crying and sobbing louder than ever before. The rain fell harder, masking the sounds of her breakdown but soaking her through to the bone. Suddenly, a strong arm hooked around her back and pulled her to her feet.

"Give me your key," Mack told her, steering her toward the entrance to her apartment building.

Sammi just turned her eyes on him, blankly staring at his face while her sobbing quieted and her tears slowed. Mack had also been prepared with his own umbrella and he shifted it into his other hand so he could cover Sammi with it, not that it made any difference by that point. He was gentle as he guided Sammi and patient with her as he waited for her to register his request to hand over her key to the apartment.

Once inside the decently warm apartment, Mack helped Sammi sit down at the tiny kitchen table before trying to find something to warm her up. He quickly discovered that her cupboards and the fridge were all bare. Shaking his head, he made his way into the bathroom to retrieve some towels.

Sammi seemed to have calmed down for the most part by the time Mack returned and handed her a towel. Her crying had ceased and there was life present in her dancing blue eyes again. She was watching Mack with curiosity and hope, opening her mouth to speak but stopping herself each time.

"Are you okay?" Mack asked with genuine concern, kneeling before her with his left arm resting across her knees.

"It is my fault," Sammi said flatly as she looked down into Mack's eyes.

"Samantha, listen to me," Mack replied, suddenly more serious than he had ever been with her before. "Nobody, and I mean nobody, blames you for what happened. Anthony is grieving just like you, and I promise you that he didn't mean what he said."

"Why are you being nice to me?" Sammi asked, leaning slightly forward toward him.

"Because I love you, Sammi. I know you're in a lot of pain right now and I know this isn't really you. But I believe you'll come back to me. I believe the obnoxiously confident, no fear, love of my life is still in there fighting to get back to me."

Sammi threw her arms around Mack's neck and slid off the chair to kneel in front of him. Mack sat back on his heels and pulled Sammi into his lap as she clung tighter to his neck and buried her face into the grey t-shirt covering his chest. He was warm and brought comfort to Sammi's chilled, rain-drenched body.

Mack could feel Sammi shivering from the cold of her damp clothes as he held her. He hugged her tighter to his body, trying to warm her up as Sammi melted into him and he kissed her wet hair.

"You should go take a hot shower," Mack said softly, kissing Sammi's hair again, so relieved to have his sweet wife back in his arms.

"Will you be here when I get out?" Sammi asked quietly, hugging his neck tighter as if she was afraid to let go.

"Of course, I will," Mack told her. "You don't have any food so I'm gonna order us something. Any requests?"

"Get whatever you want. Just don't leave."

Mack kissed Sammi once more, on the cheek this time, before releasing her. Sammi hurried into the bathroom while Mack picked himself up off the kitchen floor to look at the takeout menus on Sammi's fridge.

*

Alone in the bathroom, Sammi was joined by Eli's memory once again. Instead of the good Eli from the sidewalks and the supermarket, this was the bad Eli that had scared her out of sleeping in their bed during the past week. Sammi knew it was all in her head, feeling guilty about falling for Mack all over again, but the guilt was winning. All she could think about, the only images in her head, were from the day Eli found out about Mack and knew that Sammi was going to abandon him for Mack before she had even known it herself.

"I'm sorry, Eli, I never meant to hurt you," Sammi spoke to her reflection in the mirror after undressing.

Sammi stepped into the steaming hot shower and the near-boiling water embraced her trembling body. She enjoyed the warmth and let it wash over her, trying to clear her thoughts. But she was at her weakest when she was alone with these thoughts and Eli's memory wasn't letting her forget what she had done to him and how he'd died for her anyway.

Consumed by guilt and grief, Sammi sat on the shower floor and pulled her knees to her chest, letting the water continue to rain down over her. She remembered how she felt in the hospital in California and how all she wanted was to join her friends. That hadn't changed and tears came to her eyes as she actually considered asking her husband to do her one last favor and selflessly take her life. If anyone could get away with it, it would be him, especially since Hobbs would understand and probably support the idea so Mack would finally be free of her and her harmful influence on his life.

But Sammi realized she didn't need Mack's help as she noticed Eli's rusty old razor resting on the soap rack in the shower. As she reached for the forgotten friend, she saw Eli's disapproving face next to where it lay. She startled only slightly, knowing it was her imagination, but pulled her hand back anyway.

"Don't," Eli's voice spoke inside Sammi's head.

"Why not?" Sammi grumbled aloud to herself.

"Because cop boy needs you," Eli replied without resentment.

"He would be better off without me, just like you, Kodi, and Howard would have been," Sammi said bluntly.

"Don't be silly, Sammi."

"I want you back, Eli."

"You'll see me again one day, I promise. Just don't forget me."

With those final words, Sammi let go of Eli's image and cried into her hands. She had run the hot water cold but didn't seem to notice.

*

When the food was delivered, Mack realized that Sammi had been in the shower for quite some time. He dropped the food on the kitchen counter, walked through the bedroom and knocked on the closed wooden bathroom door. He could hear that the shower was still running but there was no response to his knocking, so he let himself into the bathroom and drew back the shower curtain.

Sammi was curled into a ball on the shower floor, sobbing under less-than-warm water. Mack hurried to turn the water off before lifting his wife out of the shower and wrapping her in the last dry towel in the apartment.

"Dammit, Sam," Mack whispered, realizing she was shivering all over again.

With Sammi wrapped in the towel, Mack picked her up and carried her out to the bedroom where he placed her on the undisturbed bed. Then he went in the closet to find her some sweatpants and a big sweatshirt to put on so she would be warm and comfortable. After laying the clothes in front of her, Mack walked a few steps back toward the closet to a spot he had noticed on the carpet. It was faint but it was definitely a bloodstain: his blood from Eli shooting him in the knee. He hadn't thought about that day in a very long while and he suddenly realized where the strange clicking in his left leg had come from. As he rubbed his sock-clad foot over the rounded square stain, he smiled.

"What are you looking at?" Sammi asked, wiping the tears from her face with the towel before standing up to get dressed.

"Come here," Mack said, reaching an open hand out toward her.

Sammi finished dressing and dashed over to her husband, taking his outstretched hand. She stood beside him and looked down at the floor to see what he saw. Thinking she had entirely missed a spot cleaning, her face burned from embarrassment.

"Do you know what that is?" Mack asked, squeezing Sammi's hand.

"No, I didn't even see that," Sammi admitted, her face still red.

"I took a bullet for you right here," Mack told her, turning her toward him and pulling her to his chest. "And I'd take a million more."

"I don't deserve you, Mack Johnson," Sammi mumbled into his chest, hugging his waist.

"You're right, you deserve way better," Mack replied with a nervous chuckle and kissed the top of Sammi's head.

Sammi wanted to kiss her husband, but she wasn't ready.

Her trauma was keeping her emotionally blocked off from him, so she just squeezed his waist tightly before leading him out to the kitchen and getting plates out for their dinner. Mack had ordered pizza from the Italian place he had ordered from the first night Sammi slept in his apartment, even though Mack never knew that she had snuck out in the middle of the night to return to Eli.

After they finished eating, Mack wanted to ask Sammi to come home with him, but he was scared. He was scared to push her and scared of the inevitable rejection. So instead, he asked if he could stay to watch a movie and Sammi gave him a strange look with no explanation before walking into the living room and plopping down onto the couch. Following his wife, Mack sat down beside her and told her to choose what she wanted to watch since he got to choose their dinner.

Once Sammi started her movie of choice, she sat back on the couch and Mack immediately pulled her closer to him. Sammi nestled into him and knew she was going to be too comfortable to stay awake and she was okay with that. She was emotionally drained and looking forward to the peace that sleep would bring her, even if just for a little while. As Sammi's head dropped onto Mack's chest, Mack massaged the area on her hip where his hand was resting, encouraging her to give in to slumber, while he reached back and grabbed the blanket off the back of the couch.

"Do you want to go to bed, hon?" Mack asked quietly when Sammi stirred as he placed the blanket over her.

"No," Sammi said abruptly. "I don't sleep in there."

Mack didn't understand what she meant by that, but he felt sad for her, nonetheless. He lifted Sammi onto his body so he could reposition himself into a laying position on the couch and made sure Sammi was comfortable on top of him. Then he moved the blanket to cover Sammi better and pressed his lips to her forehead.

"Sleep tight, wifey," Mack whispered.

*

Sammi was awake before Mack the next morning and couldn't move from how tightly he was holding her. His head was back and his mouth agape, causing him to snore and drool. Giggling, Sammi tried to wiggle his arms loose, desperate to get free from the saliva splatter zone. He finally awoke with a start, accidentally knocking Sammi to the floor on her bad arm.

"Ow," Sammi said, laughing as she sat up.

"That's it, we're sleeping in our bed tonight," Mack grumbled as he was still waking up and not thinking about what he was saying. Sammi looked at him, taken aback and speechless.

Mack was still out of it as he sat up, kissed Sammi on the lips, and got up to go the bathroom. Sammi rolled her eyes as she watched him walk out of the room, not feeling comfortable with this carefree morning version of Mack quite yet. Suddenly remembering that she hadn't bought any groceries at the grocery store the day before, she realized Mack was going to insist they go out to breakfast and then he was going to hijack the entire day and she was running out of time to decide whether she wanted to go home or not. But as they spent the day together, Sammi realized that even though she wasn't ready to be his wife again just yet, she couldn't stand the thought of losing him.

"I guess we should go get you some groceries," Mack offered, now fully awake as the afternoon approached them. They were sitting closely on the couch watching television after having a large brunch at a nearby diner.

"Do you need anything?" Sammi asked casually, making it about him to throw him off.

"No, I went shopping two days ago," Mack told her with a subtle shrug of his shoulders.

"Then we're good," Sammi said, still playing it cool but having to keep her face turned away from him so he couldn't see her giant smirk.

"But you have nothing–oh!"

Mack's face lit up as he planted a kiss on Sammi's cheek and jumped up from the couch. He hurried into the bedroom and Sammi followed to find him tossing her clothes into her luggage carriers. Sammi walked over to him and placed her good hand on his hard stomach to stop him.

"Baby, slow down," Sammi told him. "I'm not going to change my mind in the next five minutes."

"I'm sorry, I guess I got a little excited," Mack admitted as his face turned red.

The husband and wife spent the next hour or so packing up Sammi's things and closing up the apartment before making the hour-long trip home to Long Island. Sammi was upset about abandoning the apartment and all its memories, but she was trying to take everything as it came until she could feel at least somewhat normal again. She knew Eli and Kodi would want her to have faith in Mack and she wanted to be able to have that.

When they got home, Mack sent Sammi into the bedroom to unpack and take her time acclimating to being home again while he made dinner for them. Sammi appreciated his consideration, sitting on their bed in silence to collect her thoughts and feel her feelings instead of focusing on unpacking, grateful for the time alone. What really made her okay in that moment was the fact that the man in the other room wasn't going anywhere despite her attempts to push him away.

After dinner, the couple moved into the living room to cuddle on the couch and watch a movie or two. Neither of them would say it, but they were dreading going to bed. Sammi was nervous about the expectations of sleeping in bed with her husband again and Mack was scared that Sammi was going to ask him to sleep in the guestroom again, even though he had been sleeping in the guestroom the entire week that Sammi had been gone.

Two movies later, Sammi was half asleep with her head drooping lower and lower on Mack's chest. Mack ran his fingers through her golden hair, causing her to stir and stretch her arms out in front of her. Yawning, Sammi sat up and turned her body to face Mack.

"How are you not tired?" Sammi asked, upset that she was yet again the only one who couldn't keep her eyes open.

"I am," Mack said innocently, shrugging his shoulders to dismiss Sammi's attitude.

"Then let's go to bed," Sammi suggested, getting pushy.

Mack smiled at Sammi's sass before taking her hand and leading her into their bedroom. Sammi changed into pajama pants and a tank top while Mack disappeared into the bathroom. He turned the shower on to give the water some time to heat up then returned to the bedroom where Sammi was climbing into their big, comfy bed.

"I'm gonna get a shower," Mack told his wife. "Where would you prefer I slept tonight?"

Sammi looked at him, shocked. She patted Mack's side of the bed with her good hand and Mack grinned. He crossed the room to where Sammi sat in bed and kissed her forehead.

"Dummy," Sammi said, smiling as she stuck her tongue out at him.

Mack was still smiling as he went back into the bathroom and undressed. His shower was quick because he was anxious to share a bed with his wife for the first time in months. He understood that she was still guarded, but she was working with him and that was all he needed to be okay himself.

By the time Mack joined his wife in bed, Sammi was almost asleep already. But as soon as Mack snaked an arm underneath her waist to pull her close to him, she rolled toward him and snuggled into his warm body. Mack buried his face in her long hair and slept peacefully surrounded by the sweet scent of his yellow cocoon.

Chapter Twenty-Eight
Paper Heart

Sammi slept just as soundly as her husband that first night home, embraced by Mack and his love for her. It was a deep sleep and probably the best sleep she'd had since having the help of morphine in the California hospital. And her dreams were visited by memories that had been waiting patiently for her to be ready to see them.

Many years ago, when Sammi was just a child starting grade school, there was a girl in her class who was always getting into trouble. Sammi didn't really know her, but everyone seemed to think that they were sisters because of their matching blonde hair and similar styles. They were paired up one day for a project and Sammi was finally officially introduced to Kodi Sweet.

From the moment they met, Kodi and Sammi became inseparable. There were many teacher's notes to follow with recommendations to keep the girls separated because of how badly they influenced each other. They were never the popular girls, despite their breathtaking natural beauty, but they definitely weren't afraid to fight the cheerleaders in high school. They wore long and baggy clothes while they were in school so boys never noticed them, but they wouldn't have wanted that attention anyway. The girls weren't dumb, and they got decent grades when they actually bothered to do the work. Kodi was a master of math and science while Sammi excelled in English and history, complementing each other in every way possible. With barely present parents who had never wanted children in the first place, there was no keeping the terror twins apart.

In their junior year of high school, Sammi received her only award in her school career. Her English class had to write memorial pieces for a person of their choice but Sammi had never lost anybody she cared about nor did she care enough about anyone in history. So Sammi wrote about the loss of her innocence, hinting at the abuse from her mother's boyfriends. She expected to get in trouble for not following the assignment correctly or having the school counselor banging down her door because of the blatant cry for help. But her teacher was so impressed with her writing, and apparently ignorant to what Sammi was really saying, that she submitted the piece for a literary award and Sammi won. There was a hundred-dollar cash prize that would be the first money put toward saving enough for her and Kodi to get their first apartment and put as much distance between themselves and their parents as possible.

Seven years later, Sammi was planning her first major heist. She, Kodi, Eli, Shay, and Howard had robbed some convenience stores at gunpoint, but Sammi knew they could do better. Ever since her first thrill of theft, her mind had been racing with crazy ideas of elaborate planning and bigger scores. The team was resistant at first, nervous about branching out and the possible consequences, but they couldn't deny that Sammi's plans were good. And it was the way she wrote everything out for her friends to prove how well thought out the plans were that convinced everyone to listen to her.

*

Sammi woke up suddenly, remembering her dream vividly. It was still the middle of the night and the room was dark, but she could tell that Mack was fast asleep under her. Most of her upper body was resting across his chest so she very gently sat up and slid out of bed. She tiptoed across the bedroom floor, listening for any movement from Mack, and slipped out of the room without a sound.

The entire house was dark, but moonlight shined in through the few large windows on the backside of the house so Sammi didn't have any trouble getting up to the loft. Once she was up the stairs, she turned the floor lamp on that did a good job of lighting the entire loft without spilling light down the loft stairs. Then Sammi found the only empty notebook left in the house, a marble composition book, and settled onto the couch to write.

Sammi wrote all through the night, her words flowing effortlessly through the black ink pen. She wrote about Kodi, about Eli, about Howard, and even some about Shay. She wrote them through her own eyes, speaking on Kodi's beauty and warmth, Eli's loyalty and strength, and Howard's courage and intelligence. Sparing no detail, she told the pages all about her friendship with Howard, about how comparing her and Kodi as sisters didn't even begin to do their relationship justice, and spilled her love for Eli onto the paper along with her tears. It was emotionally draining, but in a good way. Her words set the ghosts of her friends free, also bringing freedom to herself.

"How long have you been up?" Mack asked groggily, entering the loft hours later. Sammi hadn't even realized the sun was up.

"Uh, what time is it?" Sammi asked without looking up, her hand still putting pen to paper.

"What...are you doing?" Mack ignored her question as he looked over her shoulder at her writing.

"Making sure the memories of my friends never fade," Sammi told him.

Mack squinted his eyes inquisitively at her, but Sammi wasn't paying him any mind. She seemed okay and Mack didn't want to keep interrupting her, so he gave her shoulder a quick squeeze and told her he'd go make some breakfast for them. Sammi completed her thought before finally taking a break, putting the notebook aside and joining her husband in the kitchen.

"How'd you sleep?" Sammi asked, sitting next to Mack at the kitchen table after grabbing a cold energy drink from the fridge and her favorite travel mug.

"Great!" Mack told her, eyeing the NYPD logo on her cup. "Although, I was disappointed when I woke up and you weren't there."

"I'm sorry, hon. Maybe we could take a nap later?" Sammi offered with the brightest smile Mack had seen on her face in months.

"You're...different today," Mack said cautiously.

"I can't even begin to tell you how much better I feel after writing about my friends and how important they are to me. It's like the heavy black cloud that's been over me since California has lifted and I can finally see sunshine again."

"Hobbs always said you wrote the best the case reports in the department."

Sammi smirked, remembering how she used to proofread Mazzeline's reports before they handed them in so her partner wouldn't embarrass her with his spelling and grammar mistakes. For one brief moment, she missed the squad and working alongside Mazzeline and her husband. But the feeling quickly passed, and she knew it was only the people she missed and nothing else.

After breakfast, Sammi hopped in the shower. She wanted

to keep writing until her friends' story was finished, but Mack was returning to work the next day and she'd have all the time in the world for it. Mack was respecting her grieving process and not pushing to read what she'd written so he deserved her full attention while he was home. She wanted to make sure he showed up at work on Monday as different as she had been that morning; she wanted him to finally be happy again.

Feeling extra cute in a pair of slim-fitting black jeans and a sexy, off-the-shoulder powder blue sweater, Sammi skipped out of the bedroom and found Mack standing by the kitchen sink. She danced over to his side and put her good arm around his trim waist, resting her head against his bicep.

"What would you like to do today?" Sammi asked with nothing but joy in her voice.

"You...are freaking me out," Mack admitted nervously, turning his head and looking down at her face. "Don't get me wrong, I'm glad you're feeling better. But this is the type of thing that happens just before someone snaps."

"No, you're right, I'm sorry," Sammi replied, looking down at the floor. "I think I'm overcompensating because I want you to be happy, too."

Mack sighed and took her hand, leading her into the living room where he sat on the couch and pulled her into his lap. He tilted her chin up so she was looking him in the eyes then kept his hands on her hips.

"I am happy," Mack said slowly, pronouncing each word seriously. "You're home, Sam. That's all I ever wanted."

"Can I ask you something that might be upsetting?" Sammi spoke softly, playing with Mack's fingers in her hand.

"Go for it," Mack told her assuredly, even though he was nervous about what could be on her mind.

"Did you even want another kid?" Sammi asked with uncertainty in her voice. The question had even surprised her as it came out of her mouth.

"Samantha Anne Johnson," Mack said, getting serious. "I,

without a doubt, would love to have a baby with you."

Mack had kept Sammi's face tilted toward his so she could see in his eyes how serious he was. Sammi smiled a weak smile as Mack squeezed her body to his and kissed her hair repeatedly. She wriggled her arm around his back so she could return his hug, still feeling too guarded to kiss him.

Displeased with how gloomy things had gotten, Sammi leapt up from Mack's lap and pulled him off the couch by his arm. She pushed him, steering him down the hall into the bedroom and told him to get dressed so they could go do something fun. Mack chuckled at how cute Sammi was when she was pushy as he swiftly changed into a pair of dark jeans and a grey buttoned flannel and took his beautiful wife to the flea market.

*

Monday morning, Sammi woke up with Mack so she could see him off to work. She made a plate of toast for him while he showered and dressed, the strong desire to send him to work happy still inside her. Mack entered the kitchen a short while later, dressed for work, looking handsome but professional. Sammi smiled at him, having not seen him in detective-mode in quite a while, and suddenly remembering how proud she was of him for his career.

"Well, hello, handsome," Sammi cooed at her husband, making him blush.

"I've missed waking up with you," Mack told her, curling one arm around her waist and kissing her forehead.

"Don't get used to it," Sammi teased and stuck her tongue out at him.

"Ouch," Mack joked, grinning. "Just for that, I'm going to turn on a few extra alarms before I leave every day."

Mack winked at his wife as he grabbed two slices of toast and headed for the door. Sammi giggled and followed him to see him off, kind of disappointed that he actually had to go.

"Say hi to everyone for me," Sammi said in the doorway as Mack stepped on the front porch and turned to face her.

"I will," Mack told her. "Hey, you sure you're gonna be okay here?"

"Honey, I'm fine," Sammi answered him. "But call me when you can."

"I love you, Sam."

Sammi ran out the door and threw her good arm around Mack's neck, hugging him tight. Mack put his arms around her and rubbed her back, resting his head on her shoulder. They remained like that for a full minute before Mack had to go.

After watching Mack drive away, Sammi went back inside and cleaned up her toast mess. Then she headed up to the loft and sat down with her notebook to pick up where she had left off on her friends' tale. It came so easily to her, flowing right from her head, down her arm, through her hand, and out the pen. She lost track of time and wrote throughout most of the day, finally stopping when Mack called her on his way home from work.

While on the phone with each other, Mack expressed an interest in taking Sammi out for a nice dinner that night and Sammi realized she hadn't even bothered to get dressed yet. As soon as they got off the phone, Sammi sprinted downstairs and took a quick shower. Then she took the time to doll herself up with a couple of curls in her shining blonde hair and just enough makeup to accentuate the blue in her eyes without making it too obvious. To complete her evening look, she chose a black cocktail dress and a pair of black strappy heels. She couldn't deny that she loved dressing up specifically for her husband.

When Mack got home and he saw Sammi, a huge smile spread across his face. He clearly hadn't expected her to go all out just for dinner, but he certainly appreciated her going the extra mile. Not wanting to let her down, he showered and put on one of his nicer black suits with a light blue dress shirt to match his wife's sparkling eyes.

"Well, we clean up nice," Sammi smirked, holding onto Mack's arm as they walked out the front door together.

"Babe, you could be wearing sweatpants and still look like you belong in a fashion magazine," Mack told her.

"I'll keep that in mind when I start looking for my next career," Sammi replied with a giggle.

*

By that Friday, Sammi had completed the memoir of her friends by working on it while Mack was at work. She felt free and happy as she snuck the notebook between a couple of large books on the bookshelf. It brought pride and satisfaction to herself, but it was personal and not for anyone else's eyes. As strange as it seemed, Sammi felt ready to finally be herself completely again now that she had written the final words about her friends.

Wanting dinner to be ready by the time Mack got home that night, Sammi ordered takeout a little less than an hour before she was expecting him. She was serving everything onto dishes as Mack walked through the door and he laughed and shook his head.

"Are you ever going to learn to cook?" Mack teased with a chuckle as he sat down in front of his takeout pasta.

"Absolutely not," Sammi told him confidently. "But I do need to figure out what I'm going to do with my life now."

"What about being a mother?" Mack offered casually, watching Sammi's face intently.

Sammi froze, dropping her silverware on her plate. Her heart felt funny, larger than usual and beating faster than normal, so much that she could feel it in her throat. She felt dizzy having not expected this conversation, at least not now. And she hadn't been prepared. She hadn't been thinking about children since the day after she moved back home, and she honestly didn't even know what she wanted anymore.

"Babe...babe, relax. It's okay," Mack said soothingly as he leapt out of his chair and hurried to Sammi's side, putting an arm around her shoulders to comfort her. "We don't have to talk about that now."

Sammi nodded and buried her face in Mack's torso, hugging him to her with her unrestricted arm. She wasn't crying; she was just surprised. And she wasn't really upset, but she appreciated the softness of her husband. Not wanting to ruin their evening, Sammi quickly straightened up and put a half-hearted smile on her face.

"Grab a beer and meet me on the back porch," Sammi told Mack with a sly sparkle in her sapphire eyes. "I want to tell you all about my cross-country adventures."

Mack raised an eyebrow at his wife. He hadn't asked her for this, and he certainly didn't want her to get upset talking about her friends. Sure, he was curious, but they had plenty of time ahead of them for Sammi to take her time and grow stronger about the loss of her friends before opening up.

"Are you sure, Sam?" Mack asked, showing concern.

"More than sure," Sammi replied, smiling more genuinely now.

Convinced that his wife was ready to talk, Mack grabbed a six-pack of Miller High Life out of the fridge and headed out to the back porch. He turned the spotlight on so they could at least see each other and about six feet of the surrounding area.

Sammi joined Mack a few minutes later with the notebook she'd been writing in all week. She sat in a lawn chair next to her husband as he handed a beer to her. Not much of a beer drinker, Sammi put her hand up to turn it down. Then she opened the notebook to where the cross-country-crookery part of the story began and dove into it. She told Mack everything and answered any of his questions, simply happy that he was showing interest in the part of her life that he had never cared much for.

When Sammi got to the part of the story about the car explosion, she got quiet and slightly choked up. But having already written everything out, she was okay sharing the details of the most horrible moment of her life. Mack listened without interrupting and had a total change of heart about Eli when Sammi told him about Eli pushing her out of the SUV to save her.

"I owe Eli my life," Mack muttered after Sammi finished talking.

"He would've stolen me back from you without thinking twice," Sammi teased with a nervous giggle.

"Oh, I know he would have," Mack chuckled, lightening up. "I'd assumed he had while you were away."

"Mack, I wanted you the entire time I was gone," Sammi told him. "I wanted to hear your voice, I wanted to see your face, and I wanted to feel your arms around me."

Sammi got up from her chair and moved over to Mack's lap. Mack held her as she nuzzled into his chest, burying his face in her hair. After a moment of peaceful silence, Sammi tilted her head up to kiss Mack passionately on the lips. He kissed her back until she jumped out of his lap and grabbed his hand to lead him inside to the bedroom.

As they fell into bed undressing each other, Mack's lips never left Sammi's. They hadn't been intimate since before Sammi ran away and Mack worried that she was going to spook, so he wanted to make her as comfortable as possible. But what he didn't realize was that she wanted this, and she wanted to throw all caution to the wind.

"Are you sure you're okay with this?" Mack whispered against his wife's lips as she straddled him, her hair falling all around his face.

"More than okay," Sammi breathed into his ear.

Chapter Twenty-Nine
We Believe

After Sammi fell asleep that night, Mack slipped quietly out of the room and back out to the back porch. Sammi's notebook was still on the lawn chair she had been sitting on and Mack's curiosity was getting the best of him. It was late and the low glow of the spotlight wasn't adequate for a long read so Mack took the notebook in to the loft and settled onto the couch with the floor lamp on.

Mack read through the story of Sammi's friends once, then twice more. He lost track of time, immersed in a world that he realized he had been only partly familiar with. These people that he had met and even one he had lived with for quite some time seemed to come even more to life on the page. It occurred to him that he had wasted his opportunity to get to know these remarkable people.

"What are you doing?" Sammi asked sleepily, rubbing her eyes as she joined Mack in the loft.

"Sammi, this is incredible," Mack announced, finally putting the notebook down to look at his wife.

"It's nothing," Sammi shrugged, settling into Mack's lap without waiting for an invitation. "I just did it for me."

"It's not nothing, babe. You should really be proud of it," Mack told her, hooking his arm around her tiny waist.

"Please don't make a big deal out of this. It's bad enough that you read it without asking."

Mack nodded with his chin on Sammi's shoulder. Although he had every intention of making a big deal about Sammi's writing, she didn't have to know it yet. Dropping the subject, he carried his wife to bed so he could get a few hours of sleep with her.

*

On Sunday, Mack snuck the notebook into his squad car, hiding it in the glove compartment until the next day. He took it into work on Monday and stowed it away in his desk until he had a minute to talk to Hobbs. At lunchtime, he grabbed the notebook and let himself into his Captain's office.

"Hey, does your wife still work in publishing?" Mack asked, dropping into the chair across from Hobbs.

"Cheryl is still in accounting like she has been for twenty-five years," Hobbs corrected his Lieutenant. "But her sister is an editor."

"I was close," Mack shrugged and tossed the notebook onto the Captain's desk. "Anyway, Sammi wrote this and it's really good."

"Come on, Mack. Haven't I done enough for the two of you?" Hobbs asked with a sigh.

"I'm just asking you to read it, man," Mack said, throwing his hands up. "If it's lame, I won't mention it again."

Hobbs sighed again and slid the notebook over to his side of the desk. Mack thanked him, added that Sammi didn't know the notebook was missing yet, and went back out to his desk to scarf down a quick lunch.

Before he left for the day, Mack got called back into Hobbs' office. Captain Hobbs was sitting in his usual spot behind his desk and had Sammi's notebook sitting open on the desk in front of him. Mack took his usual seat and waited for Hobbs to speak.

"So, let me get this straight," Hobbs said, rubbing his temples with his hands, "you want my sister-in-law to publish your wife's confession to about sixty armed robberies."

"So, you do think it should be published?" Mack asked excitedly.

"I couldn't put the damn thing down," Hobbs admitted. "I read it twice before I even realized what time it was."

"Will you at least just pass it along to your wife's sister?" Mack inquired.

"I will, but only because it's really good," Hobbs told him.

"Thanks, boss. I'll see you tomorrow."

Mack was grinning as he got up from the desk and left the office to head home. He was super happy with himself for getting Sammi's book in front of someone, but also super proud of Sammi for writing something so impressive.

*

Sammi kept busy on Monday by finally finishing unpacking her bags and moving back into the house. But by Tuesday, she was bored and went looking for her notebook so she could type up her story for something to do. She tore the loft apart looking for it and still came up empty-handed. It wasn't a huge deal, so she chose not to bother Mack at work and decided to read a book instead after cleaning up the loft.

Losing track of time, Sammi forgot about dinner until Mack had already gotten home from work. She apologized and Mack just laughed before ordering their favorite takeout. While they waited for their food, Sammi asked Mack if he had seen her notebook.

"Not since Friday," Mack said with an innocently subtle shrug.

"It's not in the loft," Sammi told him, frowning.

"Well, where else could it be?" Mack asked, trying to sound helpful.

Sammi responded with a scowl, sensing that Mack was playing dumb on purpose. She couldn't think of a reason for him to be lying so she let it go and figured she'd look even harder for the notebook the next day. But she didn't find it the next day, or the day after that, and she started to suspect foul play from her husband.

Before Sammi could work up the nerve to confront Mack with her suspicions, she was visited by a stranger at the house while her husband was at work. Sammi invited the forty-something-year-old stocky, bespectacled woman with dark hair inside and up to the loft upon her knowledge of Sammi's name without an introduction. They sat across the coffee table from each other and the stranger tossed a thick folder onto the table, providing a shivering flashback of Hobbs with her criminal case file.

"I'm sorry to just drop in on you like this," the lady began speaking, "but Captain Hobbs insisted that you'd be home."

"What is this about?" Sammi asked, growing more nervous at the mention of her old boss.

"Do you write, Sammi?" the woman responded and Sammi's face contorted in confusion.

"Uh, not really," Sammi said with a glare. "I think you have the wrong person."

The strange lady leaned forward and flipped the top of the folder open to reveal its contents. On top was Sammi's missing notebook, which Sammi snatched up in a flustered rage. Underneath the notebook was Sammi's story already typed up and printed out with editing marks in red ink. Clutching the notebook to her stomach, Sammi picked up the rest of the folder and glanced through the revision notes with a look of total annoyance on her face. At the very bottom of the stack of pages was an offer letter for a publishing contract for Sammi's book.

"I'm sorry, I don't know how you got this, but this is for me and nobody else," Sammi said with a pause. "Actually, that's a lie. I know Mack had something to do with this."

"Look, I'm not here to pry," the lady told her. "I'm just here to deliver the offer. All of my contact info is in there. I hope you at least consider it. You're a good writer, Sammi."

The strange woman then got up and saw herself out of the house before Sammi even realized she had never gotten her name. Still annoyed, she threw the folder back down onto the coffee table and watched her visitor drive away. All she could think about was how badly she wished she could call Kodi and complain about what Mack had done while her best friend took her side and justified her feelings. Angry with Mack and depressed about Kodi, Sammi went into the bedroom to lie down and try to sleep off her emotions.

Once again, something she didn't ask for was being thrown at her.

*

When Mack got home that evening, he was surprised to find Sammi sleeping. She'd had a pretty healthy sleeping schedule the past two weeks and hadn't needed to sleep during the day. But then he found the editor's folder up in the loft and knew right away that he was in trouble.

Going for a preemptive strike, Mack went back into the bedroom and sat on the bed beside his wife's peacefully sleeping body. He put his hand at the center of her back and gently massaged her until she began to wake up.

"Good morning, gorgeous," Mack said, smiling as Sammi rolled onto her back to look up at him.

"What time is it?" Sammi asked in a panic.

"Relax, it's dinnertime," Mack told her with a chuckle. "Come on, I'll order us a pizza."

Justine Klavon

Mack kissed Sammi's forehead and left the bedroom to give Sammi a minute to finish waking up. She didn't seem nearly as mad as he had anticipated but he still wanted to get a jump on the subject. He finished ordering their dinner just as Sammi emerged from the bedroom, so he quickly intercepted her and had her sit at the kitchen table with him.

"So, I saw that you had a visitor today," Mack said innocently, keeping his head down but his eyes on Sammi's face.

"I'm not mad that you tried to get it published," Sammi told him bluntly, getting right to the point. "I'm mad that you stole it and lied to me."

"Tried?" Mack asked, surprised. "So, then they don't want to publish it?"

"They do," Sammi admitted, "but it's not for them."

"Sammi, why are you so resistant to good things happening for you?" Mack challenged his wife, not completely prepared for this battle but eager to make his point.

"And why do you always think you know what's good for me?" Sammi argued.

"Because I love you and your happiness is kind of a priority of mine," Mack replied calmly and sincerely.

Sammi got quiet and looked down at her feet. Mack had never won an argument so clearly before and Sammi had never just shut up and listened to him so well. Not wanting to push his luck, he put an end to the conversation and stood up so he could kiss his wife.

*

After dinner, Mack finally changed out of his work clothes and into a pair of grey sweatpants before lounging on the couch in the living room. Sammi hadn't stopped thinking about what Mack had said and she was ready to have a real conversation about her book. So, she grabbed the folder from the loft and joined Mack in the living room, plopping down next to him on the couch. Placing the contract offer on top of the folder, Sammi handed everything to her husband.

"I don't want to keep putting up a fight against the good things in my life," Sammi told her husband. "But I need your help."

"I'll always have your back, Sam. You don't have to face anything alone," Mack replied, shifting on the couch so he could get his arm around his wife and still hold onto the folder with his other hand.

The cozy couple went through the contract together and then read the editor's revisions. Sammi got the sense that Hobbs' sister-in-law didn't realize that Eli, Howard, and Kodi had been real people and Mack couldn't really dispute the thought. He wasn't surprised when Sammi got discouraged.

"There are other publishers," Mack offered, wanting his wife to have hope.

"But none that knew Kodi," Sammi told him, disheartened. "None of them knew the warmth of Eli's embrace or the genuine kindness of Howard."

"That's what the book's for, cutie," Mack replied, squeezing Sammi to him and kissing her forehead. "It makes everyone wish they had known those extraordinary people."

"You knew them," Sammi reminded him.

"Not like you did."

Sammi felt sad and missed her friends so she curled up under Mack's arm and snuggled into his side. Mack held her tighter and turned the television on so she wouldn't feel obligated to keep talking about the book. Publishing it was a new idea to her and she deserved the time to think it through properly.

Neither Sammi nor Mack mentioned Sammi's book over the weekend. The folder remained in plain sight on the kitchen counter, so it stayed present in their minds, even if they didn't want to talk about it. The more Sammi thought about it, the more she found herself lost in daydreaming about a new career in writing. She just couldn't help but wonder if maybe this wasn't the story she should share with the world.

The following Monday, Sammi was haunted by the unmoved folder while Mack was at work. She avoided the kitchen, trying to avoid having to think about the book and making any kind of decisions. But even though she wasn't in view of it, her mind couldn't seem to think about anything else.

It was nice outside that day, sunny but not very warm. Needing to clear her head, Sammi went on the back porch with a glass of wine and sat with her phone placed off to the side on silent. But only two minutes later, she couldn't tolerate the quiet anymore and put her glass down to go back inside and get the editor's contact information from the folder.

While she was still in the kitchen, Sammi heard the doorbell ring and she dropped the folder back onto the counter to go see who was at the door. Half expecting it to be the editor again, she carelessly opened the front door and was instantly shoved backwards into the foyer. The masked intruder grabbed Sammi by the shoulders before she even knew what was going on and easily tossed her slender body into the wall, making sure her head hit first and hit hard enough to knock her out.

Chapter Thirty
Broken Windows

Sammi woke up slowly, seeing double and not having any idea what was going on. She shook her head gingerly, trying to clear her vision up, and looked around her. There was nobody around and she was actually surprised to find that she was still in her home, sitting on the floor by the stairs to the loft and propped up against the wall of the staircase with her arms tied above her head to the bars of the railing. Letting out a dramatic groan as she tugged against her restraints and felt the pain of her broken arm being free from its sling, she discovered a strip of cloth had been placed in her mouth and tied off behind her head as a gag.

It crossed Sammi's mind that she should be scared, but she was more pissed off than anything. She couldn't believe that someone had the nerve to come into her home, the home of one of New York's finest police officers, and try to hold her against her will. Her only enemy was Shay and she was still behind bars so whoever had done this probably had no idea who they were dealing with. But they would learn.

Allowing her anger to build, Sammi tugged at the zip-ties holding her wrists together a few more times before maneuvering herself so that her feet were under her and she was able to stand up. With this new leverage, Sammi dropped all her weight into the plastic ties, wearing them down slightly. The pain in her broken arm was immense but survivable. Climbing to her feet again, she intended to try throwing her weight into the restraints again, but someone appeared in front of her and she sighed in relief.

"Sit!" Christopher growled at Sammi, brandishing a fairly sized knife as he took a step closer toward his hostage. There was no trace of Australian accent in his voice and Sammi remembered that his name wasn't actually Christopher. But that's who she knew him as.

With a muffled snort, Sammi glared at him while she challenged him with her eyes. This punk didn't scare Sammi and they still had some unfinished business to discuss regarding her three murdered friends. He ordered her to sit down again so she kicked the wall behind her as hard as she could in defiance. Moving swiftly, he closed in on her and punched her in the gut, knocking the wind out of her and bringing her to her knees.

"That's better," Christopher clucked, backing away from her again. "Now where's the rest of the money?"

Sammi raised an eyebrow at Christopher, not sure what money he was talking about and certainly not sure how he expected her to answer him. The pretend Aussie must not have really wanted an answer because he just walked away. Sammi let out an angry scream against her gag and threw her body back against the wall to cause a scene, wanting Christopher to come back and fight her like a man. This man that killed her friends didn't deserve to be alive, still walking and talking freely. She wanted him dead for what he had done.

A few minutes passed and she could hear Christopher tearing apart her entire home, apparently searching for money that he wasn't going to find. Once she was able to breathe properly again, she stood up and continued trying to break her wrists free. The wooden post of the railing that she was confined to was starting to weaken under her weight and she didn't care if that broke before the plastic zip-ties did because she would still be free. But before anything could break, Christopher returned and wasn't so gracious with his space this time.

Attempting to get away from Christopher who was standing damn near on top of her, Sammi planted her butt on the floor and slid as far away from him as she could. But Christopher wrapped one hand around her neck, pushing his palm up into her chin and picking her up to a standing position. He kept his hand around her throat and used his free to hand to slide the gag out of her mouth, pressing his face to hers.

"You were supposed to die too," Christopher hissed against her cheek.

"Yeah, well, maybe if you were a real criminal, you could've gotten the job done," Sammi spat at him.

Christopher smacked her across the face and Sammi laughed. But then he pressed his lips to hers and Sammi became furious. She pulled her head back, away from him, and then rammed it forward with as much force as she could muster into Christopher's nose. That final force against Sammi's restraints broke her free as Christopher stumbled backwards roaring in pain with blood flowing from his nostrils. Only the railing post had broken so Sammi's wrists were still tied together but she was no longer tied to one spot.

Thinking quickly, Sammi ran out to the back porch with her arms down in front of her to grab her cellphone. She had a difficult time using the touch screen with her hands tied together but she managed to get through two screens to get to a call button for Mack's number. Christopher appeared in the back doorway as soon as she sent the call, so she pressed the button to turn on the speaker and tossed the phone onto a lawn chair, turning to face her intruder.

"What do you want?" Sammi asked Christopher, hoping the call had connected by that point.

"Well, first, a real criminal would eliminate all witnesses," Christopher said mockingly, holding his knife out in front of him. "But if what I took from your hotel room in Cali was just your travel money, I can only assume that there's more...a lot more."

"It wouldn't be here," Sammi scoffed, narrowing her eyes at him. "My husband's a detective, you moron."

"Then where is it?" Christopher asked, opening his arms out wide in wonder.

"In an offshore bank account," Sammi sighed in disbelief, rolling her eyes and shaking her head. "Do you know anything about being a bad guy?"

"I found you, didn't I?" Christopher retorted.

Then Christopher came at her with the knife raised and Sammi didn't run. She put her wrists up in front of her and bowed her head just as he struck, catching the blade on the zip-ties and cutting her loose. Christopher couldn't believe what just happened and paused in shock. Sammi kicked him in the shin as hard as she could and ripped the knife from his hand as he gasped in pain. Then she held the knife to his throat as she kicked the backs of his legs until he dropped to his knees. Holding the knife in place, she snatched up her phone to discover that the call to Mack had been disconnected. Uncertain of what happened, she dialed the local precinct and reported the intruder.

While waiting for the local cops to show up, Christopher made a move for the knife but Sammi just pressed the blade against his Adam's apple and he stopped.

"You won't do it," Christopher seethed tauntingly, on his knees with his back to Sammi.

"Try me," Sammi hissed, allowing the blade to dig ever so lightly into the skin of his neck. "You killed my family."

"You think you're so tough and a big, bad criminal. But

you told me yourself that you were a cop. You can't have it both ways," Christopher challenged her.

And he was right, her police training was still winning over in her mind, even though she craved to cause this man pain. She told herself that if he made a run for it that she could end him, but she knew she would do no such thing. She wasn't a killer and that's what kept her from being the true bad guy. That's why Mack was able to love her.

As soon as a swarm of vehicles could be heard in front of the house, Christopher hooked his arm behind him and around Sammi's ankles before she even saw what was coming. He swept her feet out from under her and she landed hard on her back, dropping the knife as she fell. Christopher swung around and grabbed the knife off the ground, leaning over Sammi as she struggled to breathe after the hard fall.

"Say hi to your friends," Christopher said bluntly, raising the knife above his head before driving it toward the center of Sammi's chest. Sammi had known he was aiming for her heart and was able to get her arm up just in time, catching the blade in her left bicep.

Sammi hollered in pain, knife protruding from her upper arm, as Christopher was hoisted off of her by two cops. As soon as those cops left with the intruder in custody, two more cops appeared in their place, kneeling by Sammi's side. They were trying to talk to her to keep her calm while waiting for paramedics, worried that she might go into shock.

"I'm fine," Sammi growled, even though tears of pain were streaming seamlessly out of the corners of her eyes and down the sides of her face into her hair. She was trying to sit up, but the cops kept putting their hands on her shoulders to keep her still as blood oozed out around the blade in her arm. The more movement occurring in her arm, the more it bled.

"Seriously, guys, I've been through a lot worse," Sammi told the cops, trying to laugh off the pain. She was finally able to pull herself up into a sitting position just as paramedics arrived on the scene.

"She really has been through worse," came a reassuringly familiar voice from behind the paramedics tending to her arm.

Sammi made eye contact with Mazzeline as the knife was pulled from her bicep and the wound sterilized and bandaged on the scene in a hurry. The paramedics had made the judgement call to treat her there and hoped she'd be more cooperative once they got her to the hospital. But as soon as the bandage was secure, she leapt up to her feet and into Mazzeline's arms, ignoring the two medics who were trying to help her.

"What are you doing here?" Sammi asked her favorite detective that she wasn't married to, surprised to see him.

"Mack's on his way," Mazzeline told her. "He got your call and knew I was at physical therapy up this way so he asked me to come be with you until he could get home.

Mazzeline brushed the leftover tears off Sammi's face with the sides of his thumbs as the paramedics came to separate them. They were trying to get Sammi into an ambulance to get her over to the hospital, but she was insisting that she was fine. She mostly didn't want the chance of running into Anthony, so Mazzeline reasoned with them, flashing his badge, until they agreed to let him transport Sammi himself.

By the time Sammi and Mazzeline made their way around the house to the front, Mack's squad car was speeding up the usually quiet suburban street and screeching to a stop behind Mazzeline's pickup truck. Mack leapt out of the car, sprinted up the front lawn, and nearly tackled Sammi with the force at which he embraced her. Sammi went to put her arms around her husband and discovered she couldn't lift her left arm but a few inches from her side, so she hugged him with her right arm, fighting the pain that was almost numb compared to the new stab wound, and didn't speak while Mack held her to him.

"I'm transferring precincts," Mack announced matter-of-factly, pulling away from Sammi so he could talk, but keeping his hands around her waist.

"You will do no such thing," Sammi cut him off before he could explain. "You would be bored out of your mind working outside of the city."

"I'm too far away from you when I'm working and I can't handle it anymore," Mack replied and kissed Sammi's forehead.

"Mack, I will move back to the city before you transfer jobs," Sammi told him. "I just lost my family. You're not losing Hobbs, and Mazzeline, and Palma."

Moving to Sammi's side, Mack put his arm around her shoulders and steered her toward his squad car. Mazzeline didn't need to wait for an invitation to tag along to the hospital to have Sammi's arm looked at. Sammi's last statement made it permanent that he was a part of their lives and a part of their family.

Chapter Thirty-One
I Did It for You

Mack ended up taking the rest of that week off from work to be with Sammi. Her right arm had been put back into a sling and now her left arm was bandaged tightly to restrict mobility. She was upset about how useless she felt with the limited use of her arms, so Mack set her up in the living room with her favorite movies while he cleaned the house from Christopher's ransacking. He had invited Mazzeline over to hang out, but Mazzeline had returned to work earlier than expected to make up for Mack's absence from the unit.

Fortunately, Sammi's stab wound wasn't as bad as it could have been, and she regained the full use of her left arm by the following Monday. Mack wasn't thrilled about returning to work that Monday and being an hour away from Sammi all day, but his wife insisted that she would look for places to live in the city. His name was still on the lease for his old apartment in the city, but he knew even the mention of it would make Sammi sad because of its connection to Kodi.

Upon his return to work, Mack was called into the Captain's office to talk about what had happened with Sammi the previous week, the rumor that he was transferring precincts, and the publishing offer from his sister-in-law. Mack was open and honest with Hobbs about everything, explaining how Sammi held her own against the man who killed her friends, how he didn't like being so far away from Sammi during the day in case she needed him like she had that day, and how Sammi felt like his sister-in-law didn't really get the story she had written and was nervous about the revision requests.

"I'll pass that on to Stephanie," Hobbs told Mack. Then he added with a shrug, "I guess we liked it so much because we're so close to it."

"I guess we're lucky like that," Mack snapped back at him, sounding offended and protective over the story. "I just hope Sammi doesn't give up on it."

"Like you gave up on wanting to be Captain?" Hobbs shot at him unexpectedly.

"I didn't give up on anything," Mack retorted coolly. "I realized there's more to life than the job and I don't want the responsibility. Being the husband of a thief is more than enough responsibility."

"I'd say so. But it doesn't really sound like Sammi needed you all that much last week," Hobbs challenged his favorite Lieutenant.

Mack smirked and patted Hobbs on the shoulder belittlingly as he stood up from his desk chair. Hobbs rolled his eyes and shook his head, trying to come across as if he disapproved of Sammi's fearlessness, even though he'd somehow enabled her entire behavior. The police Captain would never publicly admit it, but he loved Sammi as if she were his daughter and he never lost a night of sleep over letting her run free of consequences for her poor life choices.

Getting back to work, Mack was in a great mood, feeling good about himself and feeling a strange new pride in his wife's attitude and criminal history. It wasn't that he suddenly approved of her illegal career choice, but more that he could finally admire everything she had done. He couldn't imagine ever pulling off any one of her heists or living through any of her injuries and he had to respect her for that. His wife was strong and could take care of herself, so they didn't need to move in order for him to stay at his job. He could freely admit that maybe she didn't need him as much as he'd thought, and he was not ashamed of her or any of her decisions anymore. And that gave him an idea.

When he got home that night, Mack found out right away that Hobbs had already called his sister-in-law, who had already stopped by again to apologize to Sammi for her misreading of the story. Sammi and Stephanie had gone over the original manuscript together that afternoon to discuss which revisions Sammi was willing to go along with and those that were too drastic and wouldn't do any justice to her friends' memories. Stephanie had left still struggling with accepting Eli's violence in the story and the girls had agreed to sleep on it and chat again the next day.

"You're not going to give in, are you?" Mack asked, getting oddly protective again of the story that wasn't even his.

"Oh, no way," Sammi assured him. "What Eli did was real. And what Eli did also brought you into my life."

Sammi moved in and sat on Mack's lap at the kitchen table, kissing him with meaning. She had been grateful for the distraction of Stephanie's visit that day because she had gotten lonely in the house and slightly spooked by almost inaudible noises while her husband was at work. Mack kissed her back, entangling his hands in her long hair as she hooked her left arm around his neck. She wanted to lead him into the bedroom, but he wasn't finished talking and held her in place on his lap.

"Write our story," Mack said, softly but sincerely.

"What?" Sammi asked, more surprised than confused.

"I want you to write our story, in words that only you could put together," Mack explained. "Write about the night we met at the mall and ended up shooting each other. Write about working together and how you were the better detective but an even better thief. And tell the world how this foolish cop fell in love with the most breathtaking and goodhearted, creative criminal in the world."

*

Sammi distracted herself for the next month or so with writing whenever Mack was out of the house. She didn't like being alone with nobody to talk to and she didn't like thinking about that day Christopher showed up, so she focused on perfecting the book about her friends, with the help of her new editor friend, and starting to write the book that Mack had requested. The distraction of writing was nice, and she certainly enjoyed the creative outlet, but she could always breathe a sigh of relief when her husband came home, grateful for the companionship.

One morning, Mack gently shook Sammi awake on his way out the door for work. Sammi opened one eye to glare at her husband for disturbing her, but he just smiled at her and kissed her nose. She knew he wasn't going to leave until he was sure she was up, so she pulled herself into a sitting position, finally having the use of both of her arms again.

"Call me after your meeting, babe," Mack said and kissed Sammi's lips. "I want to hear all about it."

Sammi nodded silently as Mack hurried out of the bedroom. Then she sank back into the pillows, feeling more tired than she should after her good night of sleep. Her stomach was unsettled, and she quickly realized that she was familiar with this all-over queasiness. But she had her second meeting with her publisher that afternoon to finalize all the details of her first two printed books, and she needed to get ready.

Once Sammi showered and flattened her too-long blonde

hair, she changed into a pretty purple blouse and white dress pants and finally made her way into the city. Mack didn't know it, but Sammi didn't like the city anymore, not without her beautiful friends who were supposed to still be there. She was glad that Mack had dropped the idea of transferring precincts because she didn't want to live in the city, but she would have in order to keep Mack's squad together. This publishing company was the first thing to get her to leave Long Island since the night she returned home with Mack from Eli's old apartment, and this second trip was at least easier than the first. She often dreamt about taking Mack to see California and possibly starting a new life with him out there, but she would never ask Mack to leave his children or his job. And she couldn't really imagine leaving Mazzeline either because he was the closest thing she had to a friend anymore.

Sammi's meeting ended up being quick, not even a full hour, in Stephanie's office, which was very modern chic with low lighting and dark furniture. Sammi and Stephanie had been on the same page ever since Stephanie came to accept that Sammi's characters were real people and that Sammi wasn't going to downplay Eli's temper for her. She liked Sammi's second book even less because of Sammi's multiple brushes with death, but she couldn't deny that it was even better written than the story of her friends. Stephanie had been nothing but friendly and helpful throughout this entire process, which Sammi appreciated, and she would prefer to work with Stephanie over anybody else on any possible future projects.

"If you're satisfied with the way everything looks, all that's left to do is write your acknowledgments, which you can just email to me by the end of the week," Stephanie said at the end of the meeting.

"Wow, thank you for everything," Sammi said, shaking Stephanie's hand. "You made this even easier than you had to for me."

"I said it when I first met you and I'll say it again," Stephanie replied. "You're an incredible writer. Keep it up because I want more from you."

Sammi smiled and waved goodbye as she slipped out of Stephanie's office. She was feeling undeniably relieved, having finally taken care of all the daunting details of her first two books. But a wave of nausea crashed over her as she slid behind the wheel of her car and she suddenly remembered that she had to stop at the store on her way home. Her mind was distant as she called Mack from her car and she felt bad that she didn't return his excitement regarding her books, or at least the one book that Mack knew about. Luckily, he didn't seem to notice and had to get off the phone before he had a chance to pick up on how distracted Sammi was.

As Sammi finally returned home mid-afternoon and walked up the front walk, the sun beat down on her and caused her nausea to double-down. She wiped sweat off her forehead as she stepped onto the front porch, but dizziness took over and she missed the step, falling forward onto the cement and catching her weight on her wrists. Picking herself up with half a smirk on her face, she shook her head at the unnecessary pregnancy test in her bag. There was not a doubt in her mind that she was pregnant.

After fixing herself a quick snack to help settle her stomach, Sammi took the pregnancy test just to confirm before making any next moves. If she and Mack were going to do this, they were going to do it right this time, or at least she was going to do it right. There wasn't going to be any more running away and there wasn't going to be any more uncertainty. She wanted this. She wanted this more than she wanted to see her name on the cover of a best-selling book. But included in doing things right was planning the perfect way to break the news to Mack.

Wanting to be absolutely certain before worrying about telling Mack, Sammi set up a doctor's appointment after her home test came back positive. Still not willing to risk coming into contact with Dr. Brock ever again, especially now, she had no choice but to see a doctor in the city.

Meanwhile, Sammi also finished writing her acknowledgments and sent them over to Stephanie. Instantly suspecting something was up, Stephanie called Sammi as soon as she had read the email.

"Sammi, are you—?" Stephanie asked after the hellos were said.

"Yeah, but Mack doesn't know yet," Sammi told her quickly. "What are the chances you could rush a copy of each book for me?"

"I can get paperbacks within the week. Why?"

"I'd like to use them to surprise Mack, but I can't keep this secret forever."

"If you can wait until the weekend, I will guarantee you will have them."

"Thanks, Steph. You've gone above and beyond for me through this entire experience. I appreciate you."

"I believe we'll work together again. Oh, and congratulations, Sammi."

Chapter Thirty-Two
4 Letter Word

That Sunday, Sammi woke Mack up by kissing his face all over. He opened his eyes and immediately rolled Sammi onto her back so he could take over the face-kissing. She laughed and tried to push him away so she could talk, but he snaked his arms under her back so he could hold her close. Giving up, Sammi snuggled into him and let his warmth embrace her.

"Let's just stay like this all day," Mack mumbled into Sammi's hair, wrapping his arms even tighter around her body. Sammi started to nod, but quickly stopped herself.

"No, no, no," Sammi blurted out, wriggling free from her husband in a hurry. "I have a surprise for you so we should get dressed."

"A surprise? Is it my birthday?" Mack asked, confused as Sammi hopped out of bed and left him alone with his arms sprawled open waiting to hold his wife again.

"I think you're going to like it better than your birthday," Sammi told him with a wink before skipping into the bathroom.

Mack didn't budge while Sammi combed her hair and brushed her teeth. He remained in the same spot and watched as Sammi returned from the bathroom, changing into a periwinkle blue summer dress on her way through the bedroom. Then Sammi floated out of the room and Mack finally dragged himself out of bed, smiling to himself the whole time and thinking about how lucky he was to be Mack Johnson.

After a short breakfast, Sammi steered a still very confused Mack out to the garage to her car. Mack didn't know where they were going so he was stuck in the passenger seat while his wife drove, which was a rare occurrence for them. It had never been spoken, but it was pretty apparent to Sammi that Mack preferred to drive.

Uncertain about how Mack was going to react to the surprise, Sammi was kind of nervous as she drove them into the city. She could expect that Mack would be happy about her news, but she didn't have the best track record with sharing life-changing information with her husband. Not much in the world scared Sammi, nothing comparable to Shay on the other end of a firearm, but she was definitely scared that Mack might not get as excited as she hoped he would.

As Sammi pulled her Nissan into the parking garage, she could feel Mack's disapproving gaze on the side of her face. She knew he hadn't been to this mall since the night they'd met, but she wanted to share this with him. This place was important to their relationship and Sammi wanted Mack to be able to see it for what it was.

"Just...go with me on this," Sammi said quietly, nearly pleading after she'd put the car in park.

Mack sighed as he got out of the car, but he met Sammi on the other side and immediately took her hand in his. Sammi swung her bag over her shoulder and led the way inside the open two-story shopping mall. They walked without speaking past busy stores and happily buzzing teenagers, none of whom knew what had taken place in this mall just a few years ago. Mack was tense with a somewhat painful look on his face as they walked at a brisk pace toward familiar sights, and Sammi could sense as soon as Mack started recognizing things because his hand would begin to squeezed hers more tightly.

The first place Sammi took Mack was the tiny hallway where they'd first crossed each other's paths. It was somewhat brighter in the suffocating, small hallway than it had been years ago and Sammi leaned against the hallway wall, pulling Mack to her. She kept her hands on his waist as he stood in front of her and she studied his face as she thought back to that night when she saw this man for the very first time.

"I think you're even more handsome than you were that night," Sammi cooed softly at her husband, swinging their arms gently at their sides.

"What are we doing here, Sam?" Mack asked, dropping her hands and stepping uncomfortably away from her.

"Why does this make you so upset?" Sammi challenged him, trying to hold back her own emotions. She didn't understand why he was so closed off about certain things, especially anything involving her. "This is where we met, Mack."

"Sammi, I love you. But I am overwhelmed here," Mack tried to explain, still keeping his distance. "That night was total insanity and I still feel blindsided by it."

"I don't understand," Sammi replied, finally letting her emotions get the best of her as anger and sadness took turns showing themselves in her eyes. "There wouldn't be an us if it weren't for that night, Mack!"

"I get that, Sammi!" Mack came back, matching his wife's emotions. "But I had to turn my back on everything that I stood for that night and every day for the rest of my life! I chose Sammi the thief over my job as a cop and I don't need to be reminded of it in this cramped hallway! I could've lost everything that night!"

"But I'm not a thief now," Sammi offered to lighten the mood, keeping her head low but looking up at Mack with as much innocence in her sparkling eyes as she could fake.

"Sammi, you were, you are, and you always will be a thief," Mack replied, almost coldly.

"So...you regret this...you regret me?" Sammi asked, suddenly feeling like someone had punched her in the gut.

Mack chuckled as he finally looked Sammi in the face and took a step toward her. Sammi remained leaning with her back against the wall, trying to wait patiently for Mack's answer.

"The only thing I regret is not sweeping you off your feet the moment I looked into your eyes," Mack said, closing the distance between himself and Sammi and pressing his lips hard to hers with his hand immediately entangling in her hair. "I'm sorry that I will never be okay with your past and that I believe we were probably never supposed to be together, but I promise you that no one has ever loved another as much as I love you."

Sammi kissed Mack back, allowing her thoughts to disappear into the moment. She loved this man with everything she had, and she was grateful for the night they met, even if neither of them had made the best choices that evening. Those choices brought them to this very moment and Sammi wouldn't change a thing about that night even if she could. She would have no problem taking another two bullets to prove her love for Mack Johnson.

"Sammi, I'm not great with words but I wish I could show you how I felt that night," Mack breathed against her cheek after catching his breath. "I saw my future in your eyes the very first moment I looked at you and I knew I loved you that very second."

"It was love at first sight," Sammi whispered, then placed her hands flat on his chest and kissed his smooth cheek. "But we're not done yet."

Taking his hand again, Sammi led Mack to the crowded second floor of the mall where the two of them had shot each other. Mack looked cautiously at the floor and quickly relaxed when he noticed that the tiles had been replaced. Sammi pulled him off to the side, next to the railing overlooking the first floor, and dropped her shoulder bag to the floor. She knelt down and retrieved two books from the bag before standing up again and getting serious as she turned her body towards Mack.

"I may have thought you were the enemy the night we met, but I was never once afraid of you and that meant something to me," Sammi spoke with a purpose as she nervously played with the books in her hands. "I didn't know I was going to fall in love with you, but I'm glad I did. You're the reason I'm not afraid of anything and you're the reason I've had a life worth writing about."

Then Sammi handed Mack the first book, the one about her friends, the one he knew about. Mack looked over the front and back covers of it before flipping through the pages and curiously landing on the acknowledgments page:

For Kodi, the only friend I ever needed.

For Howard, whose genuine goodness made me a better person.

For Eli—you were right, you are my fate.

"Your fate?" Mack asked, clearly upset, just as Sammi suspected he would be.

"Mack, he saved my life," Sammi defended her choice of words. "And it was something he said after Shay shot me."

Holding onto the book, Mack looked at the floor, trying really hard to be understanding. He didn't know Sammi had written a second book, a book about him like he had suggested, so Sammi slowly held it out to him. Not expecting it, Mack looked at it with confusion and carefully took it from his wife. He ran his fingers gently across the title *Love Against the Law* as he stared at it in awe.

"When did you—?" Mack asked, somewhat in shock.

"While you were at work. When else?" Sammi said with a

giggle. She gave Mack a minute to let the title sink in before she took the book back from him, opened it to the acknowledgments page, and handed it back to him.

Mack read aloud, "To a loving father of three and the only man I ever want to call my husband."

After speaking it out loud, Mack read the sentence a few more times to himself with a puzzled look scrunched on his face. Sammi watched him, smiling, waiting for him to figure it out. Suddenly, his soft blue eyes widened, twinkling with understanding, and his mouth fell agape.

"Baby, are we going to have a baby?" Mack asked, his voice gentle but full of emotion and excitement.

"We're going to have a baby," Sammi told him, nodding and grinning widely.

Mack pulled Sammi into his arms and squeezed her tight, burrowing his face into the crook of her neck and letting her hair fall down over him. Sammi hugged him in return, her head smooshed into his solid chest. She let him hold her for as long as he needed, feeling his body tremble with happiness. People were staring as they walked by, but Mack didn't notice and Sammi couldn't have cared less. This was their moment and they'd earned it.

When Mack was finally ready to release his wife, Sammi quickly tossed the books back into her bag and hoisted her bag over her shoulder. Then she grabbed Mack's hand and started to leave their spot, but Mack stopped her and brought her back over to the railing.

"Hey, you were right," Mack said, looking serious as he made eye contact with Sammi, planting a hand on her hip. "This place is important to us. Good fell for evil that night and now they're having a child together. And no matter which side of the law that child chooses to be on, they will be loved."

*

About a year later, the Sammi Johnson book tour ended in Los Angeles, California. It was a beautiful, hot, sunny day as the ever-radiant blonde bombshell and her handsome police detective husband made their way through a large, open cemetery. Mack walked half a step behind Sammi with his arm hooked protectively around her waist from the back. Sammi walked with a purpose, effortlessly carrying a sleeping baby cradled in her arms.

When Sammi found the gravestone she was looking for, she kissed Mack before sitting down in the grass in front of the grave. Mack gave her space but stood behind her for emotional support, ready for when she needed him. Sitting with her legs crossed, Sammi readjusted the peaceful bundle in her arms.

"Hi, Eli," Sammi spoke softly to the open grassy space before her.

Then Sammi paused. She had expected this to be easier since she knew what she had come here to say. But she hadn't planned on the overwhelming feeling of missing her old friend and wanting to see him more than anything else in the world. A few tears slipped out of the corners of Sammi's eyes and she quickly wiped them away before they could fall onto her sleeping baby's face.

"I miss you, Eli," Sammi began again, slowly this time. "I want you to meet this little guy. This is Eliot Kode Johnson and, even though Mack and I agreed to let him choose his own path, he's named after the two greatest thieves I've ever met, so I think there's a good chance the criminal side will win out in the end. He will grow up hearing all about his Uncle Eli and Aunt Kodi. I promise you, your memory will never fade."

Getting choked up at the end, Sammi had to stop talking. Mack put his hand on Sammi's shoulder from behind to comfort her just as little Eliot's tiny eyelids fluttered open. The little brown-haired boy smiled up at his mother and father with the most shocking blue eyes that he could have only gotten from Sammi. There was a very specific, and very familiar to Mack, twinkle in those eyes that told his parents exactly which side of the law he was going to choose.

About Atmosphere Press

Atmosphere Press is an independent, full-service publisher for excellent books in all genres and for all audiences. Learn more about what we do at atmospherepress.com.

We encourage you to check out some of Atmosphere's latest releases, which are available at Amazon.com and via order from your local bookstore:

Saints and Martyrs: A Novel, by Aaron Roe

When I Am Ashes, a novel by Amber Rose

Melancholy Vision: A Revolution Series Novel, by L.C. Hamilton

The Recoleta Stories, by Bryon Esmond Butler

Voodoo Hideaway, a novel by Vance Cariaga

Hart Street and Main, a novel by Tabitha Sprunger

The Weed Lady, a novel by Shea R. Embry

A Book of Life, a novel by David Ellis

It Was Called a Home, a novel by Brian Nisun

Grace, a novel by Nancy Allen

Shifted, a novel by KristaLyn A. Vetovich

Because the Sky is a Thousand Soft Hurts, stories by Elizabeth Kirschner

About the Author

Justine Klavon is a 2012 English Literature graduate from Ursinus College. She lives in Eastern Pennsylvania with her two dogs, Hannah and Hamlet, who will try to tell you that they helped with the writing process of this book. Only one of them is telling the truth.

CPSIA information can be obtained
at www.ICGtesting.com
Printed in the USA
LVHW030725060821
694493LV00007B/699